NIKKI GRANT

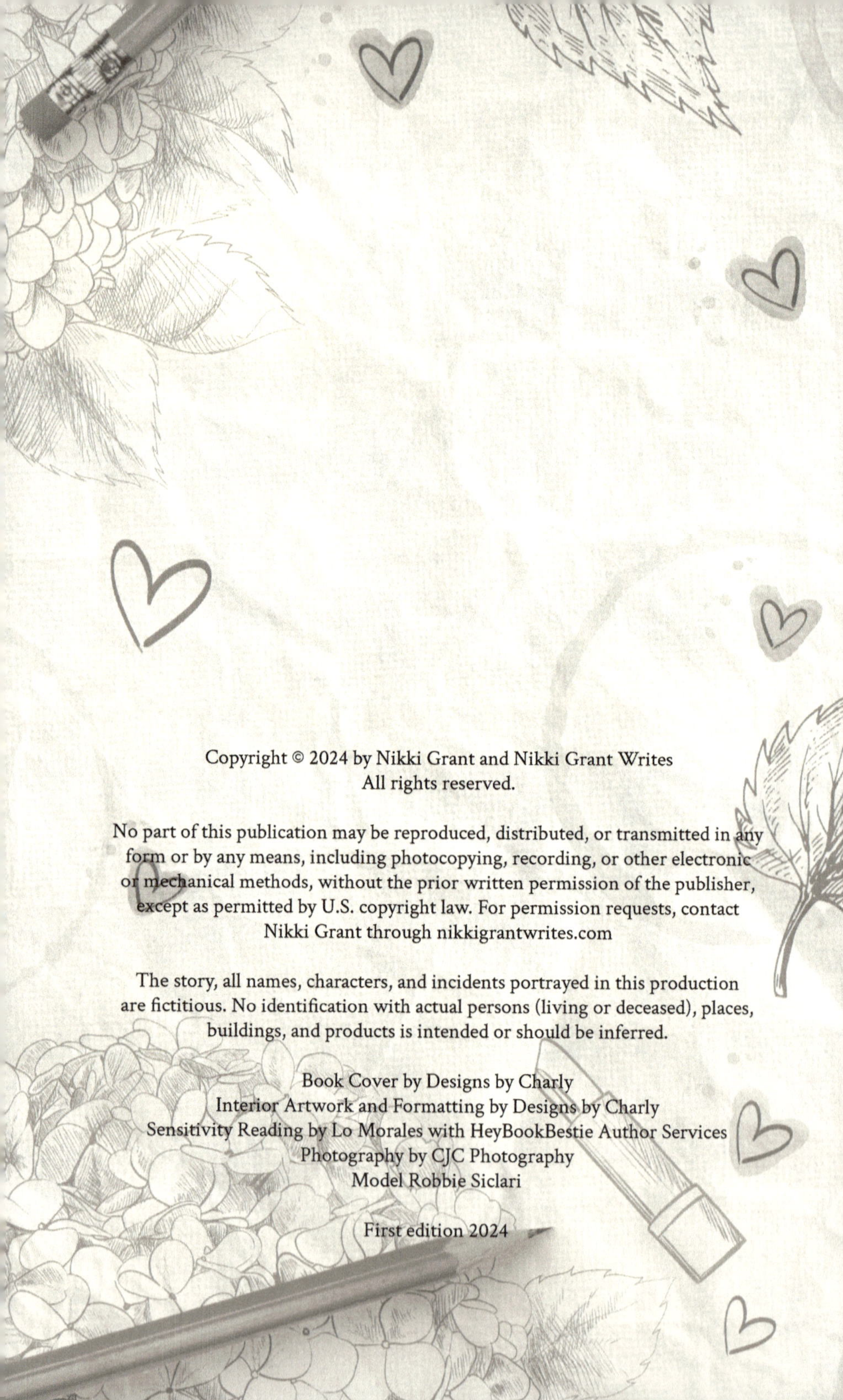

Book Cover by Designs by Charly
Interior Artwork and Formatting by Designs by Charly
Sensitivity Reading by Lo Morales with HeyBookBestie Author Services
Photography by CJC Photography
Model Robbie Siclari

First edition 2024

To the girls who wanted to see the female main character that enjoys wearing makeup unapologetically. Grab your lipstick, babe. This one's for you.

LETTER FROM THE AUTHOR (TRIGGER AND CONTENT WARNING)

Your mental health and personal boundaries are important. Please review this list before reading The Funnel to You. This is a cozy dark romance - that means that our characters may make some "red flag" decisions, but they do it out of love and care for those around them.

Sasha deals with some pretty heavy anxiety and that shows up in how she sees and talks to herself, how she responds to others, and how she processes things throughout the book. She is very "loud" in her internal talking and combines past traumas with current situations in how to handle those situations.

If you find you see some of yourself in Sasha, as I have seen myself in her, I hope this encourages you to find your own practice of finding your comfort levels and learning what works best for you.

Enjoy,
Nikki

HERE'S THOSE TRIGGERS FOR YOU

Mention of childhood emotional and religious trauma - referenced but not on page
Mention of pregnancy - mentioned in passing
Slight coffee addiction
FMC deals with anxiety - mentioned in detail on page
Sexually explicit scenes
Morally grey mmc - even though he's a total cinnamon roll
"Light" stalking including hacking, social media manipulation, and watching from "afar"

CHAPTER BREAKDOWN (WHERE TW AND CW HAPPEN)

In case you want to skip any of these pages for your own mental health or boundaries.

Childhood emotional and religious trauma
Chapter 27
Explicit sex scenes
Chapter 18, 21-22, 28, 29
Stalking
Chapter 25 (referenced)
Chapter 32, 33, 35
Pregnancy (mentioned)
Chapter 27, 37
Anxiety
Chapter 1, 7, 31, 33
Red Flag behavior
Chapter 6, 32

PLAYLIST

Espresso - Sabrina Carpenter
Better When I'm Dancin' - Meghan Trainor
Somebody to Love - Austin Giorgio
Cruel Summer - Taylor Swift
Mastermind - Taylor Swift
Bad for Me - Meghan Trainor, Teddy Swims
Don't I Make it Look Easy - Meghan Trainor
You're on your Own, Kid - Taylor Swift
Looking at Me - Sabrina Carpenter
I Wanna Thank Me - Meghan Trainor, Niecy Nash
The Alchemy - Taylor Swift
Sit Still, Look Pretty - Daya
Most Girls - Hailee Steifeld
Me Too - Meghan Trainor
Thumbs - Sabrina Carpenter
Scars to your Beautiful - Alessia Cara
You Belong with Me (Taylor's Version) - Taylor Swift
Who Says - Selena Gomez & the Scene
That's my Girl - Fifth Harmony
Rewrite the Stars - Zac Efron, Zendaya
What Make you Beautiful - One Direction
Goddess - Nation Haven
Numb Little Bug - Em Beihold
Beautiful Things - Benson Boone
Figure you Out - Voila
This is Me - Keala Settle, The Greatest Showman Ensemble
Fight Song - Rachel Platten
Treat You Better - Shawn Mendes
Confident - Demi Lovato
Welcome to New York (Taylor's Version) - Taylor Swift
Love Myself - Hailee Steinfeld

THINGS TO CHECK ON THE SITE FROM THE FUNNEL TO YOU

Sasha and other characters from this book have guest written some blog posts - these include bonus scene conversations, more insight into the videos referenced, and more! They are all on the blog at nikkigrantwrites.com.

Also, Pink Every Day is on the site as well! You'll learn more about this program throughout the book and why Sasha is so passionate about it. As of right now, Pink Every Day isn't totally a reality. But I wanted to bring it to life in my own way. You will find a whole section of Female Owned Brands on my site that you can check out and support. Have another brand that should be added? Message me directly through my website and I will get them added.

Thank you so much for your support and enjoy The Funnel to You!

VLOG POST 127: GET TO KNOW ME

I hate makeup trends.

There, I said it.

Yes, I am a makeup artist and "influencer." I'm still trying on that second one. I love makeup and trying new things. I love creating content around products and techniques and themes.

But, I hate trends.

Why?

Well first, the content becomes so saturated so quickly online. If you don't jump on the trend with a hot take, best sound, or smoothest transitions – it's really hard to get noticed.

Next, products sell out so fast! I'm not big enough yet to get PR boxes, which means I have to buy all my own products. Not complaining about that, again, I love makeup. But I only need so many pink setting powders.

Let me give you an example on that one - last year I had my friend Carter run up to the Ulta in Fort Collins to grab the new

ELF Dunkin' release for me. Don't worry, he offered. But they didn't have the full collection in the store and I missed the online release. So I missed out on the cute straw brushes. Not gonna lie, still bummed about that. When Halo Glow released, I set alarms and was on the site every ten minutes. So yes, I got that release and it is one hundred percent worth the hype.

And finally, trends are just that, trends. As soon as I start feeling comfortable with something new – it isn't in style anymore. 2016 glam, anyone?

But that's okay. Because I love makeup. And I love creating content. I just wish others could love my content too.

Hours every week spent engaging on social media, trying new products, researching trends, recording, editing, uploading…only for 200 views, if I'm lucky.

So, that's where I am right now. On a Saturday morning in a coffee shop in Windsor, Colorado. Uploading the videos for the week ahead and emailing brands trying to get some visibility. I don't want to give this up - but eventually I am going to have to decide if I am going to pursue my "real job" at Home Depot or make this makeup thing happen. Or maybe go after something else entirely.

I just don't know where the next step is going to take me. Maybe this next video will be the one to go viral.

And maybe I will just sit here staring out the window drinking my iced latte. Who knows. At least my lipstick looks good.

Bye babes. Chat soon.

Sasha x
#sashaloveslipstick

Chapter One

SASHA

TOFFEE NUT ICED COFFEE

Social Post: Finishing up some edits and then this girl is going for a walk. Do you think there's room on this water bottle for one more sticker? #coloradogirl #noco #sashaloveslipstick #afternoonwalks

Image Description: Water bottle covered in stickers next to my notebook and laptop.

"What do you mean, it's *gone?!?*"

I am freaking out right now. I uploaded a thirty-minute full makeup tutorial last night and it is gone. I cannot find it. It's not in pending uploads. And it's not in my editing drive either. Where did it go?? This took me hours and I cannot deal with this right now.

Call me basic, but I have to be super strategic about when I record content around my full-time job. And all of those hours of work are now gone.

I take a few deep breaths and look around the room. I'm at home by myself in my apartment. My roommates Kylie and Carter are at work right now so I was taking advantage of the quiet to get some content finalized.

At least that was the plan.

Now I'm trying not to have a full-blown panic attack. I can feel the tightness in my chest growing and the feeling that I need to go run around while also curling into a ball tells me I need to get in front of this quickly before it gets much worse.

"Okay, Sasha, deep breaths. Remember your visual practices. Here we go – three things that are red that I can see."

I glance around the room frantically before I spot my coffee mug.

"There's my mug," Before focusing too hard on the white floral design on my mug, I continue searching for the next item.

"My sparkly pen." Kylie gave that to me when I hit my first 5,000 followers on Instagram. She's bought me a new one at each new milestone. They write perfectly and I love having that reminder of my accomplishments close to me.

"Then there's my favorite lipstick." Is red my all time favorite lipstick color? No. But I enjoy a bold look and this red really makes my features pop.

I feel my heart rate decrease slightly. When my therapist first had me learn grounding practices a few years ago, I thought he was crazy. How can something so simple pull me out of an anxiety attack? But here I am, going through this process – and, it works.

I continue the process by finding things that are soft. My favorite fuzzy socks that I am wearing – hard surface floors mean I am always cold, so socks are a requirement. My purple throw blanket on the couch and then my Estes Park hoodie on the back of my chair finish off that section.

This last one is a suggestion I made to my therapist and he loved it so I incorporated it into my grounding practice – three things that bring me joy.

I see my little crystal elephant on my bookshelf. Its home is right next to my latest reading material – a mix between personal development books and romance books. I just finished a new cowboy series and now have fallen down the rabbit hole of reading everything from that author before I move on to the next author or series.

I walk over to the figurine and hold it in my hand for a moment while I keep looking around for my last two things that bring me joy. The picture on the wall of Carter, Kylie, and myself from our Savannah trip last year catches my attention. That was such a fun week. I miss the beach. Okay, and my coffee mug on my desk again. I focus my eyes there as I go to sit back in my chair.

I finish off by taking a few deep breaths and closing my eyes so I can focus on the feel of my socks and the smoothness of the crystal I still hold in my hand. Maybe I should make more coffee before I start working again.

"No, it's the afternoon – you need to be done with the coffee for today."

Yes, I talk to myself out loud. It's quiet at the apartment right now and I need to process things.

And no, I do not have a coffee problem.

After sitting for a few more minutes and taking myself out of my freak out moment, I'm feeling better. But I am not ready to tackle the video again. I save all the raw footage again, just in case, and grab my hoodie and water bottle then head out the door.

I need to take a walk.

This is probably one of my favorite things about living in Colorado – there are so many places to walk outside and enjoy just being. It's June and the weather is perfect. It's early evening so most people are home having dinner so the trails near the apartment are quiet. Still sunny and dry, but quiet.

I slip in one earbud and turn on my Meghan Trainor playlist and my workout tracker on my phone and start my walk. I'm not sure if this will be a two or three mile walk today, but I will see how I'm doing.

I text Kylie to let her know I am out for a bit and tell her I should be home in an hour or so depending on how things go so she doesn't freak out if I'm not home when she gets off work. I get a little nervous when I leave the house so having someone who knows where I am makes me feel a little safer, even if it's just for a walk. And Kylie tends to be the mom of the three of us. Which works since she and Carter are together. *Finally.* It took a long time for them to admit that they liked each other and they are seriously so cute together.

Is it weird for me? A bit. But for the most part, they keep it pretty PG.

Considering I haven't had an official boyfriend since high school, I appreciate it. Don't get me wrong – I've had a date here or there, but not much after that. Most guys don't really know how to "categorize" me. By day, I work the hardware aisles at Home Depot – and I'm really good at it. At night, I'm full glam and a complete girlie girl – and I'm really good at that too. One date went so far as to call my mood bipolar. I walked out at that one – let's not downplay actual mental health diagnosis, okay? *Rude.*

My passion for makeup gives me the motivation to try to do a "full beat" every day – even at Home Depot. I enjoy makeup and don't feel bad for being dressed up a bit while I'm at work. I feel like it stretches my creativity to find things that work with the orange apron, horrid lighting, and dry air of the store.

I am just not a one category person. And eventually, I will find where I will focus my time and find the person who appreciates it. And at twenty-eight, I hope it's soon. I wouldn't mind being married by thirty-two and a mom by thirty-five…but I'm not stressing about that right now.

Just then my watch buzzes. I check my tracker and see that I have already hit the one-mile mark – that didn't take long. I'm feeling pretty good so I decide to do three miles today. I look ahead and see the next marker so I know when to turn around to head back home.

Now, where was I with the internal monologue?

Ugh, I really just need to give myself a deadline. I am wearing myself out working forty hours a week plus another twenty on content. It was fun in the beginning when I was just sharing my daily makeup looks and trying new products. Once I started seeing what could happen with a social media following – trips, sponsorships, collaborations, product design – that's when I started forming the brand of "Sasha Loves Lipstick."

I tend to work backwards from my goals. It makes it easier for me to set the smaller goals to get to the bigger one. I think once I know my goal date of being done at Home Depot I will be able to create a solid plan for my social media growth and the brands and people I need to connect with.

It's June third today…. what makes sense for a goal date to be able to quit my job?

Early December should be enough time for me to see what happens with my channel and my brand. If I really focus on growth and those brand partnerships that could turn into paid promotions and possibly even positions. How I get in contact with those people is a question that I will have to answer once I get home.

I need to be bringing in actual income on my makeup content or this officially goes to "hobby" and I will focus on Depot. I can't keep doing both with full attention. Something has to give. Being devastated by so much lost work and knowing that I don't have the time or energy to devote to fixing it is not something I want to repeat. I want to be able to work on content with my full attention so things don't get missed and I don't forget to hit the save button.

By having a goal of early December that gives me six months. I can do this, right?

Now that I have a goal in mind, I can focus on finishing my walk, being present to what is around me, drinking my water, and trying not to turn this trail into my own personal dance floor. That's the one problem with a playlist I love – it's my dance party playlist at home, but my workout one as well. I just need to remember where I am right now.

I get back to the apartment an hour after I originally left and grab my favorite notebook and pen then plop myself onto the couch, cozy blanket on my lap. The texture of the blanket helps me to focus on something outside of myself – another grounding technique. It's time to map this out a bit more while the ideas are still fresh.

"Good evening, gorgeous," Kylie says as she walks in the door. She drops her keys and purse on the side table that's covered in take out menus and junk mail before unpinning her name tag from her restaurant polo and adding it to the pile. Her beautiful brown hair sways behind her as she walks over to sit with me on the couch.

I met Kylie during our senior year in college. We were both taking the same class and she started a conversation with me before every class. We hit it off pretty quickly and decided to get a place together after graduation. Both of us had steady jobs and didn't want to move back home – so this was the solution. Carter started bartending at the restaurant a few months after graduation and when Kylie heard that he needed a place to stay, we made it work.

Kylie was one of the first people I did makeup on besides myself. Her skin is tanner than mine so I love using new products on her to see how they pop on her skin compared to mine. And more than just my makeup loving self has noticed her hazel eyes. Depending on her mood, what she is wearing, and even the weather – they change colors! It's every makeup artist's dream.

She just oozes confidence. She owns her beauty and what she does.

"How are you liking the new BB cream I got you?" I ask her as she settles next to me on the couch.

She takes a sip of her water before responding, "It's good. I think I liked the last one a little better. It didn't feel like I was wearing anything on my skin. This one left my skin feeling a little tacky so I may try a different powder over it tomorrow. The restaurant wasn't busy tonight, but it will be busier tomorrow and I don't want to sweat it all off. Gross."

"How was work tonight, besides being slower?" I ask her.

"Decent. I expected it for a Tuesday shift. But I had some regulars so that made it an easy shift, even if the tips were lighter. That also meant I got to sneak a bit more time at the bar with Carter." She winks at me and I just shake my head. "How was your walk? Get the antsy energy out?"

She knows me so well.

"A little. I lost an entire thirty-minute makeup tutorial and had a mini panic attack over it. The walk helped, but I need to map some things out so I can turn this into more than a hobby. I'm giving myself until the beginning of December to actually be bringing money in with this or I'm hitting that Pivot button."

"We have a Pivot button??!" She asks with all the excited sarcasm she can muster after an eight-hour shift on her feet dealing with customers and kitchen staff.

I give her a look that tells her I'm not in the mood before responding.

"You know what I mean, babe. I just can't keep killing myself trying to do everything. I'm exhausted and not able to fully enjoy the makeup content or fully focus on my job because I am thinking about engagement or who to reach out to next. And I don't even remember the last time I was able to go out and just enjoy myself – or go on a date."

"I get it. Let me know if you need to talk anything out. And I'm always happy to be used as a product model. You do magic on my face." She laughs a bit then stands up. "I'm going to go shower before Carter gets home. He's off in like ten minutes and will be bringing home dinner from work."

She pauses to make eye contact with me before continuing, "You're gonna do this Sasha – and we are here to celebrate you every step of the way. Just don't stress about all the details tonight. You work in the morning and you need your beauty rest if you are going to be able to treat Frank with all the grace and kindness you want tomorrow."

I sigh. She's right.

Frank is my boss at work. And he is the epitome of misogynistic, boys do it better, Home Depot is for guys, why is a girl running this department – you get the idea. It took him forever to promote me to department supervisor. The last two times I went in to interview for supervisor roles, a guy was chosen instead. And I've been working there longer and doing more. He made a side comment about how 'men trust men more in a hardware store' and 'it was a better decision in the long run.' It took everything in me to smile and thank him for the opportunity and not totally lose it on him for the unfairness and inequality. He finally promoted me about eight months ago, and guess what, sales are up, customer and employee metrics are up, and I've even managed to grow some of our contractor accounts.

Yep, me. Take that, Frank.

"Okay, I'll tackle this more tomorrow. Thanks for listening, Kylie. Can you ask Carter to grab me an extra salad for lunch tomorrow if he hasn't left work yet? I can Venmo him some dollars for it."

"I already asked him to pick up a Ceasar for you." She blows me a kiss from the end of the hall before ducking into her room.

Kylie and Carter have the master bedroom at the end of the hall and I have the "extra" one. Luckily, we each have our own bathrooms – that definitely makes our mornings easier. And I need my own space for all my makeup. The huge window in my bedroom looking out at the field behind the apartment complex gives me perfect lighting to do my content and lots to look at when I just need to think.

I sit back against the couch for another minute. I just need to figure out a starting point for what to begin working on. I grab my laptop and start Googling.

Thirty minutes later, Carter is walking in the door and I am more overwhelmed than I was when I lost that video. Why are there so many sites that talk about social media growth, being an influencer, starting a website, running a social media campaign, and which foundations will be trending this fall? Okay, that last one was a slight bunny trail on my part, but really, where do I even start with this?

I slam my laptop closed in frustration and put the rest of my things on the coffee table.

"Okay...what did I miss?" Carter asks tentatively as he sets the bags down on the counter. "Do I need to pop back out and grab you some ice cream?" He's been living here long enough to know that I need ice cream right before my cycle starts – it's also when I usually get a bit on the restless side.

"No. I'm good. Thanks for grabbing food. Kylie should be out here soon. I'm just working on a problem and so overwhelmed with how to tackle it." I take a deep breath and make my way over to the bags to help him unpack everything.

"Boy problem, work problem, or makeup problem?"

"When was the last time I had a boy problem, Carter?" I ask him with a bit of a laugh in my voice. It seriously has been way too long. When was the last time I even had a coffee date with someone, much less took someone home? I don't have an answer for that. You have to actually be comfortable going out and meeting people for that. And I don't tend to do that outside of work and I have no desire to pick someone up at Depot.

Internal facepalm.

"No, I'm just trying to figure out how to map out what I need in order to grow my makeup channel into an actual income. I don't even know what I need to do first. I need to take a break from those online searches or I'm going to go crazy. What did you bring home for dinner tonight?" I grab plates and utensils so we can eat as soon as Kylie gets out here. It's approaching nine and I need to get to bed soon. I have to be at work at six tomorrow morning which means up at 4:30. Gross. Yes, I am that girl that tries to do a full face of makeup every day – even at Home Depot.

"I kept it simple tonight – chicken parm, spaghetti, and some of the garlic broccoli you girls love. And your salad, of course."

"Perfect. How much do I owe you for that salad?"

"I really don't know why you keep asking – don't worry about it. I don't have to pay for salads at the end of the night." Carter gives me an amused look and continues setting the containers on the counter.

"I know. I just don't want to assume. You know what they say about 'those people.'" I stage whisper the last two words and he laughs a little under his breath, shaking his head as he starts walking to his room.

Kylie comes out of the room just then and walks over to give Carter a kiss on the cheek and thank him for dinner. She smells like strawberries from her shower and I see the instant Carter smells it too – his eyes zero in on her and he wraps his arms around her. They are just too cute.

"Okay you two. Keep the shenanigans for the bedroom, I'm hungry."

They both laugh at me and we grab our food then sit at the table to eat. We instituted family dinner nights about six months ago. With all the work we do, them dating, family obligations – we still wanted time together. We may not be family by blood, but I see Kylie as my sister. And Carter as my brother. Which makes it weird that they are dating – I can't think about that too deeply. A few nights a week, we have dinner together at the table. No TV, no devices, just us together.

Once we finish eating, we head to the living room and sprawl out a bit – none of us quite ready for bed.

"So, I know you don't want to talk about this a ton tonight, but I wanted to ask while all those Google searches are still fresh." Carter starts then grabs out a notebook. "What do you think is the first thing you need in order to make this turn into money for you? Just start talking and I'll make some notes for you."

He really is the best. We've done this a few times whenever one of us is working through something. Someone is the note taker and we just all talk it out until we have enough to make a game plan.

I get up from my seat and pace a bit then move to the kitchen to get a cup of tea. I need to do something with my hands. And I may be a coffee addict, but even I know that I have to switch to tea at some point if I want to get any sleep. I'm not twenty-one anymore. Unfortunately.

"Well, nothing can happen until I get more visibility. I know my content is good. I love what I do and the feedback I get is good. There just isn't enough of it. I don't know how to get more people seeing my content without posting twenty times a day or spending an hour just on commenting and networking and I don't have the time or energy for that. I am NOT paying for followers or engagement. I looked at hiring someone to help me map things out, but the rates are insane. I just need to get more people seeing what I have…" The kettle starts boiling so I add hot water to my mug where my tea bag is already hanging out and then come sit back down. I already have a little tea bag holder on my side table so I can put the tea bag on there when it's done steeping.

"So, you need a funnel?" Kylie asks from the floor. She's on her phone looking at stuff. "This website says that one way to get more people seeing your online content is to create a funnel – a reason for them to get to your content and an easy way to do that."

"But how do I do that?" I ask her.

"I don't know, but that does make sense. Maybe talking to someone who does this all the time will help you know where to start." She continues scrolling through on her phone for a few minutes while I play with my tea bag and Carter doodles in his notebook. I really lucked out with these two. It's not just my problem to deal with. They are taking on part of it for themselves too.

"When you two decide to get married and get your own place, I vote we still have family dinners at least once a week." I say very matter of factly then take the tea bag out of my tea and blow off the steam.

They both look at me with amused looks on their faces. I know Carter is going to be proposing sometime soon. And Kylie knows too. Their anniversary is in the spring, so probably next March or April if I had to guess.

"That's not even up for negotiation." Kylie tells me. "Oh look, there are these guys called 'funnel experts' or 'content visibility specialists' and a few of them offer free consultations to see if they are a good fit. I'm going to send you a few of these to look over tomorrow, because it is fast approaching bed time and we need to cap this conversation or you will never sleep."

"Perfect! Thank you both so much." My phone begins dinging with messages from both Kylie and Carter – links to the expert websites, an article to read on funnel types, and a picture of the notebook paper that Carter has been working with. They really are amazing.

I finish my tea while Kylie loads the dishwasher and then we all head to bed.

I go through my nighttime routine and get on my pajamas then crawl into bed. I plug in my phone, set my alarm, and then turn the screen upside down. The fan is on so I have my white noise going. But I don't want a distraction. I need to leave this problem for tomorrow. I can only worry so much about this. I mentally go on my walk again in order to settle down and eventually drift off…4:30 is going to come early and with that a full day of work and the dive into figuring out what the heck a funnel is.

Sasha
x
#sashaloveslipstick

Chapter Two

SASHA

BUTTER PECAN COLD BREW WITH COLD FOAM AND FRENCH VANILLA

Social Post: OOTD for work at the Depot today. I'm seriously debating a petition to opt out of the orange aprons, because how cute is this?? #depotday #ootd #sashaloveslipstick

Image Description: Mirror selfie before I head out to work! Minus the apron.

Today is overwhelming.

I really have no other thought about today than that. Everyone has been having issues with the scan guns and our inventory is off on some of our most popular items. I haven't been able to put any mental energy into the whole makeup, social media, and funnel problems. Which just means I am stressed and freaking out. I am not the kind of person to put issues on the back burner until later in the day. It just sits in the back of my mind until it turns into a migraine or a tummy ache – or both.

Today, it's both.

I only have an hour left in my shift and my favorite contractor is coming in soon to review his order for a job he's starting next week. I've been working with Ryan for years and I am his favorite. I'm not full of myself – he's told me this. And he brings me coffee, so I'm not complaining.

Just before Ryan is set to come in, Frank comes up with a customer order in hand.

"Can you please pull this before you leave?" He hands it to me and immediately turns around.

"Frank, I really don't have time for this today." I go to hand it back to him. "I'm buried with the inventory glitches and I have a meeting with my contractor in twenty minutes that I need to have stuff pulled for."

Frank looks more frustrated than I feel today. His dark hair is damp with sweat at his hairline and his normal polo is untucked and covered in dirt. This man doesn't know how to handle pressure and has a minor meltdown if he has to actually come onto the floor to get work done. And apparently, he just came from the garden department by the looks of the dirt on his clothes.

"What all is in the order?" I ask him. Hoping I can at least give him some direction and he can't say I'm totally bailing on him. Although, we have two full time order pickers – why is he asking me about this?

"It's a whole bunch of random nuts and bolts. Literally one or two of twenty different pieces. And then a few basic household things like a screwdriver. It looks like someone is building a dresser or something and they aren't sure what is needed but also doesn't want to come in and look at things so they ordered one of all of the options"

I have to hold back a chuckle. That used to be me.

"Hand it over. I'll get it done. That won't take me long, but I do need to be left alone during my meeting with Ryan when he gets in. I have to finish these orders with him or he is going to miss deadlines."

Frank gives me a head nod and then walks back to his office. I seriously wonder why it takes him so long to do those reports each week. Maybe he needs an assistant.

I get all the parts pulled in ten minutes. Luckily, everything was pretty close together. I bring it up to the service desk and get it keyed into the system as ready for pickup. It's for a guy named Luca. That's a new one.

Right on time, Ryan walks in with my iced green tea matcha latte and a notebook. Ooooh, and a new pen! Yay me. We head over to the desk in millworks (doors, windows, all that stuff) and go over his latest order.

"You don't seem like your normal happy self today, Sasha. What's up?" Ryan asks after we get through the majority of the hardware order. Today he's in his signature paint covered light denim jeans and a black tee shirt. Nothing fancy, but it works. His dad handles most of the customer and client interactions and Ryan handles the actual physical work alongside his team. And the Depot trips. I'm the one that tends to get dressed up every day.

Today, I am in my black dress slacks, my sparkly silver flats, a floral blouse and a black cardigan. Plus some super cute silver jewelry. My hair is pulled back in a pink headband that matches with some of the florals on my shirt as well as my lipstick. It contrasts my deep brown hair well. I went with a subtle pink shimmer eye look today that works well with my brown eyes. I don't usually do a full glam makeup look on regular work days – I save those for corporate visits and presentation days.

"It's fine– I'm trying to figure out how to work more intentionally on the makeup account I've been growing so that it can actually turn into something where I'm making money off of it. Right now, I'm pouring a lot of attention and time into content and products and it's not really turning into much yet. I love what I get to do, but it would be nice for it to be bringing me at least a bit of free product. I only get so many new viewers because of contacts here, ya know?" I say with a bit of sass.

Ryan has been working with me for a while so he knows I am growing my makeup accounts. His wife is one of my followers and I've had the chance to do her makeup a couple of times on my channel. The connection has been good, but it isn't what I need.

"What are you looking to do to change that? I know you don't want to be here working with contractors forever."

"I have a few consultants I am planning to connect with after my shift today – trying to bring more people to my channel. I know my content is good, I just need people to see it. I'm almost done with my new paint sample inspiration looks and I want to get that series up next month. I would hate to have all of those videos flop."

"You recorded the one with the orange paint sample I picked out, right?" He immediately replies. He knows I hate the color orange. The apron I have to wear every day seriously limits the clothing and makeup choices I can do and the color does nothing for my decidedly white, winter, cool skin tone. I make do though. I understand that it's important to wear what you love and what you feel good in. And for me, orange ain't it.

"Yes, I'm not happy about it, but I think I made it work. I'm planning to do that sample for one of the first videos so my pinks and purples can really shine. By the way, have you finished the Windsor job yet? I got your punch list supplies delivered last Friday, but haven't heard from you on if that was all you ended up needing." I start pulling out the most recent purchase receipts so we can go over the items and get everything finalized on this job.

We get back to work and finish up ten minutes before it's time for me to clock out. New parts are ordered and an email has been sent to my window guy asking about timelines on a new project starting after the Windsor one wraps up. For my contractors that I've been with a lot, I do more than just their hardware orders. I'm not commission based, but taking care of my guys is really important to me. I like being able to take care of everything from the studs to the shingles and everything in between. And the free coffee, pens, and occasional new water bottle isn't too bad either.

After work, I head home to begin my afternoon routines. I'm in my room, in my comfy clothes, tea in hand, by 4:30 PM. I sent out the form responses to the different websites and experts when I got home and now I'm just waiting on the responses.

I grab my dinner from the fridge after finishing editing one of the blue makeup videos. Getting up and doing something else while I have a long editing session is important to me and helps me avoid headaches. When it feels like I have taken enough time away from my laptop, I head back to my desk. Time to see if any of the consultants replied to my inquiries. It's only been a few hours, but I'm hopeful.

"Please let this work." I whisper to myself as I begin checking them out.

After glancing through the first few replies, I realize how overwhelming this is going to be.

The quotes are outrageous and they want all of this stuff already done to make it happen. I don't even know where to begin. Apparently, I need more help than just a few buttons clicked on a website or my email list. This is going to be an actual project – like runway glam makeup look project level. Well, maybe more than that, but that's the idea. This isn't a "touch up in the car" thing that I can just wing on my way to work. I need this to be intentional.

And they're all form responses. Did any of them actually read my email or check out my content?

An hour and ten proposals later, I am ready to just say "screw it" and close my laptop. But one last reply catches my eye.

Re: Makeup Channel Views

From: Matthew Carter, Website Funnels LLC

The Funnel to You

Hey Sasha,

Thanks so much for reaching out. I took some time this evening to look over your social media, website, and YouTube Channel. It seems like you have some great content, even though it's not geared towards my specific demographic.

I've been working with other micro influencers for a few years and I would love the chance to chat and see if I am a good fit.

I've attached my calendar so you can set up a time that works for you so we can hop on Zoom and discuss. This won't be a sales call – just a time to talk through some options to see what would work best for you.

I look forward to hearing from you.

I have also linked a few other client accounts so you can see the sequence from their social channels to their websites to their other items that they offer so you can see the work I have done.

Have a great rest of your evening,

Matt

Hmmm. Okay Matt, you actually took time to look at my content, so let's give you a shot. I look over his calendar and book a slot for tomorrow evening. Then, I take a look at the accounts he linked.

One is a lifestyle blogger, another is a fitness expert, and another is apparently obsessed with kombucha. But they all have clean feeds, easy to navigate links, and I end up subscribing to everything they have. I don't even really like kombucha, but I'm intrigued.

What magic does this man possess? And how much is this going to cost me?

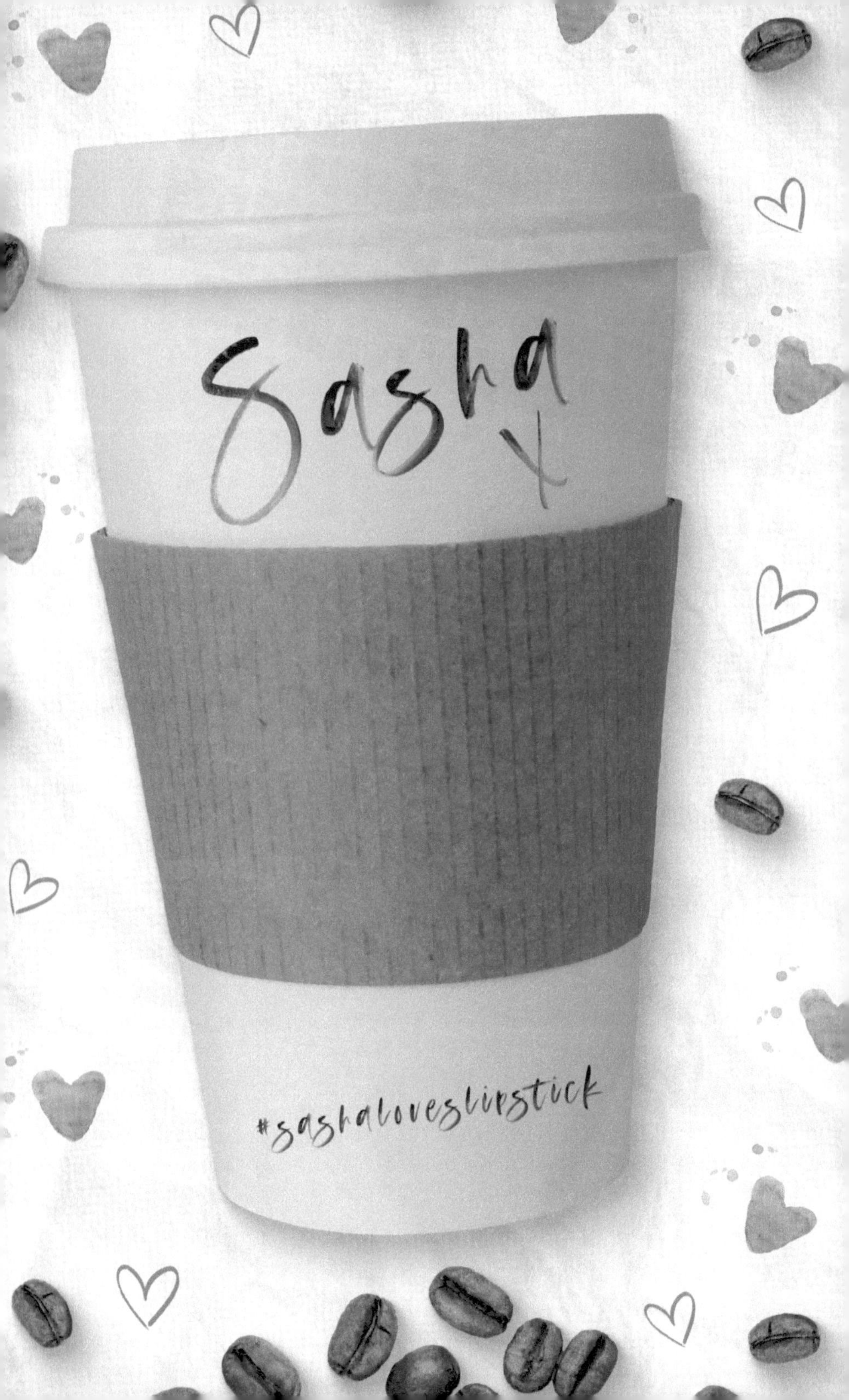
Sasha
x
#sashaloveslipstick

Chapter Three

MATT

HAZELNUT TRUFFLE MACCHIATO

I get the notification that I have a new booking – it's Sasha. I sit back in my chair and take a deep breath. I've been following Sasha on social media (through my sister) for several years. I have been interested in her for a while, but had no idea on how to approach her without coming across as the "creepy guy on the other side of the screen." I have a younger sister and she gets enough of those messages that I knew I didn't want to come across that way to Sasha. Her content is always on my sister's phone and in her stories, so I feel like I already know her a little bit. And I may have seen her out and about in town a few times. I never approached her, because again, I don't want to be creepy.

Getting the inquiry on my site was like a huge "green light" when it came through. And the fact that she liked my initial proposal, I feel like doing an end zone celebration dance – and I don't play sports, or dance for that matter. Okay, I have about twenty-four hours to finish looking through her content and make an intriguing plan. Good thing I'm already really familiar with her content and her voice (the way she talks and engages on social media) so I can really streamline this to her. And my sister is going to freak out when I tell her who I get to connect with.

Ashley is nineteen, five years younger than me, and although we don't live together anymore, we talk all the time. And she's always sending me makeup videos to show the latest trends or how things can combine to create a totally different look than what the artist started with. I may be a tech and business nerd, but it does fascinate me still. Have you seen what some of these makeup artists can do? And it makes Ashley happy. I've been watching the content that Sasha puts out for the past year regularly. And I've even gone out of my way to check out her social media channels in that time period. She draws you in during each video, each post, each email and it feels like she is talking to each viewer individually.

I feel like I already know Sasha. Her obsession with a good pen, never having enough lipsticks in her purse, and always down for a good walk on the local trails. Which, apparently, are some of the same ones I frequent.

I figured out a while ago that we live fairly close to each other and I shop in the same stores and walk the same trails. Not that I would ever have the courage to go up and talk to her if I saw her in person. She is definitely what my sister calls "model status." And I am the epitome of nerd, geek, and unsociable. You know, the guy in high school that was always off on his own reading or working on his laptop? That was me.

I'm average height at just a couple inches shy of six feet, I have dark brown hair and brown eyes and am built like a football player. I started breaking the geeky persona fully a couple years ago when I got my first tattoo. I'm now working with a half sleeve and really like how it's coming together. For Ashley's nineteenth birthday we actually went together. I got a few more roses to the end of my sleeve and she got some script work started. We'll see if that tradition sticks around for her birthdays in future years. At least it fits with my overall build and Ashley says I "pull it off well".

I'm pretty solid and am not afraid to work with my hands when needed, but prefer a computer problem to solve. Or grow social media accounts now apparently. I started working with some friends a few years ago and realized I was really good at this. Then referrals started coming in. And it's just grown from there. My business is at the point now where I can choose which clients to work with. I don't have to take on every job that comes my way and that lets me work on those projects that I really love. And maybe I can start looking to add in someone to help me with some tasks soon if this growth keeps up.

But this is one client I want to work with. I want to see her succeed. And however I can help her do that, I'm going to.

The next morning, I get up and finish the business proposal for Sasha before I go for a walk. I know she is working right now (thank you IG stories), so I go on the path by my house. I take this path for inspiration, clarity, and just knowing I am in the same space as her helps me focus on what I want to accomplish today.

I have about nine hours until our call and I am more nervous than I usually am for these calls. I usually approach business plan pitches and meetings with a sense of authority – I'm good at what I do. I get results and I know it works for my clients if they have good content. If they turn down my proposal, it's okay. The clients I should work with will come to me.

I don't pressure.

I don't push.

I don't beg.

I don't manipulate.

And I really don't want to start with Sasha. But, I *really* want this job.

I end up walking down the street until I get to my parent's

house – only a little over two miles away from my own home. I didn't call ahead so I'm not sure if Ashley is home, but I'd love to see her if she is. She's off for summer break from college. She is studying business at CSU and will be pursuing her esthetics license after graduation. So, I know working with Sasha is going to be something I'll be able to talk to her about.

I use my key and let myself in.

"Anyone home?" I holler as I walk in, take off my shoes, and head to the kitchen. There's a fresh bouquet of flowers on the island in the kitchen next to a new wooden cutting board my mom got at the farmers market last week. The space is bright and airy, even with the lights all being off. I love how much natural night is in this space. I get a glass of water from the sink and then grab a seat on one of the bar stools at the island.

Ashley comes into the kitchen to refill her coffee mug. She already has her favorite travel mug in hand so she can drink her coffee in her bedroom upstairs without worrying about it cooling down too fast. Her dark blonde hair is pulled back in a headband that tells me she was in the middle of a skincare video most likely.

"Why are you awake and out of the house this early in the morning? It's summertime and you work for yourself – sleep in while you can." She whines at me. She likes to sleep in and take it easy when she isn't in classes. I don't blame her, but if I don't get started with my morning at a decent time, the day just feels off.

"You are never going to guess who I have a business proposal call with tonight." I reply as I finish my water and place the glass in the sink next to a few spoons and mugs left over from my parent's breakfast probably. I add a bit of sarcasm into my voice hoping to intrigue her enough to join in on the conversation.

My sister just stares at me. Clearly not in the mood to play twenty questions. Once she gets fully started with her day, she is a very outgoing person who can talk to anyone. She has never met a stranger and loves making everyone feel comfortable around her. She loves word puzzles and brain teasers too, like twenty questions. I guess we haven't had enough coffee yet to necessitate that.

"I'll give you a hint – 'Always keep your purse full of happy pens and pretty lipstick.'" I prompt her, trying to act indifferent as

I finish the line, making it a point to pull out my phone and start scrolling to try to minimize how excited I am about this.

She stares at me for a moment and then I look up to see her eyes register what I just said. She screams and starts jumping up and down.

"Shut up!! You do not! Sasha? Seriously?? How is this happening? What is the plan? What does she need? Can I help? Can I meet her?" And then more screaming.

I laugh as she continues bouncing up and down in front of me – thankfully, she places the coffee mug down on the counter before reaching out to grab my arm. That would have been quite the mess to clean up in my parent's kitchen. And one I would probably end up taking care of.

"I do. Yes, it's Sasha. I'm totally serious. I have a pretty good website and she asked for a consult. I spent several hours last night and then some time this morning working on her proposal and I don't think you can meet her yet. It might be weird to start off my proposal by asking for a favor." I replied – hoping I answered all of her questions.

"I cannot believe this. Sasha is one of my favorite influencers! I would love the chance to collaborate with her as I continue growing my own channels. She's got amazing content, but I know she doesn't have a ton of time to devote to her content while she works full time. What are you planning to talk to her about tonight?"

"Yes, I know. Hence why I think she is reaching out – she wants this to be bigger too. And I really hope I can help her get there." I give her a smile. Part of me hopes that in partnering with Sasha my business will grow too. This will branch out into a new category for my business. And it will help Ashley out as she continues to grow into her own brand too. And selfishly, having some time to get to know Sasha without a screen between us is quite enticing too.

"I have a plan worked up for our conversation tonight, but wanted to see if you had any other things to share that might be helpful. You have been following her for a while and I want to make sure I help her where she most needs it right now."

"Okay, so you already know that makeup is something she first started playing with as something to do for herself when she got out on her own. She started working at Home Depot in college and enjoyed working at the store but kept getting passed over for promotions – honestly, probably because she's a girl. She didn't have the best home situation from what I can gather from her content. But she focuses on a lot of 'ready to go' looks."

"And remind me what that means," I prompt her to continue.

"She does a lot of things that fit with an everyday girl's budget and time table. Most of the products she uses are from brands that are affordable and last a long time and have a lot of versatility to them."

"That makes sense. So why hasn't she gotten brand deals or a huge following? It seems like she has a great niche there."

"She had to stop posting for a while. Work was too demanding and then she had to take a mental health break. She's made a few videos talking about her anxiety and how that has affected her content and her job. She hit burnout trying to do everything so she had to find a better balance. Since she stopped posting for close to a year, she lost a lot of momentum and has struggled with getting back on top of things again. She also doesn't hop on trends quickly, again because of the anxiety. She's done some posts about the longevity of classic makeup and it isn't sustainable to jump on every trend or every collection drop from a brand. That might have gotten her pulled from a few lists for free stuff."

"That makes sense. Knowing that background helps because I can focus on brands that target classic looks and everyday collections rather than trendy collaborations."

"Exactly. You got this, Matt. You're going to do great tonight."

"I am going to head home and shower and then get ready for my call. I've got a Zoom meeting booked for five tonight. Wish me luck. And no," I stop her before she even starts with her next request, "you may not come home with me to listen while I have my call with her."

She humphs a sigh at me and stomps her feet like she's going to throw a mini temper tantrum. She walks over to give me a hug, then decides against it once she sees how sweaty I am.

"Okay, you are gross – definitely take a shower. But thank you for telling me. I can't wait to hear how it goes. You are going to cut her a deal if cost is a problem, right? I'd seriously love to see her account take off. She deserves it. Especially with all the crap she's had to deal with over the last few years at work and starting out on her own."

Like I said, my sister is a huge fan.

"I'll do my best. Love you, Ash."

I head out the door and jog back home. I have a few hours to make this perfect. And I cannot blow this proposal. Not just for my business, or my sister, but for me too.

Chapter Four

SASHA

ICED SHAKEN ESPRESSO WITH VANILLA

Social Post: What platforms do you most utilize when you are looking at makeup and skincare content? #sashaloveslipstick #socialmedia #beautyblogger

Image Description: Light purple background with "I have a question" text on the square.

Today was better than yesterday at work, thankfully. I got the order done for Ryan and was able to redo some of the inventory issues we had yesterday. How someone could mix up PVC and CPVC, I have no idea, but that's what happened. It only took an hour out of my day to figure out the problem, adjust the counts, and get the labels fixed on the shelf. Looking at things, you wouldn't be able to tell I did anything, but I know what I completed, and the fact that the only girl supervisor in the store figured out the issue…yeah, that's a win in my book.

I make it home from work and go over the email from Matt again. I want to make sure I know what to expect on this call so I don't totally sound clueless. Content is something I understand. Makeup I totally get. But getting the right people to see my content and then go to my website to work with me in some capacity is something I need help with. And I don't want to be taken advantage of by someone just trying to sell me something.

I take a quick shower and throw my hair up in a bun before grabbing my favorite cardigan and do a quick and natural makeup look. Something that I know will look good on camera but won't be weird for an early evening business call.

I grab out my phone to text Kylie and Carter before I log on to my computer.

Me: About to get on a call, do you guys need anything first?

Kylie: All good here. I should be home from work in about an hour. Deep breaths. Take lots of notes. Can't wait to hear all the things!

Carter: Nope. Have fun. See you when we get home.

With that, I put my phone on silent and go grab my tea and water from the other room. Yes, I always have multiple drinks in front of me when I am working. I get the email confirmation pulled back up and then click the button to join the call.

"Here goes nothing." I whisper to myself as I wait for him to join the call.

Matt logs in a minute before our scheduled call time. I notice right away how handsome he is. I can't tell how tall he is from the computer screen, but his hair and eyes are the most comforting shade of brown. Comforting? No clue why that is the word I am drawn to, but there it is. He has a bit of scruff on his face, like a five o'clock shadow, and it makes him look the perfect amount of not perfect. As he adjusts a few things on his laptop, I notice a few tattoos on his arms. It looks like he is in the process of building out a sleeve on one arm and just a few small things on the other one. It's hard to make out everything without coming across as staring at him though.

"Hey, Sasha. Thanks for meeting with me," Matt says as he starts the call officially. He seems a lot more soft-spoken than I thought he would be. But I guess that makes sense if he works on computers and social media most of the time. It would be kind of weird if he was super bubbly and over excited for this meeting. That might actually freak me out a bit. "I hope work was good for you today. I saw your stories yesterday about the inventory issue."

"It was good. I got a lot done at work today and was able to get out on time so I didn't have to stress about being home before our call. Thanks again so much for looking over my content and getting back to me. You were the only response that came back that looked like you actually knew what I did and am looking to do. Makeup is definitely my passion and I want to share it with more people, but so many just see it as a hobby or something cute I do on the side. It's so much more than that to me." I respond to his initial question, then take a deep breath. I don't want to totally dump all of my emotions onto this guy that I just met. Online even. I haven't even met him in person. I don't want to come across as desperate, but I need him to know this is serious to me.

"I can tell this is important to you. Full transparency, my sister has been watching your channel and content for a while, so I recognized your name when you sent the initial email over. So, I was already familiar with your content and what you do. Do you mind if I ask you a few questions to get a feel for what you are wanting to do and your timeline and then we can go from there?"

Okay, I was not expecting that response. A guy that actually pays attention when his sister talks to him about makeup? That's new. Maybe this will work out.

"Yeah, that's fine. It's awesome that your sister likes my content. Tell her I said 'hello' when you chat with her next." I feel myself blushing a bit and continue on quickly. "What questions do you have for me?"

Over the next fifteen minutes, Matt asks me questions about my background, my training, who inspires me, my favorite type of content, my least favorite type of content, what platforms I use, my website, my goals…all of it. I'm surprised at the level of questions, but at the same time, I am feeling more at ease knowing he is really getting to know me and what I do and what I want to do. I'm not just another number to him or a client checkbox. He's listening. Like, *really* actually listening.

"So, why now?" He looks at me through the screen. "You've been doing this for a while and juggling work and social life and being casual with your content. Why are you now wanting to turn this into income that you can grow and make a full-time thing?" He says it casually, no malice, no judgment, just asking another question.

"I'm ready." I respond matter of factly. "It was kind of triggered a few days ago when I lost an entire video I had spent hours on and realized I didn't have the time or mental energy to redo it. I want the space to work this like a business during set hours and then 'clock out' so I can enjoy my friends and family and things going on around here in town. I haven't been able to explore or hike nearly as much as I want to and I missed so much this spring because I just didn't have the time. Home Depot has been fun, but I'm done trying to juggle both my job and my passion. And I love makeup. So much. And I want to share this passion with others."

I take another breath and then a sip of my now cold tea then set it back down and wait for him to finish taking his notes and give me his response.

"Okay, I got it. I think I can help you. Can I take the rest of the evening to work up a game plan and then email you in the morning? I don't want to rush this or you into a decision here, but I definitely think I can make this happen."

"Just like that?"

"Yep, just like that. Do you have any other questions for me or anything else I need to know?" He asks then waits patiently for my response.

I am honestly caught off guard. I was expecting a hard pitch or an astronomical quote from him after being on Zoom with him for over forty minutes. But no, he is giving me the space I need, even though I didn't ask him for it. Okay, I really hope his quote isn't outrageous because I want to work with Matt.

"Nope. I think I have everything I need on my end. I'll wait for your email tomorrow. Feel free to email or message me if anything else comes up in the meantime that you need from me. I am working on that new color series that should be ready to go in a couple of weeks fully. If you can let me know if we should focus on that first or wait as part of the first thing we work on together that would be great."

He smirks a bit and I realize I just agreed to work with him without him asking or even seeing a quote. *Internal face palm.* Oh well, can't take that back now.

"Sounds good." He responds. "I know that's something you are looking forward to since it combines both of the main things you do right now. I appreciate your time tonight. Have a good night, Sasha." And with that, he ends the call.

I sit back and take a deep breath, cap my pen, and finish my tea.

Now, I wait.

Chapter Five

SASHA

HONEY CINNAMON COLD BREW

Social Post: When you aren't feeling your best, find one thing that you can control to help yourself feel better. Today, that's comfy socks and a face mask before I shower for me. What about you? #sashaloveslipstick #selfcaretips #comfyday

Image Description: wrapper from my face mask on the bathroom counter along with showing my fuzzy socks on my feet in the background.

I head out to the main living area and see that Kylie and Carter aren't home yet so I grab myself something little for dinner and settle in for a movie while I wait for them. I go over the conversation with Matt in my head. Did I mess up any part of my background story or my short term goals? Did I come across as too apathetic or too eager?

There were so many points in my growing up years when I wanted to dive into something new and I was questioned on it so much that I began to question myself. I wasn't allowed to just pick a hobby or even something to read without having to answer potentially dozens of questions.

Why that one?

What is your goal with this choice?

Do you have time for that?

Is that really the best use of your time?

What could this lead to later on?

Does that conflict with something else you've already done?

You get the idea. I wasn't able to just make a choice and then move ahead with that decision. I learned to constantly second guess my desires and choices. Now I deal with anxiety over every little choice, and even more so when it affects other people – like a job change or a public outing.

This decision to move forward with my makeup channel is beyond nerve wracking. What if this doesn't work? What if my parents finally decide to look at my content and then start messaging me all of those questions all over again? What if I quit Home Depot and then have to go in a year from now asking for my job back?

No, stop. I can't dwell on this. I've already thought through all of this. I want to do this. It brings me joy and I love sharing makeup content. And Matt says he can help me. I have to trust that.

I wonder who his sister is. I pull out my phone and login to Instagram and search his name.

Nothing. *Weird.*

What about his business name? Okay, found that. How am I going to find his sister if he doesn't have a personal account? Time to start some social media stalking. I feel like most millennial women are experts at this. I spend the next thirty minutes going over his posts – the comments and likes - to see if I can find someone that looks like him with the same last name. Finally, I think I found her. Ashley Carter. OMG! This girl has been on my page for forever. She is the sweetest thing and is super supportive. I love that I recognize who this is. That's going to make this a lot easier if this ends up working out.

Would it be weird if I followed her back now after talking to her brother? I don't know why I hadn't already followed her. We've even chatted in DM's a few times. Maybe I'll wait a few days so that way it isn't weird. If Matt told her about our meeting tonight, I don't want him to be uncomfortable by my social media stalking. I shake my head and then put my dishes in the dishwasher and go wash my face. I take a quick picture for my stories: *"don't forget to take off your makeup"* is the easy caption I put on the picture.

With that done, I hear Kylie and Carter get back to the apartment and I go to fill them in on the call and my stalking. After going through everything with them, I pull out my phone to set my alarm for tomorrow morning before I forget. I don't have to work tomorrow, but I want to try to go for a walk in the morning before it gets too hot. My routine is slightly thrown off with the call and then the overthinking afterwards.

"Can I see his sister since I can't see him?" Kylie asks with a smirk. I shake my head but give her my phone anyway. She scrolls for a while until she finds what she is looking for. "Girl, Matt is hot! No offense, babe." She looks at Carter who just shakes his head and laughs. He's used to our shenanigans at this point. "And did you see this, they are local."

"Like, how local?" I ask and take my phone back from her to see what post she is looking at. It's Ashley and Matt with a few other people at my favorite coffee shop in town. How did I not notice that or the location tag on the photos before? "No freaking way. Do you think he knows? That's like really close. What if we run into each other? Do I get to ask him business questions out and about or pretend we don't know each other? Do I introduce myself or will that be weird?" I take a moment to figure out what other questions I should be asking.

"Chill. It's fine. We knew he was in Colorado, but didn't know he was in Windsor. It's a big city. If you see him in person, say hey, and go from there. And you haven't seen his proposal yet, so this may all be a totally moot conversation," Carter says – always the voice of reason. He's been with Kylie long enough that he knows how to talk either of us down from a spiral or a freak out – it was my turn apparently.

"You're right. It's all good. Totally fine. Although I really want to work with him. He seems to actually want to help me – not just have me as a client. And him knowing my content already really helps." I scroll on Ashley's feed for another moment. "You have got to be kidding me!" I yell a little too loudly and instantly lower my volume as I look at my friends. "She is going to CSU for business and has a few things here about wanting to add her esthetician license after graduation. Okay, I really hope I get to meet her now. This is awesome."

Carter laughs a bit. "I'm running to Dairy Queen – you need a Blizzard." He grabs his keys and walks out the door after giving Kylie a quick forehead kiss.

"What just happened?" I ask Kylie.

"Girl, you need to chill. Sit down and take a few breaths. And I'm pretty sure you are set to start your cycle like tomorrow with the way you are acting," She walks back from the front door where she locked the door after Carter left.

"None of this is weird unless you make it weird. And meeting Ashley would be great, but don't tell Matt you went full on stalker mode tonight. And go change into your comfy jammies because you are stressing me out." She smiles at me and goes to start the kettle again so we can have tea while waiting for Carter to get back to the apartment.

By the time he gets back, I've changed, had another cup of tea, and you guessed it, started my cycle. I curl under my blanket and enjoy my ice cream. Tomorrow is going to need to be a chill day now so I'm glad I have the day off. I go to bed with my favorite pair of socks on, my heating pad, and Taylor Swift on my playlist.

"Talk to you tomorrow, Matt. Me, please don't be weird." I whisper to myself and then cuddle in and drift off to sleep.

Sasha x
#sashaloveslipstick

Chapter Six

SASHA

CARAMEL HAZELNUT ICED LATTE

Social Post: I do not want to do anything today! Anyone else ever have one of those days? I'm seriously debating just grabbing the next book in the series I'm reading and staying in bed today. #sashaloveslipstick #todaysmood #coloradogirl

Image Description: Clock next to my bed showing 7:05, nightstand also has a book that I am currently reading in between all of the craziness of work and content.

The next morning, I wake up at seven with my alarm and immediately roll out of bed looking for coffee. Day one of my cycle is never a fun time and I am achy and cranky and I did not sleep well. Coffee then shower then back to bed. For once, my work schedule lines up with a day I desperately need off. Guess I won't be going for that walk this morning though.

It's not until thirty minutes later after my coffee and shower that

I remember I need to check my email. Should I wait until eight? He wouldn't have already sent something would he?

I login to my email from my phone. I don't want to get out of bed to get my laptop right now. And yep, there it is. He emailed me right at 7 this morning. At least I'm more awake now than I was before my shower to go through the proposal from him.

Inside is a pretty proposal done up with outlines and timelines and goal dates and even a sample content calendar. It's even in my brand colors – this man did his research. He has several ideas for funnel topics and how to tie them into my current and planned content as well as a full email sequence mapped out. Matt was not joking when he said he had a plan. Oh, and there is a calendar of brands to reach out to as well. This is way more than I wanted. I am seriously scared to see what the quote is going to be here. I keep scrolling until I get to the end with the dollar signs and fees listed.

That cannot be right. I blink and scroll through the whole thing again. Nope, that is right. $500 setup fee and then a special note at the end.

"Hey Sasha,

It was great meeting with you yesterday. I spent some time last night finalizing this proposal and I wanted to offer you something for this. Instead of my normal rates, would you be willing to do a mentorship with my sister? She will be starting her sophomore year in college this fall and wants to do what you are doing. This will give her a chance to get some hands-on experience as well as help me cater a business plan for an established channel (yours) and one just starting (hers).

I know this isn't what we talked about last night, but I think this will help both of you out and will put her in a great position to launch her career.

Let me know what questions you have and if you are open to this. If not, I totally understand. I can refigure the quote to reflect my standard work rates.

I look forward to hearing from you.

Matt"

I don't hesitate to respond back.

"Does your sister know this is part of your proposal to me? I don't want her to be blindsided and I don't want to put her in an awkward

situation if she doesn't want to do this.

Sasha"

He responds just a few moments later.

"Good morning, Sasha

Yes. I talked to her about the proposal last night if you were up to the idea. I told her it wasn't a guarantee, but wanted to see if she would be interested if you were up for the mentorship program. She already has about twenty different questions and ideas to go over with you. Like I said last night, she really enjoys your content. But again, don't feel pressured to say yes. Whatever you are comfortable with will be fine with her and I look forward to the opportunity to work with you.

Matt"

I take a deep breath and put my phone down for a moment then go see if my roommates are here and awake. They are both sitting at the table enjoying their coffee and chatting quietly.

"So, I got my email back from Matt." I say softly then pass over my phone to Kylie. They look over the proposal and their eyebrows raise at the same time when they get to the bottom.

"Um, how do you feel about this, babe?" Kylie asks me. I can tell she isn't sure about this, and honestly, I don't know how to feel about it either.

"Do you guys have any input? Because part of me is like 'absolutely, where do I sign?' and part of me is like 'this feels borderline taking advantage of the situation' – maybe for both of us. Or am I totally overreacting to this? I mean, this package is fantastic, and looking at his other clients, I know he knows what he is talking about. I'm too tired to think this through on my own." I huff out and then take a seat. Carter gets up to refill my coffee mug and I can tell he's thinking over his response.

"Do you want to mentor his sister and work with her?" He asks me. "Totally separate that from the rest of the proposal. If the opportunity came up to work with someone just getting started, would that be something you would want to do?"

"I'm not opposed to it. I don't really know her. Just the bit we have talked on social media the last couple of years. She seems really sweet and the connection is a good one to have."

"How long would the mentorship last?"

"Not sure on that one – let me ask." I pull out my phone and ask Matt. His response doesn't take long to come in.

"However long we want to set it up for. We can do six months or until she graduates and you two decide to open your own business together. (That last part was tongue in cheek by the way, totally up to you where you two go with this.)" Matt responds quickly.

"There's that." I show them my phone.

"I say go for it. This opportunity is huge and the mentorship will add another layer of what you do. Maybe it will turn into another service you provide – an internship opportunity virtually or in person to someone once a year. It doesn't sound like anything too major. Maybe a Zoom call once a week or so and then a meetup or two. It doesn't have to be a big deal. You are helping her out, she's helping you out, you're helping him out, he's helping you out…it's all the winning we talked about last night." Kylie finishes her thought and then finishes her coffee.

Once she sets her mug back down on the table she continues, "Get your boundaries figured out with what you are comfortable with and then see what he says. This is your final say. Don't let either of them have unlimited access, but I say make it happen."

"You're right. This is an amazing opportunity." I nod and start writing down my stipulations on my phone. Hours I want to work, hours I want to be offline, I want meetings planned in advance, and would like to sit down with her to map out what this looks like for six months and then go from there.

"Email sent. Now we wait."

"And if he ends up helping you in other ways…that's not a bad thing either." Kylie adds and gives me a wink.

"Girl, really? I know literally nothing about this man. And I am not going to flirt with him. This is a professional business relationship. That be that," I respond absolutely mortified and stomp off to my room. Yes, I am approaching that scary thirty mark and just pouted to my room like a petulant child and I do not care. *Really?* Rude.

A few hours later, I had taken a nap and gotten dressed. I went with my dark wash skinny jeans, pink ballet flats, and a pink floral top. My hair is pulled back in a messy bun – still a bit wet from this morning and I don't want to deal with it. I take ten minutes to do a soft pink eyeshadow look, pair it with a mauve lipstick and a light BB cream. Mascara and setting spray and I am good for the day. Will I be leaving the house? No clue. But I feel more human when my makeup is done.

I grab a salad for lunch from the fridge. Thank you, Carter for keeping me well stocked! Caesar salads are my weakness – always my first choice for a side or even a full meal. This one has grilled chicken and some extra parmesan cheese. *Perfect.* At the table I pull out my phone to see if I have anything new from Matt.

Luckily, there's only a couple of notifications on my phone. I have an email from him and a new Instagram notification from his sister.

I open the email first.

"Hey, Sasha

I went over the stipulations you had with working with my sister and she is fully on board. I told her to connect with you to set up the details for her side of things so that way you can work it out together. Does everything else work for you? If so, we can set up a time to go over what I need in order to get started and we can get this timeline going. Six months is plenty of time to make this happen, but I would love to get a few things done this weekend for you if you are ready.

Zero pressure. This can wait until next week or even later in the month. Talk to you soon.

Matt"

I kind of like how he is getting less formal with his conversations. If I had to be fully business professional for the next six months with this man, I would start to get really tired.

ANC272: *"Sasha! OMG I am legit freaking out."*

The first line of Ashley's message has me giggling.

ANC272: *"Okay, so I talked to Matt and looked over your message and everything looks good to me. Can we meet up for coffee to go over things and map it out? I do so much better with in person meetings and I know we are kind of close to each other. Let me know what your week looks like next week. Super stoked! Talk soon!"*

SashaLovesLipstick: *"Hey girl. I actually have this weekend off from work. Are you free tomorrow afternoon? We can meet at the coffee shop by the teacher store. It might be a bit busy, but it's my favorite place to go get work done."*

ANC272: *"Yeah, that's perfect. Does 1:00 work for you?"*

SashaLovesLipstick: *"Absolutely. See you then. Can you get me a list of the classes you have already taken, the ones you have scheduled for the fall, and then what you are wanting to focus on? I want to make sure we don't waste our time together tomorrow."*

ANC272: *"You got it. See you then!"*

I normally don't do in person meetings, preferring the safety and comfort of virtual visits. I've never been officially diagnosed with social anxiety – especially since I've worked in sales for so long. But I see what I do at work as totally different than socializing outside the building I work in.

I get overwhelmed easily and have to focus on what my role is. If it isn't clearly defined, I tend to shut down. So, in person events and meetings aren't high on my list of "let's do that tomorrow!!" But I think coffee in a place that I am comfortable in, will be a good try for me. With that done, I respond to Matt and tell him I'm in and to send me an invoice. Ready or not, here we go!

Chapter Seven

MATT

VANILLA RASPBERRY ICED LATTE

An hour later I get the notification that payment has been processed. It's official. Sasha Sloan is my newest client and she is meeting with my sister tomorrow. I'm not planning on showing up for that meeting. That one needs to be just the two of them and I have more than enough work to do this weekend finalizing things so we can jump right in next week.

I open up my notebook just for Sasha and begin mapping out our timeline. Six months isn't a lot of time, but I want to see what we can do to make the most of that time.

Next stop, what brands does she use the most often? A brand deal or collaboration would be the best way to guarantee visibility. After diving into that bit on Instagram and TikTok, it becomes apparent that there are so many different pitches and products going to these companies every day.

I may have done a little bit of "less than ethical" research to see how many pitches they get, and it is not easy to get the green light for these. Especially with her desire to stay away from trendy launches and really niche products in favor of more classic looks and everyday budgets.

I still take the time to make a list of her top ten brands and then ten brands that are newer to the market but still within her aesthetic.

"Let's see what we can do with a little creative suggestion…" I mutter to myself.

Over the next five hours, I work my magic. Part of me should be worried about the legality of this, but as long as I'm not hurting anyone, I figure "why not?" Boosting content, manipulating algorithms, and adding more content to search engines are just creative suggestions in my book.

By the time I go to bed that night, I know I have done what I need to give Sasha the best shot to get noticed by these brands – all twenty of them.

Tomorrow I have a whole new set of things to do to increase those chances, but I need to be fully ready for that since it will be more than just a few brands I have to play around with.

"I really hope this works."

The next morning Ashley texts me to begin the initial freak out for her meeting with Sasha.

Ashley: What the heck am I supposed to wear?

Ashley: Do I need to bring anything else besides what she asked me for?

Ashley: Am I paying for both of us or just myself?

Ashley: Should I bring a portfolio?

Ashley: Crap. I don't have a portfolio.

And that was all in about thirty seconds. Yeah, she is freaking out a bit.

I call her to try to mitigate some of the meltdown that is coming on.

"Hey Ash. First, breathe." I give her a second to do just that and then I continue, "Second, your meeting isn't until like 1:00 today. Why are you freaking out so much about this? It's coffee." I try to measure my tone so she can feel the sureness of my voice and not focus on her own anxiety.

I can hear her pacing and breathing heavily on the other end of the phone. And yep, there's the creamer cap closing…she's working on getting fully caffeinated for the day. She isn't fully Ashley until she has at least one cup of coffee.

"Because I'm about to meet with Sasha! She is my version of a mini celebrity and she wants to meet with me. Granted, it's because you worked your persuasive magic, but still. I'm allowed to freak out a bit," she huffs back at me and then pauses to sip her coffee.

"Do you want me to come over for a bit? I can work on my end of things a bit more while you get your things together so you can ask me questions as they come up and then I can drop you off at the coffee shop."

"You are the best!! Yes, please! I'll go take a quick shower and see you in twenty minutes." She hangs up without even saying goodbye or waiting for a response.

I chuckle and start packing my bag before heading to my parent's house. It's only a five-minute drive but I don't want to rush over there. I fill up my travel coffee mug that says *The best days start with coffee*" and head out the door. I may not be as addicted to coffee as the women in my life, but I do enjoy a cup or two to start my day.

It's early summer in Colorado, but because we live so close to the mountains, it's not really humid outside. But it's already warming up. August tends to be our hottest month of the year and June has been weirdly rainy this year. I wish I was able to take advantage of the weather to go for a run this morning. I'll have to find a day next week to make up for it.

Ten minutes later, I am inside my parents' house logging into the Wi-Fi and getting all my notebooks, pens, and things out and ready to go. The kitchen table has become a great work space for me and my sister. My parents really created a space where we enjoy being home and know that we can have our own space to work, but they are close by if we want to talk or jump in on a project. This table has been in their home since I was little. And the dings and random marker on the table bear evidence of a happy childhood.

It takes me a few minutes to get everything out of my messenger bag and arrange it on the table so I can see pertinent things. This is my first real work session for Sasha, so I need to get her items color coded – folders, files, notebooks, notepads, highlighters, everything. These will all work together to create my workflow and then her growth plan.

I have a system that I've been using for other clients so I already have my base work figured out. I just need to fine tune some things and adjust my task list for Sasha's brand. And then I'll be able to "plug and play" into Ashley's brand when she is ready.

I'm just getting out the last few pages of analytics that I printed out last night when Ashley comes down the stairs and into the main living space. She briefly acknowledges me with a wave before she heads to the coffee pot on the kitchen counter. She has her mug in hand and the pot is full, so she's already on a second pot of the day. I hope mom has helped her with that or she is going to be a nervous wreck from caffeine overload before we even get to the coffee shop.

"Are mom and dad out for the morning?" I ask her as she prepares her cup and heads to sit next to me.

"Yeah. I think they are heading to the farmers market and then not sure after that. There are some new artisan vendors they've been following on Instagram that are showcasing things today and they aren't done with Christmas shopping yet. And it's June so they are behind schedule," Ashley mentions. She rolls her eyes and then pulls out her phone.

Our parents are year-round Christmas shoppers. They keep master lists for everyone and have a room just full of gifts and wrapping paper and cards. It's obnoxious. But they always have the perfect gift and don't have to even enter stores during December. It's brilliant!

"Have you been with them to the farmers market recently?" I ask her.

"Not for a while…why?" She asks with a look of apprehension. She knows I am already scheming in my head.

"Just thinking." I zone out and begin making more notes. After twenty minutes of typing and searching and following, I sit back and look over my work smugly. "There it is."

"What did you do?" Ashley asks and tries to peek over my shoulder.

"I'm not showing you anything. I'm working my magic." Ashley levels her eyes at me like she is hoping I will crack under the pressure and tell her what I did. I'm a vault. That's not going to work on me.

When she finally realizes that I'm not going to tell her what I was working on, Ashley makes her way back up the stairs to her room. I start putting away everything, back in order, and in the right pouches and pockets, until she comes back downstairs. She stands in the entryway of the main space and does a little spin, arms out so I can see her outfit.

"How's this?"

"What am I looking at here?" I ask, already knowing she wants me to check her outfit.

She just gives me a look that conveys her annoyance, "try again."

"You look fine. It's just a coffee meeting." She is in denim shorts and a pink sleeveless top. Put together but casual.

She gives herself another once over and grabs her things – a backpack with her laptop and notebooks and then a simple wristlet purse for her wallet, phone, and lipstick. I've known my sister's habits long enough to know that she always has at least two lip color options on her at all times. I wonder how many Sasha keeps in her purse.

"Ready to head out?" I look down and realize it's 12:20. Time really does fly when you are having fun, or being a bit of an algorithm mastermind.

My sister doesn't even bother to respond this time. She just grabs my keys from the table and heads out the door to start my car.

"So, do you want me to come into the coffee shop and work at the other end or just come get you when you are done?" I ask Ashley as I park in the lot. It's not terribly busy, but I wanted to grab a spot in case she wants me to stay. There aren't a ton of options right here that I would want to go bum around in if she doesn't. Even the teacher store is closed across the street. Not that I need anything in there, but it's there.

"Do you mind? I know I'm a bit early and if she wants to talk to you afterwards, I want you to be here."

"This is your meeting, not mine. Your mentorship with her is completely separate from my work with Sasha." I remind her. I am not going to have time to micromanage this part of the agreement and I really hope they both know that.

"I am fully aware, Matt. I just – please – can you come in with me? I'm not nervous to meet with her, but I don't love being places by myself and I am not sure how long I will be waiting for her." There's a note of apprehension in her voice that I haven't heard before, but it's such a one-off thing, I don't focus on it. I can understand her nervousness over meeting Sasha and having this be a professional situation. From what I can tell, this is her first time showing up as a professional for a meeting and not just with friends or advisor meetings at school.

"Fine. Let me grab my bag." We head inside, order our drinks and then I head to the counter by the window as she heads to a table by the fireplace. It's not on because the weather is nice, but it's a nice aesthetic and has a bigger table so the girls can spread out their stuff as they go over everything together.

At 12:50, Sasha walks in the coffee shop and I swear, everything stops. And all I see is her.

Matt

Chapter Eight

SASHA

LAVENDER WHITE CHOCOLATE ICED LATTE

Social Post: When meeting someone for a business meeting, it's important to feel confident in what you choose – for me – that means picking a lipstick that coordinates perfectly with my shirt. And how cute is this combo?? Social anxiety is no match for a killer lip combo – okay, maybe it's not that powerful, but I feel better about today knowing I look cute. #sashaloveslipstick #coffeemeeting #coloradogirl #butfirstcoffee #dontforgetthelipstick

Image Description: Mirror selfie before I leave for the coffee shop. Full outfit shown and laptop bag resting next to me.

I love this coffee shop. It's light and airy and huge and has so many places to sit. Plus, there's a meeting room in the back that I have on my vision board to use for a brand deal conversation or collaboration meeting at some point. It's so pretty and professional! Maybe I need to bump that up on my priority list so we can start doing something there sooner. Mental note to add that to my notebook to brainstorm how we can use it.

My hair is pulled back in a bun today – it's pretty much my standard in the summer. It's super thick and I have a ton of it. And it's the most basic shade of brown. I really need to see about getting some highlights or something put in, maybe in the fall. I'm in my favorite dark denim cutoff shorts, a blue floral top, blue sparkly stud earrings, my favorite rose quartz crystal bracelet, and my brown sandals. Simple, but put together. And of course, a lipstick color that matches the pink pops in my top.

I order a lavender white chocolate iced latte as soon as I walk inside the coffee shop. It's amazing. Lavender is one of my favorite things and when it is added to coffee, another one of my favorite things, I am just a very happy person. As they make my latte, I take a look around the shop. There are a few baristas working behind the counter and the tables are about half full at this point. Couples meeting over coffee, a few individuals look like they are working, and there are a few girls around my age reading at their respective spaces in the shop.

My coffee doesn't take long and I see Ashley towards the back of the shop right as they call my name. She's over by the fireplace and I am so glad it's not on right now. She chose my favorite table! Okay, maybe I need to tone down the excitement levels – don't want to come across too strong. First meeting. And it's not behind a screen to tone down my level of anxiety and expectation this morning.

I walk over and start setting up my stuff as we begin chatting. She is super sweet in person, just like she has been online, and I love getting to know her and what she loves in the makeup space. Her favorite influencers are some of the ones I follow too and she shows me a few new accounts that I haven't found yet. We spend time talking about her favorite content that she has created in the last year and then create a shared folder for planning purposes and inspiration.

"So, how do you feel about doing a mix of collaborative posts and then working on a few specific series' for your channel over the summer?" I ask her as we continue working through our ideas together.

"I like that. I know you already have several things in the works from what you've shared on your socials, but I would love to be involved in some of the new things that you'll be working on once you start working with Matt. My schedule will be limited once I go back to school, so I'd like to take advantage of the extra time to have additonal videos recorded."

"I completely agree with that. We have to work with your schedule and make this work for you when you go back to school. Are there any specific things you want to work with me on this summer?"

"I'll look over your tentative content plan and see if there's anything that overlaps with things I was thinking for myself as well. And then we can chat later this week?"

"Perfect. I have a rough plan for the summer but I don't know how much your brother is going to adjust things yet."

"Very fair," she laughs a little at that. "He tends to rework a lot of things when he starts with a new client, but it always comes out perfectly in the end."

"Good to know," I smile back at her and then we dive back into our notebooks and ideas.

At four, we wrap things up. We have pages and pages of notes and things mapped out. And a handful of videos we are going to collaborate on over the next few weeks. Her fall semester doesn't start until the middle of August, so we are going to switch to Monday evening meetings after I finish at Home Depot. Then meet on Friday mornings to do content together – locations to be determined based on the content. It sounds like her parents have some good space we can utilize to vary up locations.

"Do you want to meet my brother in person before you head out?" Ashley asks as she puts the last of her things in her bag.

"Oh, I didn't know he was coming..." I look around a little warily, I was not expecting to meet with him today, but I guess it's a good time to get this out of the way. I try to tamp down my uncertainty and put back on my business woman face. "Yeah, sure. Is he already here or picking you up?"

"He's over by the front window. He's been working here while we were meeting. I don't love being places by myself and we got here a bit before you did." We start walking over to the window and I recognize Matt from our video call. He's in a simple dark blue t-shirt and khaki pants – the thicker ones you can work in, not the dress pants. He looks comfortable. Why does that word keep coming up for me with him? I can see his tattoos on his arms and the contrasting black against his skin draws my attention for probably a bit too long. I mess with my bracelet a bit and take a deep breath.

"Hey, Matt. We are all done. I didn't know if you wanted to say hey to Sasha before she took off." Ashley says and then heads to the coffee counter. Probably to get a top off of her iced coffee. That girl may like coffee just as much as I do. I look back to Matt to see him shaking his head incredulously. I'm guessing he is thinking the same thing that I am about the coffee.

"She has a coffee problem." He mutters quietly.

"Well then we are going to get along just fine." I reply with a smug look on my face. He looks back at me then stands from his chair and extends his hand – I guess we are going a little more professional here. I shake his hand and have to try not to linger a bit too long. I am drawn in by his eyes up close and his hair is seriously the perfect length – not too long to be messy but not too short to look like he is in the military. My dad has the military buzz cut and it just isn't my thing. He was in the Navy before I came along and some habits just stuck around, I guess.

My fingers tingle a little when I finally do let my hand drop to my side. I'm not sure if it's anxiety or something else so I use my other hand to hold onto my bracelet and ground myself a little bit. "Little hippie, little witchy" is how I like to classify myself. I have crystals and enjoy using essential oils and tinctures before trying traditional medicine. I also try to stick with the cleaner makeup and skincare brands. But I still wear polyester and enjoy a bag of sour patch kids on occasion.

"It's nice to meet you in person." I say politely. "We had a great meeting and I think this is going to work really well. We have our next in person meeting on Monday night after I get off from work. I'm sure she will tell you all about it."

"Sounds good. I think it's going to be great for both of you for sure. Let me know if you need anything from me along the way. I just finished most of what we are going to need to get started next week. Can we set up our next meeting for Tuesday? Let me know what works for your schedule. Zoom is totally fine or we can meet here. But I want to start getting some of this initial stuff going." He starts putting away his notebooks and I am so thankful that we aren't going to do any business talk today. I am exhausted and desperately need a nap.

"I work an early-ish shift on Tuesday. I can meet here at five or we can do Zoom any time after four. Let me know what will work best since you have the experience here." I'll work from six to three on Tuesday so that will give me time to get home and change before a call or meeting. And hopefully grab something little to eat if we do Zoom.

"How about we plan on five here? It may be a little easier to go over this in person. And then we can see about virtual after that if it works better for you."

"Perfect." I grab out my phone and put in the info in my calendar. "Do you need me to bring anything besides my laptop?"

"That should be just fine. I'm hoping to be able to do a lot of this for you, but I need to make sure we are on the same page." He responds and then Ashley joins us again.

"You ready to go?" She asks her brother then turns to me. "Thank you again so much for today." The pure joy on her face is visible.

"I loved meeting with you and am so excited for this! I will see you Monday, Ashley. Text me if you need anything." I give her a little hug then turn to make a quick eye contact with Matt. "And I will see you Tuesday."

With that, I head out to my car and head home. Once I get inside my apartment, I let myself relax a bit.

"Okay then, here we go. Officially counting down to December."

Chapter Nine

SASHA

BUTTER PECAN COLD BREW
Social Post: Anyone else love having a routine? That means I can color code my calendar and plan ahead for things. #sashaloveslipstick #calendar #prettypens #colorcoordination
Image Description: colored pens next to a spiral planner

The first few weeks of our arrangement go by and Matt, Ashley, and myself fall into an easy routine.

Matt: Did you have a chance to review the new product releases from the email I sent you last night?

Me: Yes. I'm not loving anything that I saw on this one. It feels a little too trendy in my opinion. And most of my target audience won't love packaging that isn't user friendly.

Matt: That was my concern with that one too. Since it's a smaller and newer company I wanted to run it by you before I put it in the "pass" folder.

Me: Thank you for checking.

Me: Did you see the number of saves on the video from yesterday?

Matt: That's all you, Sasha. Great job on the demo. Your audience is really loving the tutorials on how to do the more in depth skincare routines.

Me: Perfect. I'm thinking of doing one this weekend on "hiking proof makeup" – what do you think?

Matt: I think that's perfect. Let me grab you a few photos from my last hike so you can put in some images throughout, hang on.

Me: Matt, these are beautiful! Where did you take these?

Matt: Up at Horsetooth earlier this week. I went early so it was quiet and I was able to get some good pictures.

Me: These are perfect. Thank you! It's been so long since I've been up there. It's a really pretty hike this time of year.

Matt: Completely agree. Hopefully you get some time to go soon.

Ashley: I found the cutest art print at the farmers market with my parents last week! {image attached}

Me: Okay, that is so pretty!! Did you get the artist's info? Because I kind of want that on a notebook!

Ashley: Right? Let me see if I can find it.

Matt: Already taken care of.

Me: What does that mean?

Ashley: My brother likes to show off sometimes.

Matt: I'll get it to you at our next meeting Sasha.

Me: Get me what?

Matt: The notebook. It should be at my house tomorrow.

Ashley: See? Show off.

Matt: I found this coffee recipe when I was researching some coffee themed makeup and skincare items for you. Let me know if you try it out. {link attached}

Me: This looks absolutely incredible. And I should be able to make it at home.

Matt: That's what I thought too. Nothing too fancy, but it seems like something you would like.

Me: I can't wait to try it out. Thank you.

Mondays I work from nine until six and then meet with Ashley afterwards to work on content, go over projects, and try new products out together. Tuesdays I meet with Matt at the coffee shop or via Zoom, depending on the day. Wednesday and Thursdays are regular work days for me and we have our family dinners on those days. Friday mornings are our content times - at my apartment, at Ashley's house, or out and about depending on what we are working on. And the weekend is my catch up and rest time. It's been working and my channel is steadily growing.

It is the last week of June when I get a new email in my inbox that makes me literally do a double take and then scream. One of my favorite start up makeup brands is interested in working with me for their new product line releasing in August. Me? What? I don't remember reaching out to them, but I do use their products pretty frequently and tag them in everything. I am so excited.

I email Matt to check in and make sure this is a good opportunity to say yes to. After he gives me the green light, I email in my acceptance. I am so excited!

Literally ten minutes later, I get an email notification from the city. It's a newsletter showcasing the farmers market and the artisan vendors that are there. They are expanding into some other vendors too and have some openings for artists, performers, and influencers. I have never heard of a farmers market having influencers, but hey…it's local and will be fun to check it out.

I text Ashley to see if she would want to do a small section with me – maybe doing some mini eyeshadow tutorials and connecting with some local shops. It might be a good chance to set up an event in the fall. She's down to give it a try so I submit my application. It's definitely not something I would ever think to do on my own, but having Ashley with me gives me the courage to hit the submit button.

It's Tuesday, so I will be meeting Matt at the coffee shop in about an hour so I have time to finish checking my notifications before it's time to go. Hopefully, I will hear back about the market tomorrow so I can go get some things printed and ready for Saturday if we get approved that quickly. I pull out my phone to start making a list of ideas and things we may need before I go get changed and head out.

It's another cut off denim shorts and cute floral top day for me today. Why is it so hot? I love dressing cute for summer but I really hate this heat. At least I can get an iced chai at the coffee shop. I'm trying to cut back on how much coffee I drink after 4 PM. I'm not cutting back any earlier than that, but this is a start and I need to work on going to bed at a decent time.

I get to the coffee shop and order my chai, dirty and spicy. I never said I was cutting back on caffeine, just the coffee. Then I go to our regular table by the front windows where Matt is already waiting for me. He is sipping on an iced tea of some sort today and is wearing his signature khaki pants and dark tee. It's a dark grey today and the color seriously does beautiful things with his eyes. I wonder if he would be down to let me play with some color correcting makeup on him…maybe another time.

I set my things down on the table and start getting ready for our weekly catch up meeting. We usually go over things about Ashley first and then switch to things for me. This professional relationship has been easy to get used to and whatever magic he is working on the back end with my website and marketing, it's working.

"Did you get a signed contract back from that beauty brand yet or are they going to send it after they figure out how many influencers are working with them?" He asks me as he finishes getting his things out as well. He sets his phone on top of mine for a minute while he gets things set and then mutters an apology about not paying attention before he moves it away.

"I think I should have it back by the end of the week. They are wanting to send out packages by the beginning of next week so we have time to play with the product, do a full review, get back to them with any concerns, and then start working on content for their channels and our own. The pay seemed really good for what is included and their last several launches have sold out pretty quickly, so I am hoping this will be good visibility on both sides of things."

I grab my phone to pull up the info about the farmers market and show it to him. "This is new. Any ideas on what Ashley and I should focus on if we are able to get in this week? I won't have a lot of time to get things together for this so I want to make sure I go in prepared."

He looks at the email and then hands me back my phone before taking out his notebook again. I have learned this is his process. He has to map it out on paper to make sure he knows how things make sense together before he throws something at me. I appreciate how thorough he is. No wasted time on my part and no wasted energy on his. I tend to want to jump right in and get things done, but he makes me slow down a bit. I don't hate it.

Over the next hour we map out resources to create, handouts, a new page for my site, a few video ideas for the market, and which businesses to connect with that should be there. During that time, he also gets done a few more things on his end and I get my graphics site pulled up on my laptop to start designing the printed resources. I will need to get them printed tomorrow – even if I don't get chosen for this week. I want to start pursuing this with a few local businesses. Maybe we can even do some networking events with local influencers and content creators to collaborate together. Matt is working on a list of other local creators that would connect well with my content and things I am working on.

"Okay, I think I need to be done tonight. My creativity level is completely shot and I need to go to bed. I have work at six tomorrow morning and a meeting with one of my contractors early to help him finish his current job. Thanks again for all of this and I will keep you updated on the brand proposal and the farmers market." I tell Matt as I pack up my things. He looks up at me and I can tell he wants to ask me something, but he isn't sure how to. "Do you need anything else from me this week?" I ask him – trying to give him the opportunity. I've learned that Matt is definitely on the quieter side and doesn't initiate conversations unless he has to. I'm happy to give him an out here.

"Nope. Just want to make sure you are still taking care of you with all of this. I know it's a lot right now, but I am hoping it settles soon for you so you aren't running around so much. Do we need to cut back on this a bit?" He seems obviously concerned here. He's already looking at his calendar again and making notes about what might be able to go on pause for a little bit. I shake my head at his concern and then respond.

"No, I'm good. I really want to see what this will turn into. And I'm taking care of myself. I'm protecting my weekends and will be able to rest after work tomorrow. And Carter and Kylie bring home dinner tomorrow too so I won't have to cook or anything. Maybe you can come join us sometime." I say and then stop. Did I just invite him over for dinner? Where did that come from?

He smirks a bit, "thank you for the invite. Maybe we can set something up in a few weeks. I would like for us to get through the end of the month and have a solid plan for July before I take a breath on this. You have your next meeting with Ashley on Friday, right?" I nod.

"Okay, good. Let me know if you hear from the brand or the market before then so that way I can give her some things for you for that meeting."

"Thanks, Matt. I am planning to get a tablecloth and folding table tomorrow. Even if I don't end up doing the event this week, there are other opportunities for this, and there is an office store close to work I think. I'll have to double check. I'll see you next Tuesday." I smile and then head out to my car.

At home that night, I fall asleep quickly after double checking my email. The brand proposal and the notice from the farmers market came in within the last half hour and I am still trying to wrap my head around today. Each day I get closer to my dream of doing makeup full time. And I cannot wait. Even if it makes as me nervous as standing in a room with two hundred other people all wanting to talk to me.

Wednesday morning starts stupid early and I am not happy

about it. I am not a morning person. And it's still dark outside. Gross. At least it isn't cold outside. I am even happier when Ryan gets to the store with my iced latte. I seriously love this man.

"Your wife knows I love you, right?" I ask him as I take the latte and pull out my notebook for his company.

He laughs at me. "Yes, she knows. She loves you too. You save me money so I can spend more on her."

"Good. Just making sure. Before we dive into this I have to tell you what happened last night. I have my first brand deal signed and sent in and I'll be at the Windsor farmers Market this Saturday. This week has been incredible so far!"

"That's awesome. How long until I have to find someone else in this store that can help me out?"

"Well, no one is going to be able to handle your contracts like I can." I say with a bit of a snark to my voice. It's early and we have been working together forever. "But I'm shooting for the end of the year, but we will see. Hoping I can switch to part time by then and then fully be done by the middle of next year. It depends on a lot of things though. This is just step one. And no matter when that timeline happens, I will make sure to pass along your information to someone who I can trust to take care of your projects." I'm not sure if I can stay past the end of this year fully anymore. I am not loving it as much as I used to. And my heart is now set on pursuing makeup.

We work together for about an hour and then he heads out. I immerse myself into my work until I notice that it's lunch time. I only take a half hour lunch most days, so I head across the street to grab something at the grocery store. Keeping it simple today and just going to the deli for a salad or something. At checkout, I look up and see Matt across the way also checking out. I'm at self-checkout and he's at a register with a full load it looks like. I don't want to be weird about it, so when he doesn't notice me, I grab my things and head back to work. I didn't think he lived close to here...I thought he was in Windsor like me, and this is Fort Collins. The store is 20 minutes from our coffee shop. Maybe he was over here running other errands...

I get back to work and finish up my tasks for the day then drive over to Target to get what I need for this weekend. I was going to do the office store, but decided I should probably get a few other things for my table that won't be there. Thirty minutes, one latte, and way too many knick-knacks later, I am done and ready to head home. As I sit in my car, I get a coupon notification from my coffee shop for tomorrow. #winning!! I'll have time to swing in before my shift to grab a drink and breakfast.

The apartment is quiet when I arrive home, so I set up at the table to send in the files to be printed for Saturday. Once those are all done, I pull out my new notebook to piece together what I want for the market on Saturday. I like having a new notebook for each area that I am working on. And the new one that Matt got me with the art print from the local artist is perfect for the farmers market things.

I texted Ashley earlier since she tends to go to the market frequently with her parents to see what other vendors may be in attendance. I want to do a little research on who we may be in contact with.

Matt: I was able to get a map of where all the vendors will be this Saturday at the market. Wanted to send it to you as soon as I got it so you can see who will be next to you and which vendors you would like to chat with. Let me know how I can help.

Me: This is perfect! Thank you so much. I thought this wasn't going to be sent out until Friday though…

Ashley: Have you met my brother yet?

Me: LOL. Just curious.

Matt: I was able to get an early copy. Have fun at dinner tonight and don't forget to unplug for a bit. I know you had an early morning today.

Me: Will do. Thank you.

I take a look through the attachment that Matt sent over. It seems like we have a really good spot between a spa and a bookstore. And there is someone who makes skincare products and a honeybee product vendor across from us too! I could not ask for a better spot.

I'm just finishing up a new page in my notebook about which vendors I want to check into further when Kylie and Carter get home. Dinner is pretty standard and I appreciate the time to connect with my roommates again. Wednesday nights are our time to breathe and catch up. I hear all about the drama at the restaurant and Kylie and Carter help me go over my stuff for Saturday. Kylie will also be home Friday morning so we are going to see about including her in some content if we have time. This week just got busier, but we have a plan to make it all happen.

Thursday morning starts bright and early, thankfully later than yesterday, with me at the coffee shop at 8:30. I don't have work until nine so I have just enough time to grab my coffee and something to eat before I head out. I order a honey latte and a breakfast sandwich and then grab a cookie for later. The chocolate chip just looks so good right now. The barista takes down my name and then lets me know that my order has already been paid for. Huh, that's nice. I give her my card anyway to pay for the person behind me in case this is a "pay it forward" situation. As I wait for my latte, I see Matt and Ashley working at a table nearby so I go over to say hello.

"Hey guys. You are out early today." I say specifically to Ashley. She is like me, not wanting to be up and about before we actually need to be.

She smiles up at me. "Yeah, this dude over here decided we needed to get stuff done early today so we could head up to Horsetooth and go hiking a bit. Are you heading to work?"

"Yeah. I am. Hiking sounds amazing though! I haven't been to Horsetooth in forever. Have a good time and send me more pictures!" I give another quick smile to her and Matt and then grab my things and go. I wish I had more time to hang out or even stay here and work with them. I have enjoyed getting to work with Ashley, but I have enjoyed getting to know Matt. And between our meeting Tuesday, the store yesterday, and now here...him showing up where I am is causing him to be in my mind more than I was expecting. Is this coincidence or is this turning into a bit of attraction? No, I know this is attraction. The right question is, is this coincidence or fate?

Sasha
x
#sashaloveslipstick

SUBJECT :
DATE   /   /
WED THU FRI SAT SUN

Chapter Nine and a Half

ASHLEY

ICED AMERICANO WITH VANILLA

My brother makes me think of Taylor Swift.

Follow me for a second.

He works in advance and drops little hints of what he is working towards. It doesn't always make sense in the bits and pieces. But as it comes together, you can see all of the "Easter Eggs." There's been more than one time that I look back on something and ask myself how I could have possibly missed what he was working on.

For example, the farmers market...there's absolutely no way that he didn't orchestrate getting Sasha and me into that. My parents have gone to that market for years and Sasha didn't even know it was a thing. I didn't even think of the possibility of us going as makeup influencers. Who does that?

When I was in high school, there were so many instances where things just magically "worked out." And it usually tied back to a conversation I had with my brother. Getting a chance to audition for a school play that I missed out on because I was sick, a girl in homeroom who teased me getting moved to a different schedule, and then there was the restaurant that I got food poisoning at – they got a surprise health inspection that closed them down within a few days.

How he does it, I have no clue.

Is he the one behind it all?

I can't prove it, but I know it's him.

He's in my phone as *Mastermind* and he just keeps proving to me that he deserves that title.

Now if only he could help with some of the Karma side of things with some other of my current issues, but for now, I can handle that on my own.

For now, the focus is on as much content as Sasha and I can get out before I go back to school in the fall. Everything else can wait until then.

Ashley

Chapter Ten

SASHA

ENGLISH BREAKFAST TEA WITH A SPLASH OF MILK

Social Post: I think I might have had too much coffee this week. But I get to meet some amazing people at the farmers market tomorrow!! Who is local that I'll get to see? And what booths do I need to go check out once I'm set up?

Image description: Tote bag with makeup cards and pens next to it. #sashaloveslipstick #farmersmarket #eventprep #noco #coloradosummer

Friday morning has me working with Ashley and Kylie on the final prep for tomorrow. We have done a mock table setup and have done a handful of story posts to show off what we are working on for this weekend. Several local people are planning to stop by our booth too. I was even able to get some stickers done with my IG handle: Sasha Loves Lipstick. They're the thicker material that is great for water bottles or notebooks. The different colors are perfect and I am hoping they are a hit with my followers that are able to make it.

We also made up a few resources to share about local beauty favorites, top summer makeup trends, and links to tutorials on my site. I don't have paid services that I offer besides collaboration with brands so the goal for tomorrow is connection, collaboration, and freebies. Who doesn't love more stickers and pens?

Carter is working early today so he should be getting home at four and that will be our cue to be done for the day. I ended up taking today off from work. I went over my hours at work a few days this week so only had to take a few hours of PTO to finish off my week. I want to go into tomorrow well rested and ready for whatever happens. Will it turn into any more deals? I'm honestly not sure, but it's a great opportunity to connect with others and pitch what I want to do locally.

Carter has a couple of pizzas and salads with him for dinner so he throws the pizza in the oven to keep them warm as we pack up the car. The more I can get done tonight so I don't have to remember them in the morning, the better. We have to be at the space at nine tomorrow morning and I don't want to be rushed. Ashley is going to meet me here so we can go over together in the morning, and get coffee on the way, obviously. Kylie and Carter are going to come by the table for a bit around lunch to check in and give us a break if needed. The event goes from ten until two tomorrow, so it's not terribly long, but depending on traffic, a break may be nice.

As we finish packing up the car, I pull out my phone to double check my list of everything we need to bring. I think we are good to go but I don't want to forget anything. I shoot Matt a quick text with my list and ask if there's anything else I may be forgetting.

Matt: Do I need to bring you coffee in the morning or are you and Ashley planning on stopping first?

Me: I think we are planning on stopping first so we can take our time going over and setting up. We just finished loading the car and are going to eat dinner before we call it a night. We have extra pizza if you want to come over if you are free. No pressure, but wanted to check.

Matt: I am actually out by your place right now (Ashley sent me the address when she was over a few weeks ago ;)) so that would actually be great. Do you need me to grab anything?

Me: Perfect. I think we are all set. See you soon.

I turn to the group and let them know Matt is coming and I don't miss the little smirk that Kylie gives me. We have had more than one conversation about how easy it is to talk to him and how I'm enjoying getting to know him more. And how I wouldn't mind seeing him in a less than professional capacity at some point. But I know that isn't the focus right now. Maybe tonight we can just hang out as two adults with our friends rather than business colleagues though.

Within a few minutes, Matt drives up. He parks by the curb and then makes his way over to us. He greets his sister with a side hug and then lazily drapes his arm over her shoulder as he turns to greet the rest of us, "How was packing everything up?"

"It went pretty well. Luckily we don't have to deal with a lot of products or fragile things to worry about. I just hope this isn't a total waste of time," I am already second guessing myself so much with this. Who ever heard of an influencer attending a farmers market?

"It's going to be great. You've got your focus areas for the event and you are going to have your cheer team there with you, right?" Matt asks me. His focus doesn't stray from my face, even with the others standing around. He makes me feel like I'm the only one in the room when we talk. I take a moment to take him in and then nod in response.

"Yep, I'll have my cheer team with me. And several of our local followers are planning to stop by. So there will be some familiar faces in the midst of all the walk-by traffic."

"See, all good," Kylie pipes in. "Let's go inside and eat though because I am starving." She laces her fingers in Carter's and we follow them into the apartment.

Once we settle inside, we dive into the pizzas and I enjoy my Caesar salad with my slice. This one has grilled chicken and it's absolutely perfect. I probably eat too many of these, but I don't really care. It's a full meal and I feel good afterwards. Matt chats a bit about this weekend and some of the things that he has questions about. We show him pictures of our table set up.

Ashley will be doing our behind the scenes content tomorrow and then we will post it on both of our channels throughout the day. Photo ops and connections are a big part of tomorrow and we don't want to waste this opportunity in case the farmers market decides not to have influencers at this thing again next week.

Ashley heads out pretty early. She wants to swing by the store to grab a few more pens for tomorrow. I ran out of the pretty pink ones I love so she is going to try to find something comparable. So it's just me, Carter, Kylie, and Matt hanging out in the living room sipping tea. I'm sipping on something seasonal from Celestial Seasonings and everyone else raided my tea cabinet too. I'm not just a coffee addict, I have a slight tea problem too. And being in Colorado means I have lots of opportunities for both.

"So how did you get into social media growth, Matt?" Kylie asks as she cuddles up a bit more into Carter. If I didn't love the two of them together so much, it would be moderately gross how cute they were.

"I went to college for communications and marketing. Social media kind of branched off from there. Most of my original clients were established companies with zero social media platform so it was helping them get that established and then linking it all together. I realized I enjoyed it and I was good at it. Finding how everything fits together and then making a plan to get there with the fewest steps possible. I got to work with a few startups from there and now, here we are." He takes a breath and a sip of his drink before continuing.

"I have a few clients on retainer that I help with a monthly or quarterly meeting and planning session and then I do things like I'm doing with Sasha now with full plans and execution. I've never done it in depth before, but I'm hoping this turns into something a little more for future clients. Adding in the email campaigns and brand collaborations is new for me, but I'm enjoying the new piece." I knew some of that, but not all of it. So getting a little more insight into Matt is not something I am going to complain about.

"Are you wanting to keep doing this in the long run or do you see this changing a bit for you?" I ask.

"I'd love to get to a point where I have a few people working with me. Maybe doing the intakes or execution of certain tasks. I like doing the map outs but there are things I could delegate out. Another reason why I'm doing your account the way I am. I'm using it to outline client expectations, SOPs, and troubleshooting. Since I'm doing a few new things with your account, it gives me a good opportunity to finalize a lot of those things on my end. Not everything will work for every client, but it's a good blueprint."

"That makes sense. Do you want to keep working with startups and influencers or go back to established businesses?" Carter asks. He loves this kind of thing even if he is "just a bartender." I never liked that he referred to himself that way when he introduced himself to someone new. He was good at his job and loved it – and it shows.

He would honestly make an excellent addition to Matt's team but he loves what he does too. Social media isn't his thing, but storytelling is. And finding connections to stories is his super power. It's pretty awesome to see how he can find those little pieces. Like when I was trying to find a new video series, he was the one that suggested I do a coffee series last Christmas. I did a bunch of holiday drink inspired looks and it was so fun for my engagement and just my attitude around what I was doing. It was so perfect! And it was completely his idea. How I never thought of it, I have no idea, but it worked wonderfully.

"I'm open to either, honestly. Again, if I can have a team working with me, I could designate certain ones for each type of business coming to me and it would be a lot easier to 'plug and play' with their specific plans and goals. I like the flexibility of choosing clients, but wouldn't mind growing things a bit. Maybe in the new year once we close out the first bit of Sasha and Ashley's project." He makes eye contact with me and I take note of the first bit part of what he said. We had talked about a six-month initial, but it looks like he may want to keep working with me more than that.

"Do you see us working on more things together after this initial stage?" I ask him, a slight smile on my lips.

"If you're up for it." He responds without hesitation, never breaking eye contact with me. My smile widens as I sip my tea. And then my mind immediately starts racing. I absolutely can not have a panic attack in front of Matt. I abruptly stand up and make my way to the kitchen.

"Oh, it's getting late, we should probably call it a night," I take a look at where a watch would normally be on a wrist to distract myself, "See you all in the morning. Thanks again for stopping by Matt and the food was great as always, Carter." I drop my mug in the sink and then head to my room. Why did I get so incredibly flustered with that little statement from him? Was it the eye contact as he was talking about future plans? What if we finish this contract up and he decides I'm no longer worth his time? I have no clue, but I desperately need to call it a night and get ready for tomorrow. I cannot screw this up.

Sasha
x
#sashaloveslipstick

Chapter Eleven

MATT

SHOT OF ESPRESSO

Sasha has completely consumed every thought. In the morning, my first thought is wondering how she slept. Is she ready for the day? Did she go right to sleep after she went to bed abruptly last night? Did she forget anything before this morning? When should I show up for the event today without being weird? What floral top is she going to wear today? Will her hair be back up in her messy bun or will she have it down a bit? It's going to be hot today – it probably won't be down, although she looks so good when she leaves it down.

I check her stories and then Ashley's and notice there hasn't been an update yet. I wonder why they haven't left yet. I check my phone again and quickly realize why: it's five in the morning. They won't be up until six. I'm going to go do a quick run to kill some of this time and nervous energy.

I head out to the trail and hit it hard. I want to get my miles in early before it gets busy. With it getting hotter out, runners start earlier and earlier each morning and I don't want to really talk to anyone this morning. As I find my pace, my thoughts go back to Sasha. It's been really cool to see everything come together. I have a feeling that Ashley knows I set the farmers market thing up. Influencers at the market? Really? It was a stretch, but it worked. Today will show if it actually worked or if someone on the market planning team was just wanting to see if the stretch worked too.

Making sure that Sasha had some local connections to make her feel more comfortable took a little more work than the initial market invitation. Her social anxiety isn't something she talks about a lot, but I know it's there, and I know how to help her feel better about showing up at events. A solid plan, casual setup, and a few familiar faces really help her show up happy and ready to connect with those around her. She may still be nervous, but she won't be focusing on her anxiety.

The brand deal was a lot harder. That was several emails, well placed 'boosted' videos and a bit of finagling on my end. Totally legal? No. Creative? Hell, yes. I have a few more I am working on, but I wanted to spread them out. Doing too much too fast will be a bit suspicious for both Sasha and the brands. Looking ahead at release schedules and promotions helped me map out things through the end of the year. Which brands will start seeing her content when, who will start needing new influencers, and when it's going to be "just the right fit." This work isn't always easy, but it's a fun game finding the best way to get to the end goal.

My side quest though? Completely and purely selfish. Working together complicates this a little bit. I don't want to straight up ask her out. We are supposed to be working on her brand and growing her platforms. And I want her focusing on that, not on me. But, if she just happens to be thinking of me as often as I think of her... maybe this can happen "organically and naturally." Again, I have to be subtle about this or Ashley is going to know what I am doing and she cannot keep her mouth shut about anything – much less my 'scheming' as she calls it. It has yet to blow up in my face. This is the largest project I've ever tackled though. The most personal too. And I don't want to come across as creepy. But Sasha is everything I want and know I can't have…but maybe, I can.

I get back to my house just before six and take a quick shower. Checking stories again, I see that the girls are up and getting ready for the day. I call ahead to the coffee shop to pay for their order. It's early on a Saturday, so both of them are probably going to go for something simple for their drinks today, but I don't want them worrying about paying for it. I've done it a few times already – calling ahead with their names and my card info. With them going together it's a little easier since I'm Ashley's brother. I can use that relationship status rather than my huge crush on her mentor and my client. That might get a few weird looks. I'm not out to make anyone uncomfortable. Well, not Sasha anyways. I don't really care about anyone else.

I get myself ready and then drive to my parent's house. I had told them earlier in the week that I would go to the market with them this morning. I let myself in then head to the kitchen to get the coffee pot going for them. I hear them moving around upstairs even though it's not even seven. We still have a good two hours before they normally head out. But mom may want to work in the garden for a minute and dad is going to want to check his list before we leave. I know he is already thinking ahead for what Ashley may need for school this fall, and they should be almost done with Christmas shopping.

Mom is the first one downstairs and I get a quick kiss before she starts opening the mug cabinet to find her current favorite. Every woman in my life is obsessed with coffee. I snicker to myself a bit, but mom catches me. "And what is so funny this morning?" She eyes me with suspicion and a little bit of amusement.

"Just thinking of how much every woman in my life loves

coffee. It's a bit of a problem."

"This isn't anything new to you…" she trails off. She is fishing and I know it.

"My new client, Sasha – I've told you about her, she's as bad as Ashley is." I laugh a bit. "The coffee shop up the road just has my card on file at this point between the two of them."

"Your client is using your card for coffee?" She asks a bit incredulously. "Isn't that a bit inappropriate?"

"No. She, um, she doesn't know I'm paying for it for her. I just don't want her worrying about it." I'm suddenly a bit worried on how this may come across. The look my mom gives me is anything but worried. She seems…elated. "What is that face for? It's just coffee, mom."

"You like this girl, don't you?" She definitely has a smug undertone to her question.

"Maybe a little bit. We are working together a lot right now." I try to pass it off as not a big deal. I'm not sure if I was successful though. I try to brush it off a bit while I prepare my own cup of coffee now that mom has filled her mug – she does just a splash of flavored creamer like I do when I'm making my own at home.

"Is she the one I get to meet this morning at the market?"

"Only if you behave yourself."

"I'll be on my best behavior. Your dad on the other hand…he's the one you should be worried about."

I roll my eyes. She is not wrong.

"Okay, let's get things together and get this over with."

Matt

Chapter Twelve

SASHA

ICED CARAMEL LATTE WITH AN EXTRA SHOT OF ESPRESSO AND THEN A SPLASH OF CHOCOLATE MILK

Social Post: How cute is this?? I am already loving this setup and can't wait to see everyone! #sashaloveslipstick #farmersmarket #summerthings #coloradogirl #noco #windsormarket #tablesetup

Image Description: Table setup at the market.

It's only ten in the morning and I am finally able to sit down and take a breath. The table is set up and we have everything working really well. Even though the market just technically opened, we've already had a steady stream of people coming by to say hi – mostly other vendors, but it's been good to connect with people before it gets too crazy. It's started slow so I've been able to get comfortable with those around us and settle into a system with Ashley. She's the one in front of the table and I'm behind it so I have a bit of something to hide behind.

By eleven, my email list is growing and we have been able to connect with several local businesses in between talking with others that come up to our table. Ashley has been able to schedule a few coffee chats too for her brand and we have already met a few of our followers. I can't believe we have this many people close to us that have been wanting to meet us in person. I double check that Ashley is good to go and then take a quick walk through the market. I want to see who all is here just as an attendee and not a vendor and I am ready for another cup of coffee and probably something to eat.

It takes me longer than expected to even find where the food vendors are and I'm enjoying looking at the different tables on my way to the far end of the market. I've stopped at a jewelry stand that makes earrings out of Aspen leaves and am seriously debating buying myself a pair when I hear a familiar voice close by. I know that voice. I smile to myself as I turn my head to meet Matt's gaze.

"Did you see the copper ones?" Matt asks me over my shoulder.

"No, where are they?" I ask as I spin around, grinning even bigger when he hands me an iced coffee. "What did you get me this time?"

"It's an iced caramel latte with an extra shot of espresso and then a splash of chocolate milk. The barista was very excited about it. And the copper ones are over there." He points at a display on the other side of the table. "You wear a lot of silver jewelry already, and the copper will stand out when you start switching over to fall makeup looks."

"Well, that's quite the observation." I chuckle to myself a little bit. This man really does pick up on everything. I don't understand how he does it, but he does. In such a short amount of time, he is understanding who I am, what I like, and what I need even before I ask for it. Not gonna lie, I'm not mad about it. I go to pick up the earrings, but he is faster, grabbing the earrings and then looking for a coordinating necklace. He hands them to the lady behind the table and pays before I even have time to register what he is doing.

"You really didn't have to do that, Matt. I could have paid for those." I mildly scold him.

"I know. But these are a Colorado staple and they are going to look great on you. Now you can't say I never got you anything." He winks at me before handing me the bag. "Are you wanting to wander around a little more or head over to the table again? I checked on Ashley when I first got here and things were looking good over there."

"Let's head back. But I want to find something to grab for food first. I'm officially starving."

"Did you not eat this morning before you left to head over here?" He asks, stopping mid stride to make eye contact with me. If I'm not mistaken, he is now the one taking on the mildly scolding tone.

"I had a granola bar and then an apple. I ate. I'm a big girl that knows how to take care of herself," I remind him as we make our way back to our table. I spot a booth making breakfast burritos with a very big sign proclaiming "smothered in green chili" and I squeal. "Okay, another Colorado staple right here. And don't even think about it, I'm buying this time." He just shakes his head at me and then puts his hands up in mock surrender.

I purchase a handful of burritos, all in individual covered bowls to accommodate the sauce from the chili, and then we are on our way back to the table where it looks like a few others are now hanging out at the table.

"Do you know who's over at the table with Ashley?" I ask Matt as we get a little closer to see that they're having a full conversation and not just looking at the table.

"I guess it's time you met the parents." He says, then leads me over to the table. I don't even have the time to process what he just said before I'm being introduced. "Mom, Dad, I want you to meet Sasha. This is the client I have been working with for the last few weeks and she's been helping Ashley out along the way too."

His mom immediately gives me a hug. Okay, guess we aren't shy in this family. I have to mentally tell myself to relax and that this is okay. "It's so good to meet you! Ashley has been so excited about working with you and about the market today. I really appreciate you helping her with her content."

"Absolutely. It's been amazing working with her, and Matt too," I quickly add, making sure I am making eye contact with everyone.

His dad is looking at me like he's trying to figure me out and I honestly don't know what to do with that. Matt nudges him a bit and then his dad steps forward.

"Nice to meet you, Sasha." He extends his hand and I shake it. "Is this your first week at the market?"

"Yes! I am surprised I haven't been here before, and honestly have no clue how we got selected to have a table here, but I'm hoping we get enough good feedback that this becomes a regular thing. And I found burritos," I say as I hold up the bag, "do you and your wife want one? I got plenty!" I am so awkward and I know it. This man is not breaking eye contact and I don't know what to do with it. I make a quick glance at Matt and Ashley signaling for some help just as they both burst out laughing. "Okay, whatever the joke was, I apparently missed it. Do I get to be clued in yet?"

Ashley comes over and puts her arm around my shoulder. "Dad likes to make people uncomfortable with borderline inappropriate eye contact. He's been doing it for at least ten years and it's a great way to see who wants to maintain a conversation and who scares easily. I think you passed." She looks over her shoulder to her dad who simply gives her one nod of his head. Okay then, guess I passed that test.

"So, can we eat now?"

The day flies by. By the end of it, I'm sweaty and sore and so insanely happy, but completely emotionally drained. My bag is filled with business cards and notes from other businesses and creators. My phone has so many texts to follow up with. And my calendar has five new coffee chats booked over the next two weeks with local businesses wanting to talk about what a collaboration with a makeup influencer may look like – one of which is a local spa! My heart is so full right now, and even if I don't get invited back, today was amazing.

"Is this the last of the boxes that need to be brought to the car?"

Matt asks as he comes back from his last trip to the car with the signs and table.

"Yeah, that's it. I have everything else in my bag. I am so glad we don't have to deal with a bunch of product on top of all of this," I fall into stride next to him as we head to the parking lot where the other vendors are doing the same.

"I think it went really well, and maybe one day you'll have your own products to show at something like this," he sets the box in the trunk and then latches it closed before leaning on the trunk to look back at me. We aren't uncomfortably close, but closer than usual when we talk in person.

"I don't know about that, that feels like a completely different undertaking than talking about makeup or connecting with business owners," the thought honestly freaks me out. There is so much that goes into product development. Sourcing and manufacturing and packaging and fulfillment and social media – plus consistently coming out with new products that will fit the target demographic.

"It's definitely not something you have to figure out right now, but maybe one day," he smiles at me gently then takes the bag from my hands to place in the backseat of my car. "Do you have plans for the rest of your night?"

"Um, I don't think so. Probably just home for a shower, nap, and then ordering in something. I do not want to cook tonight," I chuckle softly at that. Even the thought of a hot shower right now is unpleasant – maybe a cool one would be a better choice. God, I hope I didn't burn today. I hate sunburn, but I think I forgot to reapply as often as I usually do.

"You should come over to my parent's house with us. We usually do a family dinner on Saturday nights after the market so mom can use the new produce and dad grills out."

"Would that be okay? I don't want to intrude on your family time, but that sounds amazing," I open my driver side door and lean in to start the car so it can begin cooling off.

"Absolutely, my mom actually texted me when she left earlier to remind me to invite you, open invitation."

"Yeah, okay. Can I run home to shower first and then meet you there?"

"You got it. I'll text you the address."

"Perfect, see you soon." I get in the car and take a moment to feel the AC on my skin.

It isn't long before I'm parking in the driveway next to Matt's car and making my way into the house. Matt's mom opens the door before I even have a chance to decide if I'm going to knock or ring the doorbell.

"How can I help, Mrs. Carter?" I ask as we make our way into the kitchen and I wash my hands in the sink. It's one of those really nice brushed stainless-steel deep farmhouse ones with a beautiful pulldown matching faucet. The countertops are a white and grey quartz that compliment the slate blue cabinets and light grey backsplash. I may work in hardware, but I love a good kitchen design. "This kitchen is absolutely stunning!" I tell her as I come over to the counter she is working on.

"Thank you so much. We redid it a couple of years ago and I am still in love with how it turned out. So glad we went with the classic stainless steel everything even though they tried to sell me on black hardware and sink. It would have looked awful with the blue."

"I completely agree. When I'm not doing makeup, I'm living at Home Depot, so this kitchen definitely makes me happy."

"That's right," she nods slightly like she's reminding herself of a conversation, "my kids told me that. And, on that note, you are not allowed to call me Mrs. Carter. You may call me 'Momma' or 'Martha' but none of that Mrs. stuff allowed, *capiche?*" She looks at me with such a stern expression, I get the feeling that I did something wrong.

"Oh, absolutely, I can do that, Martha. Is there something that I can help with in here?" I need to get busy with my hands or I am going to continue overanalyzing my interactions with her up until right now.

She puts me to work chopping up tomatoes, cucumbers, onions, and garlic for a salad and then moves on to slicing the veggies for the grill. The fresh zucchini looks amazing and I can't wait to see what she does with it. We talk for the next fifteen minutes or so about their shopping habits at the market, their next home improvement project, and Ashley going back to college. Just as we hit that topic, Ashley comes downstairs to join us. As soon as she notices what we are talking about, she visibly stiffens a bit.

"I'm not ready to go back." She admits quietly as she settles onto one of the stools at the island and picks up some sliced cucumbers to munch on. "This summer has been amazing and we aren't even halfway done with it yet. I need to connect with my advisor soon to finalize my classes for the fall semester."

"You get to stay home while going to classes, right?" I ask her, trying to get her talking about it a bit. Every time college has come up with us in the past, she has strategically changed the subject or brought it back to me. I don't know what she isn't wanting to talk about, but I want to know more about her, so I try to give her an opportunity to open up to me if she wants to take it.

"Yeah. I had been debating staying on campus this year, but it's not a far drive and I save money staying at home."

"And it keeps you out of trouble too." Her mom pipes up.

"I don't get in trouble, mom. I'm a perfect angel, remember? Matt is the one you have to worry about." She says that last statement with a smirk at me and I wonder how I'm supposed to take that comment.

Chapter Thirteen

MATT

UPSIDE DOWN CARAMEL MACCHIATO WITH OAT MILK

Having Sasha at my parent's house, doing dinner prep with my mom, and laughing with my sister is amazing. It just feels right. I came inside to get the tools for the grill and the meat out of the fridge to see her chatting away with them while they cut up the vegetables. She fits in here so well and I can't help but feel comfort in knowing that she is here. With me. Mom obviously loves her and she got the thumbs up from dad too. Not that I had any doubt. Sasha is amazing. Seeing her here with everyone just solidified that for me.

"Once you ladies finish chopping all of that, do you want to come outside under the umbrella while dad and I grill?" I ask as I make my way to the back patio door.

"Yep, I'm going to grab some drinks and then we will be out shortly, don't leave the patio door open long – you're letting all the cool air outside." My mom scolds me playfully so I quickly close the door behind me and join my dad over on the patio. It doesn't take the girls long to come out and join us with drinks, the salad, and a few other extras in hand.

While we finish cooking and prepping for dinner, conversation moves to childhood memories and vacations. We both enjoyed our time at Estes in the fall and beach days at the Outer Banks. We both went around ten with our families, her going a few years before I did. My mom is visibly amused when she realizes that Sasha is older than I am. I already knew that though. Luckily, we are able to make it through nostalgia without breaking out the embarrassing elementary program or teenage acne photos. *Thank you, Lord!*

Dinner comes and goes without any issues or awkward conversation, and then I offer to drive her home after we are done cleaning up in the kitchen. She had a seltzer with dinner and I don't want her stressing over finding a ride. I don't usually drink over at my parent's house in case I need to pop out for something, so that worked out well. We say our goodbyes and Sasha promises to come by again for another Saturday night dinner sometime soon. Then it's off to my car to make the short drive back to her apartment. Dad offered to bring her car back to her place tomorrow when my parents head out for some errands so she doesn't have to try to figure that out either.

"So, how do you think today went?" I ask her as I pull out of the driveway. My Civic provides a bit of room for her to stretch her legs, but not so much that she feels far away from me. Seeing her get comfortable in my car has me thinking of summer drives with my hand resting on her thigh instead of on the steering wheel.

She lets out a deep sigh and leans her head against the headrest, looking out the window. "I am hurting absolutely everywhere and I am exhausted, but I think today went really well. I don't know if anything is going to come from the contacts I made today or the conversations that were started, but it's a whole new group of people, so I'm hopeful. And I had a great time tonight with your parents. Thank you again so much for letting me tag along. How do you think this morning went? Ready for the next steps with my project?" She asks me. I can sense the tiredness of her voice and know she is going to crash hard tonight. I have to keep my eyes and mind focused on the road and the question she just asked me and not on her getting in her bed tonight.

"You did incredible today. Seeing everyone with your cards and talking about your table was really neat. And you finally got to meet mine and Ashley's parents." I smile at her quickly before bringing my attention back to the road. "I think we can take tomorrow to recover and then we will reassess next week to see what next steps would make the most sense. Take tomorrow to make a list of contacts and who you want to connect with as a potential client or collaboration and we will start there at our next meeting."

She nods at me and then goes back to staring out the window.

"You good?" I ask her. She's quieter than normal and I don't know how to fully read her right now when I can't see her face clearly.

"Yeah, just tired. I guess I'm a little worried that today wasn't enough and all the work we have put into everything is going to be a waste. But I really want to make this work. For me and for Ashley. And for you too," she gives me a little smirk then continues, "I guess I'm just not wanting to get my hopes up too high but still patiently optimistic. Does that make sense?"

"Definitely. I want this to work for you too. And I enjoy spending time with you too, if I'm being honest. So, if this turns into more Saturdays spent together at the market and then grilling out afterwards, I won't complain about that." There. That's out there now. I've kept my interest pretty subtle up until now and even that comment can be deemed as a friend thing, not necessarily more. But I want to start letting her know that I am interested in more. More than interested, desperate for it. I hear her take in a breath and then grab her purse. I didn't even realize we were almost to her place already. That went way too quickly.

I pull up next to the sidewalk and put on my hazards so she can exit safely.

"Thanks, Matt." She says as she unbuckles and pulls her keys out of her purse. She takes another few breaths before turning to make eye contact with me. I take a moment to just appreciate how beautiful she is. Not a drop of makeup on right now and she couldn't be prettier to me. I have to stop myself from telling her that and instead just nod my head and smile in acknowledgment. She smiles back at me then opens her door and starts to get out. "I'm enjoying spending time with you too." And then she steps out and closes the door. I wait until she is inside her building before I give myself a little congratulatory "YES!!" Quietly of course, because I don't want someone hearing on the sidewalk. Once the light goes on in her bedroom, I head for my place and start working on the next phase of growth – for her business, and for us too.

The next morning, I take some time mapping out the week ahead. This includes ordering her coffee for the week, some mornings at the shop and then a few mornings as a delivery to her work when I know she has to leave early. I hope having a note to leave it at the Service Desk and then call her is enough to actually get it to her each morning, but I will hopefully find out soon.

Then, I work on compiling a list of everyone she met with yesterday. She had a list going on her phone of the connections she made and little notes to go back to for reference, so I have a master list to go off of. At least until she goes through this list and decides who she wants to prioritize.

I'm excited to see what comes of these and how many of them will be collaborations or even full product deals. I get creative with Sasha's ads for the next week and then the suggested videos. I use some money on ad spend so that enough of this is legit on her end to make sense. I've been watching who engages with her content for months, so this part is becoming easier and easier to manipulate.

What's going to get my creativity going is the collaborations. I can't just cold message all of these places. I need it to be their idea. So, the spa that connected with Sasha is going to start seeing a lot of content about color theory and makeup brands that also feature skincare. One of those makeup/skincare brands is going to start seeing Sasha's tutorials from last fall on transitioning skincare to winter skin needs as well as the benefits of connecting with smaller influencers. And the permanent jewelry company is going to get several requests for a lipstick charm this week. Social media "suggested" content has become my favorite thing to play with – especially in a target demographic that pretty much lives on social media channels. It doesn't take more than a suggestion or two before the clicks start coming in.

Will all of them go the way I want them to? I can only hope. But my success rate with this is very good. My sister doesn't call me "Mastermind" for no reason. Yes, I know about that.

It's finally a decent hour, so I send a message over to Ashley.

Me: Hey. Are you recovered enough to get some work done today?

Ashley: No. I am dead. Everything hurts. Please tell me we don't have to do this every Saturday!

She follows it up with several gifs that convey how sore she is and apparently, with quite the mess of hair.

Me: You don't have to do this every Saturday. I'm thinking of giving you a week off and then going back into it. What all do you have planned for Fourth of July content this week? With everything planned for the farmers market, I didn't get the final content plan from Sasha and I want to double check it against what I am working on.

Ashley: Yeah, give me a sec.

A minute later she sends me a picture of a notecard with the content schedule for the week. It's all videos and pictures that are already done and scheduled to post. Part of what they have been working on is getting ahead of the content schedule. Batch creating, recording, and scheduling it out so that way they aren't stressing about consistency.

They're going for a traditional and classy Americana look series this week with basics in summer skincare, all day makeup looks, and pool friendly eyeshadows, liners, and mascaras. Perfect. I'm glad they are going simple with this. Ashley did an all-out look last year and then borrowed one of my hoodies. That thing still has blue glitter on it. And my mom has even tried to wash it. Twice!

Me: Thank you, Ash. I will see you later. Rest up and let me know if you and Sasha need anything with your meeting tomorrow.

Ashley: Sounds good. Do you want to meet up at all tomorrow before or after my meeting with her or wait until Tuesday morning like normal?

Me: Let's do Tuesday morning at the coffee shop. I have a full day planned tomorrow.

Ashley: Okie. Love you.

Me: Love you too. Thanks again for the pic.

Matt

Chapter Fourteen

SASHA

ICED RASPBERRY LATTE WITH CHOCOLATE DRIZZLE

Social Post: Something that people don't chat about a lot as a side effect of social anxiety – the intense exhaustion that comes after having to "people" for extended periods of time. I feel like the market yesterday went really well, but my entire body hurts today. I may spend the day in bed today and just rest. If you saw me yesterday, make sure you tag me in your photos! #sashaloveslipstick #thisisanxiety #farmersmarket #noco #coloradosummer

Image Description: lazy Sunday morning selfie holding my coffee mug in the kitchen

Sunday is spent in bed. My body is absolutely paying for yesterday. It was a long day, physically, mentally, emotionally – all the things. And I need a reset day. I make my way to the couch for part of the day and watch Star Wars with Carter for a bit before he goes to work. I make it thirty minutes into Episode Four before I pass out again. I am just too tired to even function today apparently.

I wake up to my phone buzzing with a text notification

Matt: Just want to tell you again that you did great yesterday. I know you're probably beat today, but you did good. Get your rest and I'll chat with you soon.

I smile at my phone as I read the message, debating how to respond so it doesn't seem like I'm ungrateful or fishing for compliments.

Me: Thanks, Matt. I appreciate all of your help and the encouragement too. See you Tuesday.

At eight, Kylie gets home with dinner and we eat on the couch, watching Friends reruns until Carter gets home at ten. I never even got out of my pajamas today, a cute silk set with lipstick kisses all over it. I'm predictable with what I like, no shame in that at all.

I finally drag myself back to my room to shower, change into clean pajamas, this one a simple blue nightshirt with "coffee queen" on the front, and climb into bed. I set my alarm for work the next morning and promptly pass out again. If this is how event days are going to go, I don't know how many of these I can commit to. I'll have to chat with Matt about this at our next meeting.

Monday starts really well. It's the last day of June but the first day of our July as far as the Home Depot calendar goes, so it's a reset for metrics. I love starting a new month so I can try to hit goals all over again. I dress in my dark wash skinny jeans, a white short-sleeve shirt with light pink flowers on it and then grab my dark pink cardigan to go with it. It's a little chilly this morning so I am thankful for the layers as I head to the coffee shop before my shift. I seriously love this place.

I run inside and smile at the barista.

"Hey, Sasha. I have your order ready to go." She smiles at me. I stare at her for a second, trying to understand what she just said.

"Um, thank you, but I didn't order anything ahead of time today..." I drift off as she hands me a bag and a drink. "What is it and who ordered this?" I ask her.

"Um, it was in our system this morning with your number and name on it and the time you would be at the shop to pick it up. It's an iced raspberry latte with chocolate drizzle and then a sausage breakfast sandwich on a bagel. I can get you something else if you would like, but this was made like three minutes ago for you."

"No, that's okay. This is great. Thanks, Sarah." I grab the items, leave a tip, and then head back to my car. Last week with the order paid in advance was a once in a blue moon moment, this, I don't even know how to respond to this. But I'm not turning down free coffee and this is so very good!

Work is unremarkable. I go through my reports, prepare for my meetings, place orders, check inventory, eat lunch, walk my department, grab carts from the lot, and run a register for a little while when things get busy. By the time I'm clocking out, my feet hurt and I am ready for dinner. I text Ashley to see if she's okay meeting at Panera so we can eat something while working on things for the next month. Since it's the start of a new month, we are going to go over analytics, trends, and overall content plans. It's a good check-in time.

Twenty minutes later, Ashley meets me and we both grab a salad and lemonade then find a quiet corner of the restaurant to work. We split up the list from the market and start sending emails and messages. I go through the social media tags from the weekend and re-share a bunch of pictures to my stories and then post a quick recap video too. Ashley does much of the same on her own accounts.

At 8:00, we call it a night. We are both drained and have gotten so much done. Content is mapped out through the middle of August and we have a solid plan to get there for both of our channels. This week is going to fly by at this rate.

Tuesday is my early day at the store so I am walking in as the doors unlock at five. We open early in the summer for contractors so I'm back on the floor just a few minutes later. The one downside of Tuesdays, I am here before my coffee shops open. Except for one, but they burn their beans and I don't want a sugary drink this early in the morning. At 6:30, I get a text from Carol at the Service Desk.

Carol: Hey love, you have a delivery up here when you get a moment.

Me: Thank you. What is it?

Carol: Smells like coffee and something yummy.

What? I head up there as soon as I finish putting away my returns from last night. Sure enough, there's a hot coffee and cinnamon roll waiting for me. The coffee has two sugars and two creamers in it, just like how I take my regular coffee.

"Any idea on who brought this by?" I ask her as I look it over. There's no notes on it except for my name, phone number, and the store address.

"Nope. One of the girls from the coffee shop down the street just dropped it by saying it was for you. I didn't think to ask. I figured you ordered it with it being so early when you got in today."

"Huh, nope. Not me." I shake my head and then my phone is buzzing again with a call to head back to the department.

The rest of the day goes by in a blur and it takes me nearly two hours to finish my coffee. It's one customer issue after another and complicated returns that I have to go deal with. Why people can't look at warranty information or use power tools for their intended purpose, I will never know apparently.

As I clock out early that afternoon, I am thankful that I have a few hours before I'm set to meet Matt. I need a breather before I go talk business. Can I just turn my brain off for an hour? Is that an option? I go sit in my car and check emails noticing that one came in from a new salon and spa not far from my apartment. It has a coupon for half off a pedicure. Don't mind if I do. I call and they have the space to fit me in with enough time for my meeting with Matt.

I walk into the space at 2:40. My appointment is at 2:45 so I have a minute to grab a water bottle and look around. The waiting area is beautiful, open, and has a water feature in the corner. I head over to the wall of polishes to pick out something fun for the warmer weather. This may be my only pedicure this summer, so I need to make it worth it. I grab a really pretty raspberry pink from the wall and head back over to the check in desk. As I wait for the girl to check my information with the computer, I look out the front window. There are several businesses in this plaza, including a gym, and Matt is leaving the building right at that moment. It takes me a moment to notice that it's actually him. I'm not going to try to get his attention from across the parking lot, I'm going to be seeing him in just a little while anyways.

As he reaches his car, he looks up and we make eye contact. Well, I think we make eye contact. It's across the parking lot and I have no clue how bad the glare is over here. But I still smile and give a little wave just in case. He waves back then heads to his car. I hope that wave was for me, otherwise, that would be super awkward.

"Okay, we are ready for you at chair two." The receptionist brings me back to what I'm here for and I head over to the chair and stick my feet into the warm bubbly water. The scent of peppermint feels amazing on my senses as I sink into the water and the comfy chair. An hour later, my feet feel incredible, I've enjoyed a calf and foot massage, and my toes are painted a lovely shade of Far Out Fuchsia from OPI. I love this color!

I head home and grab my work bag and then head to the library to meet up with Matt. I told him I need someplace that I won't spend money today since I have been going out a lot. I get there right on time to find him already working at a table. He looks up and smiles at me then hands over a bag from the grocery store.

"I know we are meeting at dinner time, so I grabbed you something little." He says as he finishes up his email or whatever he was working on a moment ago.

"You did not have to do that, but thank you." I know eating in the library isn't really something we are supposed to do, so I'm thankful when it's a snack box that I can eat easily without making a mess – hummus, carrots, pita bread, grapes, and a hard-boiled egg. "I didn't know you went to the gym over in the plaza with Lotus." I bring up seeing him earlier once I am sitting and situated.

"Yeah, been going for about a year now. I sit at a computer for hours every day, if I don't make it a point to go a few times a week, I would not be very healthy." He chuckles as he answers me. "I thought I saw you at Lotus when I was leaving, it was hard to tell from how far away I was."

"Yeah. They just opened so I got an email blast from them with a coupon, so I got a pedicure and just chilled for a bit. By the way, please tell me I won't be this tired after every event." I tell him, absolutely exasperated.

"No, it gets easier. There will be less prep going into them and more people coming to you at your table rather than you going to network around. And I'll be there to help provide some breaks next time hopefully."

We work together for a few hours, setting up my email campaigns to my newest extra on my site that is set to go live in two weeks. Now is the time to make sure all of the automations are in place so it is ready when it's scheduled. And we can start thinking ahead to fall and winter content. Content creation is a lot of working ahead at least three months. The goal is to have the bulk of content and campaigns mapped out six months in advance and then add in the other things as needed.

By the time we are done, I'm feeling like we are in a good space with things. He walks me to my car and helps me get everything inside.

"Have a good night, Sasha. Things are looking good on my end. Analytics are showing that this last campaign is working how we were thinking it would. I will see you next Tuesday unless something else comes up. Text me if you need me." He smiles at me then walks off.

This is just too seamless. The conversation. The growth. He really is that good with what he does. And I am enjoying spending time with him – both the work side and the leisure side too.

The rest of the week is more of the same routines.

Wednesday I have a new coffee order waiting for me at the shop.

Thursday I end up waking up late and an order is delivered at 7:30, half an hour after I clock in at the store.

Friday morning, Ashley comes over to the apartment for content and has coffee with her that she picked up on her way over.

Friday afternoon I head to work for my closing shift. I'm scheduled to work from one until ten tonight and I was running late, so I forgot to pack a lunch for myself. I clock out at 5:30 to run to Subway just as I hear my name over the intercom. I head to the Service Desk to find a sandwich waiting for me.

Okay. This is officially getting weird. Again, no one knows who ordered it. It's just here. I shake my head and go back to the breakroom to eat and then finish off the night. I'm going to miss fireworks, but that also means it should be a quiet night. At least my eyeshadow is still sparkly and shining. I'm so ready for a quiet weekend after this week. And all the content from this week is doing really well. I'm glad we went for summer technique and weather styles rather than full Americana this year. It's going to have a longer "life expectancy" than the traditional holiday makeup. And it's easier to take off when I get home that night too.

Life continues with our regular routines – spending time at work, with my roommates, with Ashley, and with Matt. I start getting more texts from Matt of things he sees when he is out running errands that make him think about me, or a package showing up at the house from Amazon with things I didn't order. There's usually a note attached to those.

A pink pillow with a bunch of lipstick swatches in a pattern on them: "This popped up on my suggested purchases lists last week and I immediately thought of you. Have a great day. – Matt."

A pack of makeup inspired stickers and notecards: "I know you are sending out some follow up messages to those you have been connecting with at farmers markets and collaboration inquiries. I figured these would be a nice touch to include with those notes. By the way, you are starting to look a lot more comfortable at those events. I'm proud of you. – Matt."

A variety pack of coffee flavors from a new company in North Carolina: "My parents brought home a bag of this from their last trip and I really enjoyed it. I wanted you to be able to experience it too and maybe try something new. Let me know which one is your favorite. I think it's going to be the Raspberry Creme – try that one iced or cold brew. – Matt"

He was right – the Raspberry Creme was spectacular and when I told him that, he promptly set up a subscription for me so I get a new pound of coffee every two weeks, usually with another one to try or a refill of one of the others that I liked. I feel incredibly spoiled. And seen. He notices those little things and takes care of them. He does it in a way that I don't feel like I'm bothering him though – it's like he wants to make this effort. Effortlessly.

It continues like this throughout July until early August when we meet up at our regular space for our weekly check in. I'm going to be meeting with Ashley tomorrow, so we are meeting earlier so I can help her with some back to school shopping and prep. And a last girl's day out too before the semester starts in a few weeks.

I walk into the coffee shop at four and smile when I see Matt waiting for me at our table, and no surprise, there's a drink there waiting for me.

"What did you get for me this time?" I ask as I set my bag on the ground and start pulling out my notebook and pen. He passes the cup to me along with a small package.

"It's a dirty chai but I asked them to add a little more cinnamon to it. Kept it simple for you today," he smiles at me as he waits for me to take a sip. He does this every time too, waits to make sure I like what he picks. It feels important to him.

"This is perfect. Sometimes going with a classic like this is just what I need. What's in the box?" I don't want to assume it's for me, but I'm pretty sure it is. He holds it out to me and waits for me to grab it. I look at his eyes again and he gives a subtle nod to encourage me to open it now. Awkward, okay.

I open the lid to find a beautiful pen set. They're rose gold and metal. I look back up at him to see his smile on his face. How he could ever be worried about giving me a pen I have no idea.

"Take them out, test them and see how you like them," he encourages me.

I do and they feel amazing. The weight is perfect in my hand and I immediately start writing with one to test the ink.

"It writes like my favorite ink pens!"

"I know." And with a wink from him and a blush from me, we get back to work.

The time flies by and pretty soon, the shop is closing up, but I'm not ready to be done. We've spent the last thirty minutes chatting about our own college days as Ashley gets ready to go back.

"Do you want to grab dinner and head back to the apartment with me for a bit? I don't have to meet Ashley until noon tomorrow and I'm hungry," I ask as we head out to the cars with our bags.

"Yeah, that sounds great. I can go pick something up and meet you there if that works for you, what are you in the mood for tonight?"

"Surprise me." I smile at him and then head off for the apartment. I need to double check that there's no random dirty dishes around and see if everyone else is still at work. And maybe light a candle or something. And text Kylie to see if she has time for a five minute pep talk. She wasn't able to answer my call, but she did send all of the best gifs and reminders to breathe and just enjoy a chill night.

It feels like I'm going to wear a line into the rug in front of the couch by the time I hear Matt's footsteps approaching the front door. I wait a breath after he knocks before I walk to the door, not wanting to seem too eager, even though I am. I open the door to a smiling Matt. He holds up the takeout bag from one of the local places.

"I was in the mood for pad thai. I grabbed a few dishes so we can do family style if that works for you," he makes his way into the kitchen and begins removing the containers from the bag as I pull out dishes and utensils.

"That's perfect. Let me grab the Sriracha out of the fridge. I like to spice mine up just a bit."

"I would not have pegged you as a Sriracha girl," Matt muses behind me as I find the bottle on the door.

"Only with pad thai. I don't like it on anything else," I shrug a little as we begin plating what we want. "Do you want to sit at the table or on the couch and watch a movie?"

"Let's do the couch. I picked dinner so you can pick the movie."

We get settled into comfortable silence as the movie starts and we work through our plates. He surprises me a bit when he reaches over to snag a bite of my pad thai. I playfully tap his fork away, "What do you think you're doing?" I ask in mock alarm as I hold my plate away from him.

"I was curious. I've never put hot sauce on my pad thai before. Please?"

I smile back at him and offer my plate, "It's not hot sauce, it's Sriracha, and of course. Definitely interested to see what you think, but I won't be offended if you hate it. I'm the only one except for one of my coworkers that I know that does this. I saw one of my friends at work do it a year ago when we got food for the team and I've done it ever since."

"That's actually pretty good. What else did you do besides the hot sauce, I mean, Sriracha."

"I add a little bit of lime juice too. Most of the time they have the limes cut up in the containers so I just squeeze one over the dish and then mix it in with the Sriracha. Lemon is not the same – don't do that. Made that mistake once and it was ruined."

He leans back a little on his end of the couch and laughs. "I love how passionate you are about things that you love. You've got it all figured out."

I turn my body a bit so I'm facing him as I mess with the rest of the food on my plate, "I don't know about that. I don't have much figured out. Pad Thai and lipstick, yeah I got that, life, not so much."

"You seem to be doing okay with what you have figured out though, Sasha. Don't diminish what you are doing. I'm amazed at all that you have done so far over the last few weeks. I don't know if you have others telling you that, but it's true." He holds my gaze for a moment before he finishes his last bite then stands. "Can I bring your plate to the kitchen?"

As he brings the dishes into the kitchen and sets the leftovers in the fridge, I take a beat to look back at this year. I have done a lot. And no, my life isn't perfect. But this moment is. He finds his spot next to me again and we find an easy space between us. The movie continues and we chat through it a little – life, school, the approaching fall coffee drinks. Matt tells me a little bit about his friends that he went to school with and their hobbies. He shows me pictures of some woodworking projects one of them recently worked on and I start building a perfect coffee cabinet in my head.

Before long, it's approaching ten and the tv has shut off because we didn't pick another movie.

"I should probably head out. I'm meeting with Luca tomorrow to help him deliver some new pieces to my parents. They wanted to upgrade some things in their house so I need to get the old table and chairs out and get the ones Luca made. Thanks for letting me hang out a bit tonight." We make our way toward the door, he grabs his keys and I pull my cardigan a little closer. I always get a little cold towards bedtime.

"Sounds good. I'd love to see a picture of it all set up if you think of it."

"If you want a picture, I can send you a picture," he smiles at me as he opens the door. He leans on the doorframe as I do the same to the other side.

"Thanks, Matt. Tonight was nice." I don't want it to end. I have to force myself not to say that last part out loud. Getting to know Matt outside of work conversations has been so good.

"I enjoyed it too," and there's the awkward moment. We both just stand there, alternating between looking at our feet and each other. Like we are both waiting for the other to do something. What? I don't know.

"Have fun with Ashley tomorrow. Goodnight Sasha."

"Goodnight Matt. Drive safe." And then he was gone. And I find myself thinking about why I wish he would have given me a kiss or even a hug goodnight. Where did that come from?

Chapter Fifteen

SASHA

SALTED CARAMEL COLD FOAM COLD BREW

Social post: Back to school shopping for someone else is a whole new experience. Look at how cute these cups are that we found today!! #sashaloveslipstick #backtoschoolshopping #coloradothings #augustishere #cups

Image Description: Selfie of me and Ashley holding up our new travel coffee mugs covered in lipstick swatches.

It feels like just a few moments later and then I'm going shopping with Ashley to get things that she needs for back to school. She's staying at home again this year, but still needs a few things for the new semester, and she didn't want to bother her mom or her other friends to go out today. This is our last week to meet with our regular schedule, so I'm happy to go with her for this. And I also get to take a look at the new planners and pens for the season too. And no, I don't have an office supply problem.

Three stores and four hours later, we are both completely beat and my car is at capacity with bags.

"Hey, I hit my step goal for the day." Ashley tells me as we get back in the car and I can't help but laugh at her.

"I think I hit my goal by the time we finished at the first store. My feet are killing me." I get my bag settled in my car and put my phone in the stand then adjust my sunglasses. In Colorado, sunglasses are a must. It's so bright here all the time. Not complaining though. "What do you say we find some dinner then head back to your house to sort through everything? Any requests?"

She shakes her head then scrolls in her phone for a minute, "How do you feel about sushi? There's that Poke place in Johnstown we can go to. It's a bit of a drive, but that sounds really good right now."

"Perfect! And then we can get Boba too!"

We drive in comfortable silence for a bit before Ashley starts the conversation up again. She's been fidgeting in the seat next to me for the last ten minutes, playing on her phone, and moving things around in her purse. I could tell she wanted to bring something up, but didn't want to push her. I've had enough of those uncomfortable conversations before that I don't want to put her in that position.

"So, do you like my brother?" I can feel her eyes on me as I focus on the road and take a breath before responding.

"Um, where is that coming from?" I am genuinely confused because who knows where this is going. I haven't been flirting with him, have I? I mean, we are together several hours every week, and we text almost daily. He's starting to open up to me a little more and I am getting to know Matt, not just him as the funnel guy, but him as a person too.

"I don't know. You guys just seem to fit really well together. He's comfortable around you. I'm going to be busy with school soon, and I like seeing you guys together. Just didn't know if you see it going somewhere or if you are curious about it going somewhere..." She lets her thoughts drift off and then waits for my response. I sit in the silence for a minute, thinking it over.

"Honestly, I don't know, babe. I do enjoy spending time with him. If he decides to ask me out, I will probably say 'yes.' Does that answer your question?" I really hope that answers her question. Because I don't want to tell her that 'yes, I wish your brother would have kissed me last night when he dropped me off at home and we spent twenty minutes talking about life and hiking and my excitement over fall coffee drinks coming back before he left.' I totally wanted him to. And I thought he was going to for a moment, but then he just smiled at me and told me to sleep well and have fun with Ashley today. Moment: gone.

"Yeah, I guess so. He gets so consumed with his projects sometimes that he forgets to look at the actual people around him. I'm hoping that with me in school again, he will be able to see you a bit more outside of work projects and see if it's something he wants to pursue. He hasn't had a girlfriend in a while, and from what you've told me, you haven't had anyone for a hot minute either."

"Let's not start playing matchmaker please." I laugh at her a little bit. "If it happens, great, if not, that's okay too. I like where we are and the friendship we have been able to grow along the way."

"I won't push him either way. But I make no promises aside from that." She winks at me and then turns on the radio so we can jam out to Taylor Swift all the way to dinner.

"You didn't pick this restaurant because Ulta happens to also be in this plaza, did you?" I ask her when we park in front of the strip mall. I had forgotten that there was one here along with a host of other places we could do some shopping and walking around later if we wanted to.

"Maybe..." She smirks at me. "And Matt may have given me a coupon that expires tomorrow for us to go check out what is currently drawing attention at this location." She waves the coupon at me.

"Is that a thirty% off full purchase coupon? How on earth did he get that?" I almost scream at her. I was not prepared for that level of potential spending to come out of her purse right now.

"I don't question him anymore. I just take his gifts and smile and remind him that he's my favorite. Now can we please go get food before we go play with the makeup? I need fuel before we tackle that craziness." She gets out of the car and starts to head inside. I shake my head and follow her. Some good spicy tuna sounds just about perfect right now.

Two hours later, we are both immersed in the skincare section of Ulta. We have been working on our winter skincare routine videos and Ashley wants to do a series on quick college skincare and budget skincare, so we are working through some options that we want to get.

"Any brands that either of us are hoping to partner with before the end of the year that we should try to prioritize with our purchases today?" Ashley asks me. I grab my phone to check our list from Matt and then check that against our social media favorites. It's a strategic process, but hopefully this means we have a more curated follower list and collaboration list when that happens too.

I show her the two we are each shooting for – one higher end and one more budget friendly for each of us. We wanted to have a variety, but still brands we could stand behind with products we already know and love. It's still August, but we are already looking ahead to potential holiday collection collaborations. Matt has us working with specific hashtags, smaller creators, and curated content on my website to try to attract the attention of these brands. We've done a couple more farmers market events and I'm working on planning a back to school night at a spa close to campus later this month. I'm finding I love the education aspect of these events and get so excited when I can answer questions about products or specific skincare or application problems.

We go back to shopping the skincare sections and I find the vegan skincare collection I have been looking for. One of the employees is stocking some facial mists in the collection so I wait for her to finish before I go over to see what all they are carrying in the store.

"You're *sashalovesmakeup* aren't you?" She asks me after staring at me for a moment.

"Yep, that's me! How's it going?" I ask as I grab the sampler pack from the top shelf.

"Great. It's so awesome to meet you in person! My name is Tilly! I've been following you for like two years. You're the big inspo for why I'm working here now. I just turned eighteen and am hoping to become a professional makeup artist in a few years after I get my esthetics license. Oh, put that one down." She reaches for what I am holding, plucking it out of my hand and promptly putting it back on the shelf.

"We have gotten so many returns of that sampler pack. I think one of the bottles is defective and it leaks everywhere. Get this one instead." She hands me a different collection from the same brand, the bottles are a little bigger, but the packaging looks so much better. I can see why – the price point is considerably higher.

"Why do brands do this?" I ask her. "It's great to meet you by the way. You definitely need to chat with Ashley. She is in college for business right now and will be getting her esthetics license after graduation. She would be a great person to connect with." I point to her at the end of the aisle then turn back to the two packages in front of me. "It's so annoying to love a product but have to tell my followers that you can't buy the smaller size because it breaks or you don't get your investment back."

She thinks about it for a moment and then shrugs, pointing back at the first set I picked up, "I'm not sure, but this one does it all the time. Have you checked out this one though?" She motions to the smaller brand display just next to the one I had been looking at. "It's a newer brand and they are actually Colorado based, woman owned, and the owner comes in like once a month to stock this herself. I got a sample pack last month and really love it. I've been recommending it to everyone and haven't had any returns or complaints yet." I look over the package and add a few of their items to my cart.

"I haven't seen this one yet, but you just gave me some more homework for this week. Thanks, Tilly. Please go chat with Ashley and exchange info so we can meet up once you get started with school!" She smiles and walks off while I add a few things to my to-do list on my phone. If I don't do it right this second, I am going to forget.

Check reviews on retailers for these two brands - specifically on sample sizes
Follow and research COBeauty brand
Do unboxing and first reactions to COBeauty brand products from Ulta

With my list updated, I go grab a new lipstick (obviously) and then head to wait for Ashley at checkout. It looks like I may need to chat with Matt about pivoting the content plan for the fall and go more on the "can we try to fix this problem" side of things instead of the "send me free stuff" plan. And I think I am very okay with this pivot.

Sasha
x
#sashaloveslipstick

Chapter Sixteen

MATT

AMERICANO WITH SUGAR FREE WHITE CHOCOLATE POWDER AND SUGAR FREE PEPPERMINT SYRUP

As Ashley transitions back to school, we transition content to learning more about brands with better sustainability and customer experience in mind. Apparently, the market for makeup and skincare has grown considerably fast in the last few years, thanks, in part, to social media. This means that a lot of brands have had to add to their catalog without being fully ready for that growth. Outsourcing, cutting corners, and just poor choices have been the result.

Since October is breast cancer awareness month, Sasha wants to do a Women Owned Business focus and then collaborate with a few smaller companies to donate to some local resource centers that are helping women with reproductive and female health concerns. I am more amazed by her the more I get to know her. I wasn't expecting this pivot from just makeup tutorials to campaigns to give back and even promoting industry changes across the board, but it is something I am absolutely on board with.

The random coffees and lunches continue to show up at her work or apartment. I think she may know it's me. I know the weekly packages she gets from me are appreciated because I get a text every time one shows up. And the things I send her are showing up in content too. I know Ashley knows about more than Sasha does, but I'm not sure if Ashley has told her or not. I definitely know she hasn't figured out how I am conveniently where she is at least twice a week. I told you I was good at what I do. She gets nervous when she is out and about without a familiar face, so I want to make sure she doesn't have to deal with that anxiety when I can help it.

Tonight, I plan on asking her out for the first time. Like, an actual date. Not just grabbing dinner after a meeting. We've been working together for several months now and I think she sees me as a friend as well as a business colleague. And I really want the chance to ask her out and see if this can go somewhere. Even if that means taking it slow. I have some big things in the works for her for the holidays this winter, and I would love to show up on her arm to those events to support her and see all of her hard work pay off.

That night, I show up at Home Depot right as she's clocking out. We make eye contact as she heads up to the front desk holding her cardigan and her purse. And the smile she gives me when she sees the iced coffee in my hand says I made a good choice.

"Long day today?" I ask her.

"It was not ideal." She smirks at me. "Drama with employees and random customer issues kept me going all day. I feel like I got nothing done and I am just so ready for food and a movie. I'm so glad I don't have work tomorrow."

We walk out to her car, parked right next to mine. The parking lot isn't dark yet so I felt okay having this conversation out here rather than inside where a coworker might make her uncomfortable.

"I was thinking." I pause as she starts pulling her keys out. "Do you want to go grab dinner with me? And then maybe we can watch a movie together? We are a bit ahead of schedule on some things so it doesn't have to be anything work related tonight." I bring my eyes up to meet hers and I honestly don't know how to read her at this moment. She takes a moment to consider my offer.

"I want to make sure I am understanding you here...are you asking me out on a date or just want to hang out as my friend? Not a problem either way, but I am so emotionally drained right now and I don't know how to interpret what you just said. And I know we've done the dinner and a movie thing a few times after a meeting, but I really need you to just tell me what you mean right now." She has a slight smile at the end of her lips, and I notice that she must have recently reapplied the color because it is flawless.

"I am asking you out on a date, Sasha. I've wanted to for a while, but wanted to make sure work was settled and we could really take some time getting to know each other outside of work stuff. Is that okay?" Again, I hold my breath. This could either go really well or I can get politely refused and continue working with her until the end of the year and have to pretend not to be a lovesick puppy dog around her.

"I would actually really like that." She responds lightly. She smiles at me then asks, "Who's driving?"

Fifteen minutes later we are settled in at Olive Garden enjoying breadsticks and people-watching. I may have made sure to plan this for when they were doing the endless soup and pasta this week for the date night. Sasha loves carbs and isn't afraid to order what she likes, and I absolutely love this. Over an hour goes by of us talking and laughing and I find it is so easy to get out of my shell with her. She is so easy to talk to, and not just behind a screen. I feel like I already knew her before tonight, but seeing her relax and just be present with me is amazing.

"I *so* needed this." She admits as she uses a breadstick to sop up the rest of the sauce in her bowl. "It's been crazy since Ashley went back to school and I needed a night to just not be 'on'. Does that make sense?"

"It definitely does. I've been waiting for a good time to take you out and just let you have a night to enjoy yourself. Where do you want to head to go watch something? Or is there something else you want to do?"

Her eyes light up as she connects with mine – "Boba?"

After finding a place that is still open with Boba, we head back to Home Depot to grab my car then off to my house to watch something before we call it a night.

"So, this is the first time I'm at your place, Matt. It's honestly exactly what I expected." She says to me as I let her inside and then make my way in after her.

I have a simple layout space, and I like to keep it clean. My kitchen is an open concept style opening up to a breakfast nook area that I've turned into my full dining area. My living space has a couch, a comfy chair, and a massive rug on the floor in front of a wood-burning fireplace. The floors out here are plank flooring that looks like real wood, but definitely isn't. The dark color shows quite a bit of dust so I stay on top of cleaning, but it contrasts nicely with the light green walls and my throw blankets on the couch. Ashley made sure I had plenty of "cuddle fabrics" at the apartment for when she comes to visit me. Down the hall I have a full bath in the hallway, my office, and then my bedroom that also has an ensuite. The office has a couch that converts to a bed for when I have friends over. All in all, it suits me well and I'm close to pretty much everything I need.

I haven't quite decided on what I am going to put on my walls, so right now it's pretty stereotypical with cityscapes and mountain pictures that my parents have found for me at the farmers market. My office has some neat schematics of different sci-fi ships and stations – it's where I let my inner geek out to play. But out in my main spaces, you have to look closer to find those parts of me.

I have mini Spiderman figures and symbols all over the place, you just have to know where to look. I smile as I notice Sasha finding a few as she peruses my bookshelf and window sills. The planters with my succulents have little figurines inside of them holding up the plants. Well, at least it looks that way. The throw pillow on my couch is black against the grey couch, but the pattern on it is a web if you look close enough to see. I have several book ends that are nods to Spiderman in other ways too and Sasha chuckles lightly as she sees those.

"So, there *is* a geek inside there somewhere, isn't there?" She asks me as she grabs her water bottle then heads to the couch. She looks right at home as she grabs the oversized throw blanket and cuddles up underneath it. "What are we going to watch tonight?"

"I am glad my geekiness doesn't offend you. I try to keep it kind of subtle out here so I don't come across like a six-year-old obsessed with their favorite superhero. I have several streaming services, so whatever you want to watch, we can probably make that happen." I tell her as I sit next to her on the couch, leaving plenty of space between us, even with her feet curled up beside her.

"I don't want to have to pay attention too closely to anything today if that is okay. I want to be able to zone out a bit so maybe something we have seen already – are you opposed to a Disney movie?"

"How does Big Hero Six sound?" I grab the remote and start making my way to the appropriate app on the TV.

"Absolutely perfect." She responds with a smile.

An hour or so later, I've popped popcorn and we are halfway watching the movie and halfway chatting. I'm impressing her (at least I hope that is what I am doing) with the little Easter Eggs throughout the movie nodding to other Disney movies or Marvel characters. At some point, she stretched out a bit so I was able to grab her feet and put them on my lap and start giving her a bit of a foot rub.

"Is this okay?" I ask her as I start tentatively rubbing the soles of her feet.

She groans softly. "It is very okay. Standing on concrete for nine hours today is not kind to my feet." I chuckle back at her as I rub her feet and ankles, taking my time to work out the sore spots and help her relax a bit. I make a mental note to start researching more supportive shoes that she can wear that will still go with her style. And maybe some at home oils or soaks that would help too.

By the time the movie is over, she is fully laying out on the couch, her legs spread across mine and a lazy smile on her face.

"Feeling better?" I ask her and she nods back at me, her hair a bit messy from being up against the couch and in the blanket. "Do you want me to follow you home or do you want to hang out for a bit longer?" It's fast approaching midnight and I don't want to push my luck tonight. This is new and I don't want to pressure her at all. But I definitely wouldn't mind a little more time with her so close to me like this.

"I should probably head home. This was amazing, but I want to get some content prepped in the morning. Oh, or maybe we can go for a hike and then work on content when it warms up?" She suggests as she stands up. She folds the throw blanket and places it back on the couch as we walk towards the kitchen.

"Sounds good. I can pick you up at your place at seven and then we can head out?"

"That will be perfect. We should be able to grab breakfast on the way up if that works," She smiles at me. I know she has been wanting to go hiking this summer, but with all that we have been working on, we haven't had the time to devote to it like we wanted. Normally I go out a few times a week in the summer rotating between Horsetooth trails and some of the others in the area. And I usually finish off the summer doing the incline at least five times and I haven't been down there once this year.

"Perfect." I agree with her as we head towards the door. I unlock it and open it as Sasha shrugs on her cardigan and puts her things back in her purse.

"This was an amazing night, Matt. Thanks for the low-key evening. I really enjoyed it." She smiles up at me in the doorway.

"Text me when you get home, okay? I want to make sure you make it home safely."

"Will do. Thanks again, Matt." She stops and lingers for a moment. Waiting.

"Am I allowed to kiss you goodnight, Sasha?" I ask her quietly, as I lean in a little bit, so my voice is almost a whisper. I hold my eyes on hers as I wait for a response and her shy smile tells me it's probably a 'yes' but I want to make sure before I assume and get smacked in the face. It's been a long time since I've attempted to date anyone, and I don't want to ruin this.

She doesn't respond with words. Instead, she steps a little closer to me and goes up on her tiptoes as she places a tentative kiss on my lips. Her right-hand rests on my shoulder and mine comes to her waist to keep her steady. The touch is soft, almost barely there, but the reaction is immediate. I smile up against her lips and then place my other hand softly on her neck, brushing her hair with my fingertips. I lean in again and press my lips to hers. I take the reins this time. It's not hard or desperate. It's soft and intimate and just us. I take in her scent of berries and bits of wood that lingers from her day at the store. She smells like summer and I hope my blanket smells like this when I go back inside.

A moment later I lessen my hold on her and she steps back. The smile she gives me is one of contentment.

"Goodnight, Matt. I'll see you in the morning."

And then she's gone and apparently, so am I.

Chapter Seventeen

SASHA

ICED AMERICANO WITH CARAMEL DRIZZLE

Social Post: If you're wondering if the new lip stain from COBeauty is kiss-proof...it is. #COBeauty #lipstain #kissprooflipstick #sashaloveslipstick #whatimwearing #latenightpost

Image Description: Selfie taken in a car mirror of the lower half of face with bright red lipstick still in place, it is dark outside.

I kissed him.

Like, I actually kissed him. He asked, but I initiated. I never am the one to make the first move physically like that, but it felt so insanely right. I needed to feel his lips on mine. And then he came back for more. And the way he held me close while he kissed me was absolutely perfect! If I didn't leave when I did, we probably would still be making out in his doorway. Which would not be a bad thing, I decide.

I text him as I step inside my apartment letting him know I

made it okay. I am so excited for tomorrow already and can't wait to see how our day goes. It will be a nice mix between work and pleasure. I have missed hiking this summer and want to get up to Horsetooth while it is a weekday and there won't be as many people up on the trails.

My relationship with Matt changed at some point this summer. It isn't just work anymore. I can definitely see things moving in a more relational direction. I enjoyed our time together tonight. It is so easy to be around him. And I feel very seen with him. I don't have to be "on camera perfect" or ready to sell or take care of people like in the aisles at work. I can just be. He seems to like taking care of me, and I won't say no to more of those foot rubs. That man should be paid for those massages. I chuckle to myself at that thought then go get ready for bed.

The house is quiet so Carter and Kylie must already be asleep. I had texted Kylie that I was going out with Matt so she wouldn't be worried, but I am a little bummed she's not still up so I can go over everything with her.

I take a quick shower and then get my bags ready for tomorrow so I don't have to stress in the morning about where my hiking shoes and good socks are. I put my hiking water bottle in the fridge and prep some ice cubes too. I'm not sure if they will be fully frozen, but it helps to have some extra cold things in my insulated bottle to make it last longer. Especially since it will be in my car for a few hours in the morning. The weather is set to get in the high seventies tomorrow, so I grab some shorts, a tank top, and a lightweight long sleeve top for if a breeze blows in. Adding my hat, scrunchie, and sunscreen to my bag, I think I am finally set for tomorrow.

Now I can get some rest before another long day tomorrow. A fun day. A day with Matt. But it's still going to be a longer day.

The morning comes too early, but I am thankful that I have everything ready to go. Kylie is up in the kitchen with her coffee and a book as I bring out my bags and go through my mental checklist again.

"Hiking today?" She asks me. She recognizes my bag and the extra stuff I always have in my car for hiking days.

"Yep." I let the 'p' pop a bit as I stand up and put my hair in a bun on top of my head. "Matt and I are going to head to Horsetooth and then get some work done this morning."

Kylie raises her eyebrows at me as she abruptly stops reading. The look tells me she knows exactly what I am thinking, and remembering from the doorway last night.

"Again? Is this another date or just hanging out together since Ashley is at school?"

"It's a date. And last night went really well so I'm excited to get to hang out again today" I trail off a bit as Kylie seems to be a bit shocked. I guess it's to be expected, this is new. I fill her in on what happened last night, keeping it brief to just the overview. She's not having it though.

"So…did anything fun happen on this impromptu date last night?" She teases me, a little wiggle in her eyebrows.

"He gives amazing foot rubs. Like, I'm pretty sure he massaged my feet for a solid twenty minutes. And there might have been a couple kisses goodnight at the door before I came home." I can feel my face heating with a blush. That's definitely new. I don't get embarrassed with my friends – not that I've had a guy to be embarrassed about in a while.

"Oh my gosh! Kisses? Foot rubs? Who is this man and why are you only just now telling me about this? You should have woken me up when you got home last night!" She practically screams at me.

"I knew if I woke you up last night we wouldn't go back to sleep until like three this morning and that would not be good for either of us. And I don't want to build it up too much too fast. It's new. And he is super reserved, so I don't want to scare him away by reading too much into things. Yes, I like him, and I really enjoyed last night, but this is new."

Kylie nods in agreement. "So, how are you feeling about it all now that you've slept on it?"

"I think I want to see where this goes. And if it includes another foot rub after our hike today…I won't say no to that either." I wink at her as I grab my bag and head out the door. Her laughter follows me as I close it behind me.

I make my way downstairs to the front of the building and stop at the front door for a moment. The windows look out to the street and I take a moment to compose myself. I am surprised that I'm not super overwhelmed right now. I'm a little nervous, of course. I can tell by the little tingles in my fingers and the needing to consciously settle my breathing pace. I double check that I have everything I need in my bag one more time and then peek out the window to see if Matt is parked close.

He is. His car is right outside and I must have impeccable timing because I get to see him step out of the car and begin making his way over to the side of the car closest to me. He leans against the vehicle and pulls out his phone, and the vibrating in my pocket tells me he is checking on me to see if I'm ready. I take another deep breath and then head outside, a very genuine smile on my face as I head over to meet him.

I'm not surprised at all when he opens the door for me and then motions for my bags, "I can put these in the back, your laptop should be okay in the trunk while we are hiking, there's some good shade at the parking lot before we head for the hike." I nod at him in agreement and then get settled into my seat, pulling out my sunglasses to wipe them off before putting them on – why is it so sunny already this morning?

"Just a warning - I am not caffeinated yet this morning so I am going to need that soon if you want me to be any sort of pleasant this morning," I mention to Matt as he slides back into the seat and starts the car. Soft music plays as he buckles up and looks over at me.

"Good thing I know what you need then, huh?" He asks with a smirk on his face as he reaches behind me to the cup holder that I didn't even notice was there. He passes me an iced coffee and then a small paper bag. "It's an iced Americano with caramel drizzle, let me know what you think of that one – and then some egg bites.

Some protein to get you started and soak up some of that caffeine."

I am barely able to get out a thank you before I'm sipping on the drink. Why is this so good? We sit in companionable silence for a little while as Matt navigates to the park. Horsetooth is a pretty decent hike and shouldn't take us too long. It's about two miles each way so it's enough of a workout that I won't be upset if I spend all of tomorrow in bed. Which may happen because I haven't hiked at all this season.

The roads are quiet this early in the morning and I giggle a bit when we pass the llamas in a few of the farms.

"I don't know why but it still makes me laugh when I see llamas here. Growing up I always pictured them somewhere in the mountains of Europe," I muse, mostly to myself.

"As opposed to the mountains of Colorado?" Matt teases back.

"You know what I mean. I know they must be in other places, but I just remember being little and learning about them and it never clicked that they were something that could survive locally."

"Makes sense. Have you ever seen one up close?"

"No. I don't particularly love the smell of farm animals. But they're cute from afar. And make for a good phrase to use in content."

He looks at me in confusion.

"Drama llama?" I prod, and he just shakes his head a little. "How have you never heard that? 'Don't be a drama llama,' nothing?"

"Nope. But it is catchy. I can see why it has taken off a bit." He chuckles quietly and then we are pulling into the gated off area to park and start off up the trails.

Chapter Eighteen

MATT

ICED VANILLA HAZELNUT ALMOND MILK LATTE

I take the time driving up to the park to calm my racing heart. I've seen pictures of Sasha in hiking clothes from last summer and when she posted videos after just finishing yoga with Kylie or Ashley, but in person is a totally different experience. And it is an experience. I know my eyes are lingering longer than they should be, but I can't bring myself to look away.

She's in her hiking boots and white socks that come up a bit above her shoes. Her shorts are like a second skin and a navy-blue color. Her tank top is a light pink and I can see the dark blue sports bra under it. She's topped it off with a lightweight grey hoodie and a ball cap. I had no clue someone could look hot in a baseball cap, but there she is. Her hat is the same pink as her tank top and it contrasts well with her bright pink lipstick. I swear this girl is always wearing lipstick and it's amazing. Her ponytail is the perfect amount of messy from being in a bun this morning, I'm guessing. She looks effortlessly beautiful, even with a full face of makeup.

We park in the shade so the car isn't an oven when we finish the hike and start getting our things settled. I have a hard time not staring at her body as she adjusts her backpack and applies her sunscreen before putting the small bottle back in her bag. When I finally make eye contact again, I can tell she knows I was checking her out. And from the smirk on her lips, she's not mad about it. I'm in lightweight pants that will keep my legs covered if we go off trail and a dark blue tee.

It doesn't take long to get geared up. This is a fairly easy hike at just over two miles each way, so we didn't need to do hiking sticks or a bunch of extra water and food. The weather is nice and the lot is halfway empty so this should be a pretty nice hike up to the falls. Maybe the end of the trail if we are feeling up to it.

Sasha goes ahead of me on the trail and we start making our way up. We offer the obligatory "good morning" to other hikers on the way up and stop a few times to take some scenic pictures for social media. When we are fairly close to the falls, I notice a space that has some amazing lighting. Being the brother to an up and coming influencer has taught me how to find these spots and take advantage of them. Ashley has told me more than once that I will make an excellent "Instagram husband" once I find someone to settle down with.

"Hey, let's take a few shots right here." I point it out to her and we start making our way off trail. I pull a small blanket out of my bag as we find a good space with lots of color from the trees and flowers. You can see the blue sky in the background and the sound of grasshoppers is still in the distance. I spread the blanket down on the ground and give Sasha some directions on how to stand so she is backlit for a few photos that we can use on the website. After several minutes of her looking over her shoulder and laughing at me as I pretend to be a professional, I have her sit down to reapply her lipstick.

Of course, she's wearing her signature pink color today, so this is perfect. I have her take a few applying the color and then pretending to take a selfie. Then some of her with her favorite lilac water bottle. I really need to see about getting her a new one – this one is completely covered in stickers and she uses it almost every day.

"Why don't you take off the hat for a few of these?" I suggest and I am not prepared for the eye contact I receive as she does just that. She takes off the hat and then loosens the hair tie so her hair falls down along her shoulders. She takes a deep breath like she is composing herself, all the while not moving her gaze from my own.

"What next, Matt?" It's almost a whisper on her lips, but I don't miss it.

And I don't know how my brain continues to work. I just stare at her for a moment while the soft brown of her hair settles around her shoulders and her tank top straps.

"Lie back on your elbows a bit." My voice is soft to match hers as I come closer to adjust her hair. She stares at me with a soft smile and then adjusts to a look that I don't know how to interpret. I want it to mean that she wants me to kiss her lipstick off of her face, but I don't know for sure. I can read an algorithm like the genius I am – women, not so much. So, I tentatively place my hand back on that spot on her neck where I held her last night when I felt her lips on mine for the first time. I take a picture of her, showing her hair falling over my hand and her lips slightly parted. Neither of our faces are fully in the picture, but the subtlety of it has my heart racing. I turn my phone around to show her. Part of me thinks of those "soft launch" photos that Ashley is always showing me and wondering if maybe this can be ours.

She smiles at me and then takes my phone out of my hand and sets it next to her. And then she's got her hand on my neck and is dragging me down to her lips. And I decide in that moment, I will never get tired of kissing this woman. Several moments later I shift so my arm is under her and she can lay in my arms as I continue to explore her mouth with my own. Learning her little noises of contentment and pleasure as I press my tongue against hers. The intake of breath from her as I do this encourages me to keep going.

My hand tangles in her hair so I can deepen the kiss and I feel her hand going down my shoulders to my back. I'm not a small guy, and I don't want to crush her, but it seems like she wants my weight on her a bit more.

"You're not going to crush me, Matt. So, unless you think I smell sweaty already, I don't mind you on top of me. I think I might like feeling the weight of your body pressed against me." She says on a breath as she stares into my eyes again and that's all the consent I need to roll us a bit so she is flat on her back and I am staring down at her. Her lipstick is a little messed up and I place my thumb next to her bottom lip to clean her up a bit. I follow my finger with my lips. Going from the corner of her mouth to her chin, to her ear, then down her neck. Once I hit the space where her neck meets her shoulder, she gasps a bit.

"Did I find something you like?" I ask her softly, smiling against the warmth of the pulse point I found as I do it again. My voice comes out a little rougher than I expected, but I can't get enough of her underneath me like this.

"Yes. Please don't stop, Matt."

So, I don't.

I continue exploring her exposed skin with my fingers and my lips, finding what she likes as she continues to run her fingers through my hair and down to my shoulders. I get a little more confident the more I see that she is enjoying this. I run my fingers up from her hands to her shoulder and then lightly stroke her collarbone. My lips come back up to her ear as I quietly ask her, "Can I touch you, Sasha, please?"

She makes a soft moaning sound as she arches into my touch. And I'm not sure if it's from my fingers or my mouth or my words. "Yes, Matt. I need you to touch me, please." I smile against her neck.

"Was it the touching or the words that got you all breathy for me, sunshine?"

"All of it. I think the 'please' was pretty amazing. But can we stop talking and get back to the kissing and touching please?" She smiles at me as my lips meet hers again and my fingers continue their exploration. My hands roam down the torso of her tank and

I am starting to be annoyed at the sports bra choice today. It will keep me moderately well behaved out here though, so that may be a good thing. I can feel her hardened nipples through the bra, and that does more to spur me on than I was expecting.

"Someone is liking this," I mumble to her as I continue to explore her curves. I love that I don't feel like I am going to break her. She feels incredible underneath me and the way she arches into my touch shows me she is liking this. Just confirming the words she has already told me and the way she guides my hands and lips to where she wants by her subtle movements. I adjust over her so I can get better access to her other breast and then freeze – because I am very hard, and Sasha can now feel just how hard she is making me.

"It appears we both are." She responds to me, an obvious smile in her voice, as she drags her hand down my shirt to start untucking it. I take a few deep breaths to steady myself as I look into her eyes.

"I'm not sure we should do this out here where anyone can walk up. It is the middle of the morning and we are not alone out here." And the timing could not have been more perfect because suddenly, there's voices approaching. We scramble apart quickly and get ourselves adjusted before a group of teenage boys comes around the corner. I'm picking up the blanket and Sasha is placing the hat back on her head just as they get close enough to chat.

"There's no snakes back here, right?" One of the boys asks us.

"Not that we've seen." I respond and then grab Sasha's hand so we can make our way back to the trail. Her giggles follow me as we hurry away from other potential questions. I'm definitely feeling like a teenager almost getting caught making out behind the bleachers rather than a fully grown consenting adult right now. I love it though. This woman does amazing things to me.

"So, are we going to finish the hike or head back?" I ask her.

"Can we head up to the falls and then head back? I wouldn't mind going back now, but I desperately want to at least see the falls before we call it a day."

"As you wish, Sunshine." I wink at her as we continue up again.

"Where did the Sunshine come from?"

"You have a light in you that makes me happy. I enjoy talking to you and you bring joy to those around you. People gravitate towards you and it's obvious that you have a positive effect on them. So, Sunshine." It's obvious to me but it might not have been obvious to her so I have no problem sharing my thoughts with her.

She smiles at me then takes a few steps ahead of me on the trail.

"Enjoy the view on the way up, mister." And she takes off. I chuckle and then I am right behind her. And I absolutely am enjoying this view.

Matt

Chapter Nineteen

SASHA

VANILLA SWEET CREAM COLD BREW

Social Post: Don't forget the facial sunscreen! Skincare and healthy skin practices should start before you are actually worried about wrinkles or skin cancer. And there's so many amazing options out there right now. #skincaretips #summerskincare #sunscreen #dailyskincare #sashalovesmakeup

Image Description: Outside photo of me in my hat and sunglasses and signature pink lipstick holding up my water bottle.

The falls were absolutely spectacular. Horsetooth isn't a very long hike and the falls are small, but it's a quiet place in the middle of the busy college town of Fort Collins. The college campus isn't far away, so it's full of college students taking a break from the beginning of class and teachers who are doing the same. A few photographers of all ages and backgrounds come to use the space for both nature photos and portraits. Surprisingly, there were no families at the falls today. I'm sure that will be different on Saturday morning. Since it is an easier hike, many local families use it as a way to help their little ones learn how to hike and prepare for the more difficult trails nearby.

And having Matt standing beside me, looking at the water, his hand in mine – that was quite possibly my favorite hike I've made up to Horsetooth Falls. It wasn't my first time there with someone I have been dating, but this one felt different. He feels different. I feel so at ease with him, like he actually knows me. Not just what he thinks he knows about me. But who I am truly and completely.

We finish up our hike and head back to the coffee shop to get some work done, I head inside to change while Matt grabs us a table. I need to wear more than my booty shorts to be in "work mode." I touch up my makeup a little then head out into the main space. Matt makes eye contact with me and I can feel the blush come up on my cheeks to match the same color on his.

"You look refreshed, this is for you." He says as he hands me the one of the cups of coffee in front of him.

I sit down and take a sip of the coffee. Why are these always so good when he orders them? "For someone who doesn't drink much coffee, you seriously know what you are doing when you order for me."

"As far as the coffee orders go, I know the basic things of what you like and don't like and have spent a bit of time looking up coffee orders that you may like and I'm just gradually going through the list."

"So, there's more that I haven't tried yet? I thought I had already tried most of what was out there as options." I ask with a bit of surprise in my voice. He chuckles softly before looking up at me over his laptop screen.

"Yes, there's a lot more that you haven't tried yet, at least from my list that I know of. I know you prefer a hot latte first thing in the morning. You don't like overly sweet drinks. You have recently switched to tea after four pm unless you have had a long day or only had one cup of coffee in the morning. Lavender is your favorite surprise flavor in the summer and you don't love pumpkin spice very much, but you will order one or two once fall flavors come out. You prefer hazelnut and almond over caramel and vanilla. There are only a few shops you will order dark roast at because the other places burn the beans. And about once every month you will ask the barista to surprise you with something yummy."

My mouth is open. Fully. Totally unladylike and obnoxious. But I am speechless. What in the actual heck did he just say?

"How?" I finally manage to pull out of my empty brain.

He just smiles back at me and asks me what I am working on this afternoon. And we get to it. I start working on more research for the Colorado Beauty Brands I am working with. I decided I wanted to create a bit of a collaboration with local brands and creators to have a network to connect with and we are going to work together on the October Women's Health Initiative. There's a lot that is going to go into it so I've been talking about business plans, pitches, social media campaigns, new product launches, collaborations, events, and blog posts. It's extensive, but the overall goal is going to be incredible. And hopefully, we will bring awareness to local creators and brands as well as funds for local initiatives.

An hour into our work sesh, my watch buzzes to remind me to move around. Fine. I walk to the bathroom and then come back to fill up my water bottle. As I sit back down, Matt is also walking back to the table. He has a refill for me and a bagel. It has been a while since I've eaten so I guess it's a good thing he remembers to feed me. I sometimes forget to take care of myself. Okay, more than sometimes. And he knows that.

"I kind of figured you would be ready to eat something." He says to me as I start breaking the bagel into smaller pieces so I can eat without making a mess, "and the coffee is half-caf for this one but they had some of the creamer you liked up at the bar so I added that. How much have you gotten done so far with your list?" He takes a sip of his drink, which is probably not coffee at this point, then pulls out his notebook.

He likes to take notes while I talk through things and think out loud so he can help me find the areas I may still be missing or follow up questions. We learned quickly that I work better if I can talk through a project fully out loud before he interjects any questions or suggestions. And if I don't have to worry about catching every thought on paper, even better.

We spend the next several hours working on the initiative together and make a good way through the list of the project. Everything is at least outlined and lists have been made. Goals have been drawn up and initial messages have been sent to the brands, companies, creators, and local areas that I would like to be a part of for the give back portion of the campaign. This is going to be extensive, and if it works, hopefully it stays around for longer than the month of October.

The next weeks are filled with lunch dates, coffee meetings, and weekend hikes. We work on content planning together and then have our own work hours outside of those meetings too. Before long, it's time to start the fall promotions and reach outs. Christmas is fast approaching (at least when it comes to marketing) so fall has been in the works for a while.

September brings me lots of work at Home Depot with new store and product promotions, layout changes, and district meetings, so I am not able to spend much time with Matt just as us. We text and have a few moments together during our meetings or on walks after I get off of work. But I find myself craving to be under his body again. It's been weeks since our hike and while we've had some pretty passionate make out sessions, there just hasn't been the opportunity for more.

The first week of October brings cooler weather, but not much change in foliage. That's one downside of Colorado. The leaves only change for a week or two – and usually just yellow thanks to all of the Aspen trees. Going up to Estes is a yearly plan and this year, I am going with Matt and Carter and Kylie. We have planned to get a cabin for one night so we can get some content done, but also just have a relaxing day enjoying the leaves and just being tourists for the day. Yes, even as semi-locals. There's just something about the fudge you can get up in the mountains.

But it's not the weekend yet. It's Monday. And I have to go to work. I seriously can't wait until I can turn in my notice. It's getting harder and harder to show up here every day. My numbers are steadily growing online. But the bigger part that has been in the works – the Women's Health Initiative – that has been taking up a lot of my time, and I seriously love how it's coming together. Our big fundraiser campaign kicks off this weekend online. I have been pleasantly surprised at how many brands have jumped in to support this.

We've gotten donations from many companies for local resource centers in the form of actual products and a few of the bigger companies have even done some grant donations. It amazes me how fast it has come together and the right people have jumped in. A few other influencers have also joined to do something similar for their communities.

Part of the push this month is "pink every day." Not just in wearing pink, but supporting a woman owned business every day. The campaign is already trending on multiple platforms and Matt has hinted that he is working on a media release, but he hasn't filled me in on much of that yet.

Compiling the list of all the brands we could support this month was amazing! We started putting up posts in August asking for people to nominate their favorite brands and we had over one hundred submitted! I got to reach out to most of them personally to connect with the owners and main content creators if they have had a chance to hire out already. And even those that aren't going to be featured this month on our channels will be working with us in some capacity. Our blog is full of posts talking about the brands. So many interviews have taken place, samples have been tried, reviews have been shared, donations have been distributed. I am so overwhelmed with how amazing it has been.

And I got to do it. With Ashley. With Matt. We did this! My income hasn't changed much in the last few months, but the fulfillment in bringing awareness to a cause that I am passionate about and helping so many women owned businesses grow this month has been so incredible. Some of these brands just needed a little more visibility to really take off.

Another reason why I just really don't want to wear this orange apron anymore. I'm not able to do as much while I am here. Matt has really helped by pulling together information for me so I can just sit down and do the reach outs when I get home from work. But I know I am not putting my whole heart and energy into this project because my time and attention has to be split. And I feel like he is acting as my personal assistant as well as the expert right now. Which just isn't fair to him.

Tuesday afternoon I am practically dragging when I get to the coffee shop to meet with Matt. I'm in a simple pink floral top and leggings today along with my pink lipstick and some cute pink earrings. The content scheduled for this week is highlighting women owned skincare brands and I'm loving the products I've gotten to try already. And I've been able to share several of them with Ashley, Kylie, and Tilly. We've been chatting with the Ulta employee quite a bit and she is enjoying being a part of things from her perspective as a "broke college student." It's helping us make sure we are featuring products for every budget and need throughout this campaign.

It's no surprise Matt has a drink for me waiting at the table when I get there.

"What's my surprise today?" I ask him as I sit down and start getting things out of my bag.

"Spicy dirty chai. Figured you would want something warm with a bit of a caffeine kick to it. It's not as spicy as the place you go to in Fort Collins, but they do a good one here. I got one for myself too." Matt passes me my drink and I gladly take in the smell and the warmth of the cup.

"Have you been up to Estes for an overnight before?" I ask Matt. I haven't either but I want to make sure we are having some non-work conversation. We try to split our time together between work and personal topics. That way, we are getting to know each other better outside of those work labels while still making good use of our time together.

"I went when I was little with one of my friends' families. His family rents a cabin up there twice a year for a week each time and I got to go once. It was nice to take a break from school for a bit and it was gorgeous up there. And the uninterrupted video game time wasn't half bad either." He smirks at me a bit.

"I don't think I've had a chance to meet any of your friends yet. Maybe we should set up something for later this month – maybe for Halloween?"

He thinks on it for a moment. "Yeah, we can probably set something up. It will be at the end of the campaign and we can keep it lowkey at my house if you want. That way we keep the guest list small and not too many new faces."

I love that he remembers my social anxiety. Although, it's getting easier to go places when I know he will be by my side. He keeps me steady. He's my comfort in all of the crazy changes that have already happened this year, and I seriously don't know if I would have made it this far without him.

We get back to work and I pencil something in to chat with the girls about a party at the end of the month – lowkey, fun, and maybe a movie to finish off the night. I wouldn't say no to cuddles on the couch and another foot rub.

"Do you have a time in mind that you want to leave on Saturday to head up to Estes?" I ask him. I want to plan ahead so I am not rushed with packing and can touch base with Kylie and Carter when I get home after we finish up here.

After a moment of thinking it through he responds, "I think if we leave around ten it would be good. That way we can check in at the cabin at noon and get settled before we wander a bit and get some dinner. And then we don't have to check out until two on Sunday. I was able to get us some extra hours on each end of the reservation so we could sleep in a bit or wander around town some more without paying for parking."

"You really do think of everything."

Chapter Twenty

MATT

TIGER SPICE CHAI WITH CINNAMON INFUSED OAT MILK AND CINNAMON WHIPPED CREAM

Social Post: So, I guess I'm on Instagram now as me and not just my brand. #thisisme #coloradolife #thefunnelguy #firstpost

Image Description: Spiderman figurine next to a water bottle on my desk.

My phone is ringing practically moments after I hit the "Publish" button on the post. I can't believe I'm doing this, but it's a big deal to Ashley and Sasha, and I want to be a part of this piece of their lives. I am not even able to get a greeting in before Ashley starts talking.

"Did someone hack your information or did you finally cave and get an Instagram account for yourself?"

I chuckle a little, "I did not have any of my information compromised. If that ever happens to me, I am failing at more than just a username choice. I set up an account. Don't make it a big thing. I just want to be able to interact with you and Sasha from an actual account and not just my business one."

"As opposed to…" she drifts off so I will fill in the blank.

"Plausible deniability, my dear sister. What are you up to today?"

Over the next fifteen minutes Ashley fills me in on how the semester is going so far. We chat about the Halloween party and she asks if she can bring a friend.

"A guy friend?" I prod a little.

"No, it's Tilly from Ulta. We've done some content together and I need someone else with me that won't be drinking."

"None of us are really heavy drinkers, Ashley. If anything, it will be a one drink night for most of us. But yes, that should be fine. I will be inviting Luca and Jonathan so there will be a few familiar faces there as we start introducing everyone to the group."

"Oh, so this is actually moving forward then? We are merging friend groups?" I can hear the amusement in her voice.

"Don't make it a thing, Ashley. You know Sasha and I are doing a bit of a double date overnight trip with Kylie and Carter this weekend, right?" It's Thursday and I cannot wait for Saturday to get here. It will be our first "sleepover" together and while I may not be putting any expectations on Sasha, I can't wait to have her in my arms for longer than a greeting hug.

"Yep, you guys are going to have a blast and I can't wait to see pictures. Just make sure you guys keep it down in the cabin – you are going to have roommates." She jokes with me. I wish I could see her face so I could give her a look that shows my amusement.

"I don't think anything noisy will be happening in the bedroom. We are adults and still figuring this out. And I don't really want to be talking about bedroom activities with my younger sister."

"Bedroom activities? You are twenty-four not fifty. Who even says that? Just don't wait too long, brother. You may forget how to…" I cut her off.

"And we are done with this conversation. I'll text you before we leave on Saturday. Love you."

"Oh fine. Be good. I'll throw some shiny silver packets in your backpack before you leave just in case." And with that, I disconnect the call knowing she isn't talking about Ghirardelli chocolate. Although, I should probably get some for Sasha – she loves those things.

Friday evening I text Sasha to see how she is doing with packing. I tend to be a "pack the week before" kind of guy and I am honestly not sure how Sasha packs. I probably should have texted her earlier in case she needed anything or I could help with running to the store.

Me: Hey Sunshine, how is packing going over there?

Sasha: Decent. I'm keeping it simple. Not having to bring my entire makeup kit for content is making this a lot easier than I thought.

Sasha: So, I'm assuming for sleeping arrangements that I will be sharing a room with you…but I wanted to double check. I haven't talked to Kylie and Carter because I wanted to ask you first and I kept freaking myself out when I went to ask you earlier this week.

Me: I would love to share a room with you, beautiful. No pressure. But I would love to hold you while we sleep on Saturday night.

Sasha: I would love that. So comfy jammies it is. But you have to pick: lipstick or coffee?

Me: You have lipstick and coffee pajamas?

Sasha: Yes, and I will hear no disparaging comments about my sleepwear. Pick.

Me: LOL. Coffee.

Sasha: Perfect. Goodnight Matt. I will see you in the morning.

Me: Goodnight Sasha. I'll be over there at nine to help load the car with coffee in hand.

Sasha: You are amazing! Sleep well.

Matt

Chapter Twenty-One

SASHA

COCONUT MOCHA

Social Post: Road trip ready – even if it is just forty minutes. Can't wait to spend the next little bit up in Estes. Don't forget to share your "pink every day" posts today!! #roadtripday #coloradogirl #estespark #octoberincolorado #sashaloveslipstick #pinkeveryday #womenshealthinitiative #supportlocalbusinesses

Image Description: Full mirror selfie. I'm wearing a pair of black leggings, comfy shoes, and an oversized blush pink sweater. Makeup is softer today and my look is finished with an over the shoulder bag from a local company.

Right on time, Matt shows up at the apartment at nine – coffee in hand. He doesn't even wait for me to ask.

"Coconut mocha this morning for you. I kept it simple so you could have your caffeine fix while we load the car up while still trying a new combination." I smile at him as he hands me my drink and he returns the smile before dropping a kiss on my cheek.

I never knew I was a "sweet kiss" kind of girl, but Matt has changed that. It's a lot of sitting close moments, holding hands, foot massages, and forehead and cheek kisses. They aren't big elaborate gestures, but they show me that he is thinking about me and is making an intentional move to make sure I know that.

"You two are beyond adorable." I hear Kylie behind me. She drops her duffel on the floor next to mine. Carter follows her out into the hallway. It's been non stop since early August. Ashley went back to school so our work schedule has changed quite a bit. And then Carter got a promotion at the restaurant so he is working longer hours and Kylie has been hanging out with him during any "off the clock" moments. This weekend is going to be good for them too. Not being called in for any emergencies is going to be helpful for all of us I think.

The guys start bringing things to the car. Luckily, it's only a few bags and a cooler. There is definitely a benefit in us staying close to home. Carter filled up the gas tank last night so we won't have to stop on the way up the canyon. It is the height of the tourist season in the mountains, so the earlier we leave and the fewer times we have to stop, the better.

I finish applying my sunscreen and pass it to Kylie so she can do the same, fill up my water bottle one more time, and then we are on the way.

Okay, one stop on the way up isn't bad. We stop at the Cherry Store on our way up the canyon. It's a tourist stop for sure, but the Colorado Cherry Company has some amazing products! Sweets and sodas and a whole lot of local options. It's a spot I come to every time I am in this direction and we load up on sodas and muffins before continuing the drive.

From the apartment to Estes Park is only about an hour. Conversation was easy and traffic was light so we made good timing. And I love that on our first "casual outing" there aren't any arguments or tense moments. I had friends in college that had to make choices between friends or boyfriends when they went out because the two groups didn't get along. I didn't think it was going to be a problem, but knowing that everyone gets along makes me feel better.

The cabin is beautiful! It's close to the river and we will have to drive a bit to get to downtown Estes Park, but it's going to be quiet and beautiful out here! Matt goes to check us in at the main house and then we head into the house. Kylie and Carter claim the back bedroom so we have the one up front. We walk in and I immediately start laughing.

"Guess this isn't an 'only one bed' trope situation."

Matt just looks at me totally befuddled and then takes a look at the room.

"I must have missed the two twin bed situation on the listing."

"I think they are upgraded to doubles. So are we pushing them together, squishing into one, or taking this as a sign to sleep separately?" I ask him with light amusement in my voice.

"I may not have expectations of us doing more than second base tonight, but there is absolutely no way that I am not sleeping without you in my arms tonight, beautiful." He says as he walks closer to me, gently pushing my body up against the door that we had closed behind us.

"I wouldn't be opposed to third base..." I trail off as I take note of his body pressed against mine. I love feeling his weight on me. It settles me and turns me on all at the same time.

He smiles down at me as he rests his hand on my neck, softly stroking the side of my face as he lowers his lips to mine. I let my purse fall to the floor so I can put my hands on him. I decide to play with him a bit and nip at his lip a little bit. I can feel his smile against my lips as he pushes into me further. There's no space between us as he deepens the kiss and grips my hip and neck a little harder.

I want this man so badly. And I'm starting to regret the decision to have roommates just a few feet down the hall.

"I am starting to wish we took this trip on our own." I tell him breathlessly as he takes a break from my lips to start kissing down my jaw line to my neck.

His only response is a small hum as he continues his exploration.

"I mean, it's nice having them here, but I want to do more than a quick make-out session behind the door."

At that comment, he raises his head to meet my eyes. "Who said this would be a quick make-out session? We've got time." He has a hint of mischief in his eyes as he reaches behind me and locks the door before picking me up and carrying me to the closest bed and lays me down gently.

Sasha
X
#sashaloveslipstick

Chapter Twenty-Two

SASHA

DIRTY CHAI WITH A SHOT OF WHITE ESPRESSO WITH CINNAMON AND NUTMEG

Social Post: I may be used to Colorado, but heading up further in the mountains is always a bit of an adjustment with the altitude. #altitudethings #coloradovacation #estespark #coloradogirl #weekendtrip #fallincolorado #sashaloveslipstick

Image Description: Photo of my purple water bottle on the deck of our Estes Park cabin – Yellow aspen leaves in the background

"Is this okay?" Matt asks me as he reaches down to gently pull off my shoes.

"It is very okay. Are you going to tell me what you are planning to do, mister?" I ask him with a bit of amusement in his voice. I am so worked up and have no idea what he is thinking right now, except that he looks very pleased with himself at the moment.

"Mister? What's that about?" He asks me as he slowly crawls up my body, letting his fingers gently touch my body all the way up until he is laying on his side next to me, with his right hand laying gently on my stomach and his left one holding up his head as he looks at me.

"It seemed to fit the situation but if you don't get back on top of me and kiss me I may go crazy."

He chuckles a little and then slowly lowers his fingers until they are teasing the bottom of my sweater. I breathe in a little more than I was expecting, almost a gasp. His fingers feel like they are charged with electricity up against my skin and I arch into his touch. *"More"* my mind screams at him, but I refrain from begging out loud.

"Can I take this off, Sasha? I want to see you." He asks, his fingers steady just under the hem. This man and his constant asking. Why do I love this so much?

"Yes, please. I like feeling you touch me." I am breathing harder than his touches dictate, but I want his hands all over me. And why is he taking so long peeling this sweater off of me? It's like he's memorizing each new inch of skin he reveals. Finally, it's off me and I'm left in my pink lace bralette. I'm a solid C cup so I usually wear full bras, but I knew with the sweater that I wouldn't need a ton of structure and support today and I am greatly appreciating that decision when I watch Matt's eyes as he takes me in.

His fingers gently explore the lace and the lines up against my body. Then his mouth follows. In that moment, I am not self-conscious of my tummy that isn't flat or the light stretch marks at the top of my hips that he hasn't revealed yet. I am not thinking about what he is thinking of me. I am just here, in this moment, with him. I am enjoying his fingers and his breath and his lips on my skin. And I could stay like this for hours, and from the way he is taking his time, he is thinking the same.

I arch up into him again as he teases along the edge of the lace again. My nipples have pebbled and are aching for his touch, for his lips, anything. And he doesn't make me wait long. He peels the cups down so they are against my body just below my breasts.

"You are absolutely beautiful, Sasha. I could stay here worshiping your body all afternoon."

"You will get absolutely no objection from me." I breathe out. He uses his hands to feel and touch and explore while his mouth does the same on the other side. He gives me the attention I need and the care I want. It isn't rough. It isn't hurried. But it is perfect.

My hands get lost in his hair as he continues his exploration. It's so soft and thick and I love teasing him with my nails. I start to pull on his shirt so he sits back just enough to pull it off of his torso and lays it next to me. And he is just as beautiful as I was expecting. Strong shoulders, broad chest, and just the right amount of dark chest hair.

"I need to feel you on top of me, Matt. Please." And he obliges me instantly. Settling one leg between my own and the other caging me in, he lays his body on top of mine and begins kissing me. A path from my aching breasts to my neck to finally, my lips again. His kiss is deep and the warmth of his body against mine is perfection. Could this get any better?

Oh, it can. And it does. He adjusts a little so that his thigh is pressed against my center. And I don't think. I just react. I press myself against his leg as he kisses me and takes control of my mouth with his tongue.

"Feeling good, Sunshine?" He murmurs close to my ear as he reaches down and holds my thigh close to his own. "What do you need? How can I make this better for you right now?"

"You are making me feel so good, babe. Please, don't stop. I need you kissing me and more pressure where your leg is." I try to press against him to put the pressure where I need him. I am so worked up that it won't take me long, even with all the layers between us.

"This leg?" He teases me. Drawing his legs closer to each other so that there is more pressure on the outer one. "Or this one?" He growls in my ear. At that moment he inches closer to my core and the friction is right where I need it. His right hand is holding my hip so I can stay steady against him and the left hand is gripped in my hair as he kisses and nibbles along my neck and shoulder.

"You can use my body, Sasha. Take what you need. I want to see you fall apart for me. Give me a preview of what I can expect." And with that he brings his hand from my hip to my breast and begins tugging on my nipple as he grinds his solid thigh up against where

I need him the most. Within moments, I am detonating and he knows it. He meets my mouth with his own to keep me quiet. His touches soften, but he doesn't move until my breathing steadies. Then he pulls away and smiles down at me.

"You are absolutely gorgeous. And seeing you let go for me is something I will never forget."

"If you behave, I'll give you a repeat performance later." I reply.

He grabs his t-shirt and pulls it over my head after fixing my bra back in place then holds me close to his chest as we drift off for an afternoon nap.

Sasha
X
#sashaloveslipstick

Chapter Twenty-Three

MATT

BROWN SUGAR LATTE

Social Post: Am I the only one worried about hot tubs at rental properties or hotels? #vacationthoughts #thefunnelguy #coloradothings #estespark

Image Description: Picture of a hot tub with a cover on it on a deck. Background of Aspen trees with yellow and green leaves.

"I am not getting in that. I am happy to be on clean up duty after dinner, but no." I tell Carter as we finish getting dinner plated up. We went simple tonight with pasta and chicken. We brought stuff up with us in the cooler so we didn't have to eat out every meal while we are up here. He suggested we open up the hot tub and spend some time out there with the girls tonight, but I don't love that idea. I'm not a germaphobe or paranoid, but this isn't my house and sanitizing a hot tub is a whole lot harder than cleaning a set of sheets.

He laughs at me and shrugs. "More room for me and Kylie then. What movies did you bring for tonight?"

"A couple rom-coms that Sasha mentioned that she loves, the newest Marvel movie, and then a couple classics that I think we have all seen for some background noise if we want to play a card game or something."

"I'll go set the plates on the table if you want to pour drinks and we can see what the girls want to do after dinner."

A little less than an hour later we are all sitting on the porch, watching the stars come out and enjoying the quiet. It may be tourist season in Estes Park, but we are far enough away from the main strip that we don't hear the noise from the shops. And most things close when it gets dark anyways. I didn't think to look if they are doing any fireworks or anything this weekend, but I don't think it's going to happen. It's October – not really a fireworks kind of holiday.

"So, do we want to open a bottle of wine and the hot tub?" Kylie asks. We've been sipping on coffee and tea to keep us warm out here. It's not too chilly, but just enough that a blanket on my lap while Sasha snuggles into my side makes sense. And, having her close to me like this is definitely not something I am complaining about.

"I don't really want to turn that thing on if it isn't already going. And I didn't bring a suit with me either." Sasha responds. Carter makes eye contact with me and I get the hint.

"Why don't we go inside and pop in a movie or something and these two can hang out in the hot tub. I'm not big on hot tubs that are open to public groups anyway." I stand and grab the blanket then reach back for her hand. "And I brought up some of the hot cocoa you love too."

That's all the encouragement she needs before she is up and telling Kylie and Carter goodnight. I hear her tell them not to stay up too late so we can go exploring tomorrow and then her hand is in mine and we are heading into the cabin.

"Do you want to pick a movie while I get the kettle going?" I ask her. A moment later, I am surprised to feel her body up against my back with her settling into me. Her arms come around my waist and I just take a moment to feel the weight of her against me.

"Can we put the movie on in the bedroom and just cuddle? I liked being in your arms on the porch and wasn't quite ready to be done, but I know Kylie and Carter needed some quiet time."

"Absolutely, babe. Do you want the hot cocoa or any snacks or just want to go get in bed?" I turn to face her so she knows she has my full attention. I love having her in my arms like this – close enough that I can see every small variation in her brown eyes and I know she is examining me the same way.

"Hot cocoa is great. And maybe some popcorn?" She waits for me to nod before she steps towards the bedroom. "I'm going to go get changed while you do that. Did you bring any candy with you?"

"I think there's a few options here – M&M's or Sour Patch Kids?"

"Both." She smiles at me then ducks into the bedroom, closing the door quietly behind her.

When I go into the bedroom a few minutes later, she has put her bag on one of the beds and is under the covers on the other one.

"You okay getting a little cozy with me?" She asks as she pulls the covers back next to her. She has taken off her makeup and her hair is up in a messy bun. Knowing that I get to see her without any filter on her face is something I don't take lightly.

"Absolutely. And in case I haven't told you yet today, you are absolutely gorgeous." I set the hot cocoa on the nightstand next to the bed along with the snacks and climb onto the bed. "And now I'm going to kiss you like I've wanted to all night before I go change and you eat all of the chocolate without me."

"I'm not going to eat all of the – ," but her words are cut off because my lips are on hers as I make good on my promise.

An hour later, Kylie and Carter have come back inside so we locked up the house and I am back in bed with Sasha. Her being comfy next to me, cuddled into my side, is one of my favorite things to experience. The movie is playing quietly in the background while I run my hand up and down her arm, feeling her skin under my fingers. Sasha has grown more relaxed in my arms, and since there isn't a lot of room to spread out, she's on her side curled up into me as I am propped on the pillows. At least there were plenty of those to use between the two beds.

"Do you want me to go into the other bed before I fall asleep?" Sasha asks me quietly.

"Do you not want to sleep right here?"

"There's not really a lot of room, and I'm not sure how much I move around in my sleep. And it's been a long time since I've slept in the same bed as someone else, well, except for Kylie on the random sleepovers when we fell asleep watching a movie, but that's different. And I don't know if I'm going to be weird while you are sleeping, like, what if my hands wander a bit or I drool on you?" Her voice gets a little faster and the worry in her tone is evident by the time she finishes.

"Take a breath, Sunshine. You're rambling a bit. Now look at me." I lower my voice as I raise her chin so she is looking at me. "I want you here, in my arms, while I sleep. I know there's not a lot of room, and that's okay, because I fully plan to have you sleep on top of me all night long. And as far as drool goes, that's a sleep thing and won't bother me at all. And your hands, well, you can put those wherever you want and I promise I will move them if I don't like where you are touching me, but I don't think that's going to happen. Okay?"

She nods slowly and then smiles softly at me.

"I love that you are comfortable enough to be in my arms while we cuddle, but I would love to sleep here with you just like this too." I remind her. And I hope she says yes, because I am so gone for this woman already and all I want is to wake up with her in my arms.

"I would like to try. But are you okay if I end up moving to the other bed in the middle of the night?"

"Would it be so that you could sleep better or that I can sleep better?"

"You."

"Then no, if you move to that bed for my benefit, expect me to carry you right back over to this one so you can sleep in my arms. I'm going to sleep best with your body on mine, with your legs wrapped around me, and the scent of you all over my pillow and my shirt. Don't think otherwise. Now come here so we can get some sleep." I pull her close to me and she settles in on my chest. One of her legs sliding between mine and the other coming to rest on the outside of my hip. I can feel all of her against me and she is perfection. This is perfection. And I don't know how I will sleep unless she is in my arms after this.

Chapter Twenty-Four

SASHA

ICED CHAI LATTE, WITH PUMPKIN CREME

Social Post: There's something about the quiet of the mornings when there isn't all the city noise in the background. It's so beautiful up in the mountains. And I slept so well last night! Anyone else sleep better in the mountains? #sashaloveslipstick #mountainretreat #weekendgetaway #nocogirl #estespark

Image Description: Coffee cup in my hand while I'm bundled in a blanket on the porch.

It is so quiet out here and I wish I could be up here for another week. I have my laptop out so I can check on the October campaign and respond to a few emails with the brands I am collaborating with for the donations and product highlights this month. Everything we have been doing has been keeping me busy, and I am loving it. Especially with the new campaigns to help women owned brands with more sustainable and user-friendly packaging as well as supporting local resources. I get to do what I love with those that need help and resources. And being the person to connect them, it makes me so incredibly happy.

I'm still sharing a bunch of makeup tutorials and skincare tips. But it's also become a lot more than that in the background. Working with a few local businesses has been new too.

There is a spa that is adding in "girls' night in" events and is wanting to use these as a way for local women to connect with each other and also get resources they may need. We helped a single mom with things she needed for her son for the upcoming colder weather last month. She got so many things as hand me downs and brand new while we all got mini facial samples from the spa. And I got to do a tutorial on how to prepare skin for colder weather and what products to switch out over the coming months. It's been a great collaborative effort and is so incredibly rewarding.

There's another new skincare and makeup brand looking to launch in the area early next year and they have been talking to me quite a bit about options for their first launch and what would be most beneficial for their target demographic. Part of me really hopes that one turns into a job offer. Working with a startup company, especially one that is already jumping into the campaigns that I am running for the October Women's Health Initiative, is something that I could absolutely get behind.

Before long, Kylie comes and joins me on the porch, two cups of coffee in hand.

"Figured you would be ready for a second cup pretty soon." She hands it over to me and sits next to me on the couch. "How's it all coming?"

"Really well. I'm excited for how things are going and working with a few of these brands and companies is going really well. They're seeing good growth and new business partners and I'm hoping this brand that's launching next year will have some good momentum going into their launch. Most of my content is set through the end of the month so I'm able to spend more time working with them and the spa for next month's event."

"And how did everything go last night?" She asks suggestively. She wiggles her eyebrows at me and we both start giggling.

"It was actually really nice. We cuddled and I slept so well. I hope he did too. He woke up and went for a run while I got some work done. He should be back soon so we can go explore the town."

"Have you guys done more than cuddle yet?"

"A bit. We are taking things slow and honestly, I'm okay with that. I don't want to rush into things with him, especially because we work together. I'm just enjoying where we are right now and he is taking this whole dating me thing very seriously. I'm not mad about it."

"And he's someone you don't wear makeup in front of, which isn't normal for you. I mean, how long was I dating Carter before you came out of your room without a full face on?" She laughs at me a little, but it's true. I'm a full face of makeup girl. I like the way I look without makeup too, but it's a confidence thing for me. That's what I need every day to be ready for what's coming and show up my best.

"I don't feel like I have to 'get ready' to see him. I'm ready just as I am. And he looks at me like I'm the most beautiful thing he's ever seen whether I'm all done up or not. He saw me in my coffee jammies last night and this morning and I still got a reaction out of him." And with that, I'm remembering just how big his reaction was this morning. It wasn't a verbal one, but his body definitely did the talking.

"And with the way you are blushing, that reaction must have been a good one." Kylie responds. "Why don't we head inside so we can start getting ready, the guys should be back from their run soon and I want to braid your hair today." Bringing our coffee mugs to the sink and the blankets to the couch inside, we start getting ready.

The weather is cool today, so I grab my favorite pair of dark wash skinny jeans and another blush pink sweater. My wardrobe is pretty simple once it gets colder outside. I do a simple makeup look that plays with the pink of my sweater and will pop a bit against my brown eyes. Then Kylie comes in to braid my hair. I can do it myself, but it's a calming thing for her and I can tell she needs a little bit of normalcy before we head out to go be tourists. Her hair matches mine with the braid, but the color, texture, and what we are wearing are very different. She is in a pair of black leather like pants and a bright red oversize tank with a grey blazer over it.

"Going for biker chic today?" I ask her. It's outside of her normal look and I'm curious.

"Trying something different. I wore these pants a few weeks ago and Carter about choked on his drink, so wanted to see what happens when I push it a bit. Plus, I feel amazing in this slouchy blazer. Definitely think I need more of these – or at least an excuse to wear it more often. It's not exactly waitress approved." She smiles at me as she pulls out a tube of red lipstick. Oh, she is going hard today and I am absolutely here for it.

Walking out of the bedroom, I can hear the guys talking and I peek around Kylie so I can get a look at Carter's reaction. And I am not disappointed. The man is absolutely speechless as he takes her in. Matt chuckles a bit as he watches the scene unfold too. Carter walks closer to Kylie and reaches out to play with the blazer a bit.

"This needs to be a date night outfit at some point when we aren't doubling with those two."

"'Those two' have names, Carter." I playfully remind him.

"Don't care at the moment." He replies as he leans in to kiss her.

"Do not mess up my lipstick, Carter." She warns him.

"Oh babe, let's go set that so you don't have that problem." And I grab her hand to bring her to the bathroom to set her lips. Red lipstick stains are great when you want them, but horrid when you don't. And Carter is one of those guys that hates lipstick stains on his skin or his clothes – one reason why Kylie doesn't wear it very often. I'm glad she tried today though, but I would hate it if Carter bugs her about wearing it after today.

Sasha
x
#sashaloveslipstick

Chapter Twenty-Five

MATT

LONDON FOG LATTE

Social Post: Halloween is being hosted by me this year – do I need to decorate or can we keep it simple?

Image Description: Spiderman figuring next to a pumpkin on my kitchen table.

I'm hosting Halloween.

At my house.

With my friends.

And Sasha's.

And Ashley's.

Okay, I can do this.

I've been mentally preparing myself for this for weeks, but with tomorrow being the party, I'm a little nervous. And if I'm nervous, I know Sasha is too. She stresses in new social settings. Which is why her doing the monthly spa nights is such a huge step for her. I was hoping that her gradually meeting people at the farmers markets would be what she needed before jumping into something steadier on her own, and I was right. Those first few Saturdays were a big step for her. And then she started meeting each of the business owners she would be working with, and she became more and more comfortable.

I think part of that was because I was at her side for each of those introductions. The first spa night was totally on her own. She had Ashley with her and Kylie too, but she was the one running the show. Was it part of my idea before we even started the farmers markets? Yes. I knew it was something on her wish list of things to do that she didn't think would be possible. So, I found out what businesses locally would be the best fits, and made sure that a new one got the market invite each week. Several weeks later, all the introductions had been made. And the stage was set for the spa nights.

The new business starting next year was a happy surprise. I was doing some research in our first weeks of working together and found the LLC application. Some more digging led me to the owner's information, business plan, and warehouse location. It could not be a better setup. Getting them to see Sasha's work wasn't hard at all. By then, she had a few of the smaller collaborations under her belt and had started sharing more of the local businesses on her page. I may have sent out an inquiry on their site as Sasha asking for a reach out. From there, it was her show. And she has excelled with it.

Seeing her joy as she shares more about what she is working on and where she hopes this goes is amazing. Will I ever tell her my part in all of it? Probably not. I'm happy with the growth she has seen and if a few prompts on my end helped her get there, I'm ecstatic that she has this platform now to do what she does best.

And for some reason, Ashley and Sasha thought it would be best for me to host tomorrow night. I shoot a message to my friends and hope that between the three of us we can figure this out.

The following day, my house looks like Pinterest and Instagram threw up the entire search bar for Halloween. Well, not exactly, but it's close.

Ashley ended up coming over with Tilly while I had Luca and Jonathan here too. Sasha was working so I was overseeing the craziness by myself. Having two college girls who are a little craft crazy, and then my friends, made things a bit interesting.

Luca enjoys working with his hands on things, so he ended up crafting a few decorations out of wood that look like spider webs and will act as décor hangers in a bit here. He also used a bunch of random leftover hardware pieces to construct a makeshift graveyard on my table. In between the markers are the bowls of snacks and signs for drinks.

Jonathan is the odd one in our group. He was the one that played sports in high school and at twenty-six, he is getting ready to take over his dad's auto body shop a few towns over. He loves working on cars, especially classic models that are used for car shows. He gets to travel all over the world for certain shows with his dad and clients. It's his thing and I'm glad he will get to take over the shop soon. It's been his dream since we were teens.

At seven, I go over to unlock the front door. People will be arriving soon and I don't want to be held at the door. I have all the snacks and drinks set up. There's a mini bar set up too and Carter offered to oversee that. I grabbed a couple cases of seltzers and a few mixers. I figured having two "signature drinks" for tonight would be enough. Plus, we have mocktail options and sodas. Ashley and Tilly aren't old enough to drink and most of us don't drink much. We have work to do tomorrow and classes for the girls, and I don't want to have to deal with people getting rowdy, or weepy.

I open the front door to see the most gorgeous version of Spider Man I have ever seen. Sasha dressed up as Spider Gwen. And I am officially speechless. Her hair is pulled back in a white headband

and the white bodysuit she is wearing only accentuates her curves. White tights, black heels, black lipstick, white bracelets, black corset, white eyeliner – this woman is trying to kill me.

"How did I do?" She asks when I finally make eye contact again, doing a little spin so I can take in the full outfit. "I know Spider Man is your favorite but could not bring myself to wear red and blue so I went with someone in the same universe. That's what it's called right?" She's nervous. She did this for me. I'm wearing a simple Spider Man t-shirt and black jeans. I don't tend to dress up for these things, but I wore my favorite tee.

"You look absolutely perfect, Sasha. And yes, you got the word right, it's universe. I am not going to be able to keep my eyes or my hands off of you tonight." I shake my head softly as I continue to take her in. "I have never seen a sexier cosplay of Spider Gwen before and I am speechless. Where did you find all of that?"

"Surprisingly, I thrifted most of it. I'm always looking for an excuse to break out the black lipstick and the graphic liners so this seemed perfect. And with that look in your eye, I'd say it's worth it."

"Please tell me you set your lips with that thing you were talking about before."

"You mean where I make it kiss proof?"

"Yes, that."

"I did."

"Can we test how well it holds up before everyone gets here?"

"If you feel strongly about it." She gives me a challenge with her eyes.

"I feel very strongly about it." And with that, I pick her up enough so she can wrap her legs around my waist. I press her body up against my front door and show her just how much I love the effort she put into this for me.

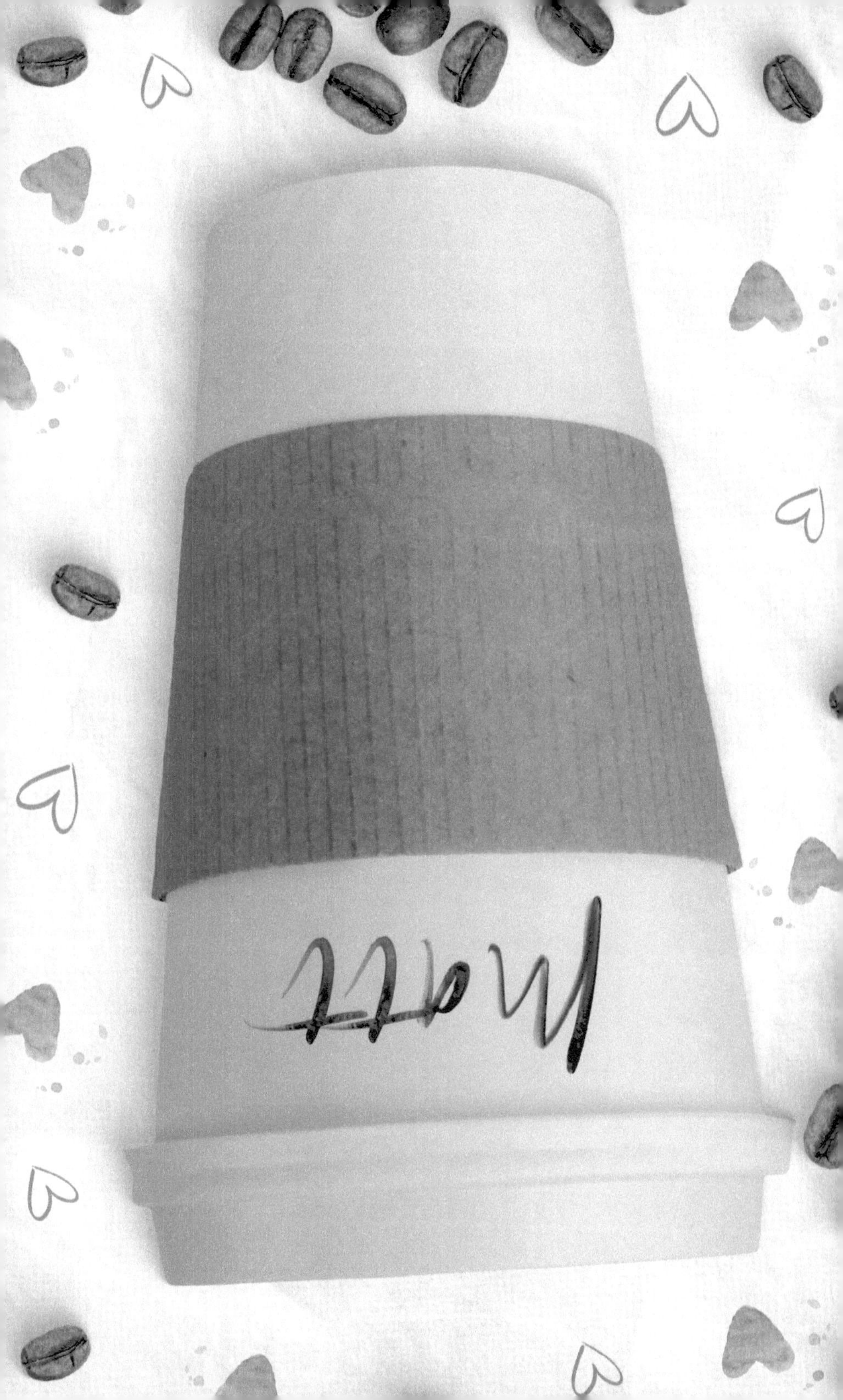

Chapter Twenty-Six

SASHA

VANILLA AND CARAMEL BLONDE WITH OAT MILK

Social Post: Bold lipstick choices are as much of an attitude choice as they are an outfit choice. Be confident in what you choose, even if it's outside of your normal. Black lipstick for me is one of my favorites to play with. It's totally outside of my normal, but it's a whole look for me and the finished look is always one I feel confident in. #sashaloveslipstick #graphicliner #boldlipstick #cosplay #blacklipstick #partyreads

Image description: Lipstick bag opened up on my makeup counter with the black lipstick open next to my coffee mug.

I'm pressed up against Matt's front door looking down at him. The look in his eyes is one of admiration and hunger. This man wants me. And I want him too. I was hoping this was going to be as much for him as it was for me today when I got dressed. It's sexy and way outside of my normal, but this corset does wonderful things for my boobs and the heels just accentuate my legs in the best way. And apparently, Matt noticed all of that when I walked into his house just a few minutes ago.

He lowers his lips to where my neck meets my shoulders and I can feel him breathing me in. His lips follow just a moment later as he kisses that place that makes me shiver. One of his hands is holding my hip to him and the other is bracing his weight on the door behind my head. My legs are wrapped around him, and I can feel how hard he is through his jeans. I should have shown up sooner than ten minutes before everyone else is going to get here.

I tilt my head back as he continues his exploration around my neck, shoulders, and collarbone.

"I thought you wanted to try to mess up my lipstick." I prompt him while trying to press my body further against his. I am needy and I know it.

"I had a better idea." He says as he nips at my shoulder and I arch into his touch further.

"What's that?"

Someone knocks on the door and I groan. He looks at me as he slowly lowers me down and helps me fix my skirt.

"I'll mess it up tonight when we are alone." He whispers in my ear and then he unlocks the door like I'm not a total pile of goo standing next to him.

While he lets the guests inside, I sneak down to his room to drop off my purse and my other bag. I was hoping I wasn't being presumptuous when I packed an overnight bag. If nothing else, I can change into something else after the party and I for sure am going to want to take this makeup off. It's not full costume makeup, but it's definitely heavier than I am used to and I don't like wearing makeup when it feels like I'm wearing makeup. I can see my eyelashes. That's not normal. Falsies are great, but they mess with my depth perception so I don't wear them often. I'm good with just good mascara.

When I come back to the main room, everyone has arrived for the most part so I head over to help get the rest of the snacks out of the fridge. It's not even 7:30 and we are planning to be wrapped up by ten at the latest. Most of us have tomorrow off from work, but late nights are not our thing. Several of us have other plans for later

I think, at least I hope *we* have plans for later.

By eight, everyone is here and having a good time and pretty much everyone has settled in. Kylie and Carter are dressed as Princess Kate and Prince William – in casual clothes because Carter "didn't want to rent anything special for one night." Fair. Tilly and Ashley are dressed as Influencer Barbie and Makeup Barbie and it's honestly pretty amazing. Both of those girls pull off the Barbie pink lipstick really well! Matt's friends are in superhero tees like Matt is so they look like they probably planned that. Nothing too fancy, but it works well.

There's another bartender from the restaurant and then Tilly's roommate from college too. It rounds out to be a pretty good group with everyone being between nineteen and twenty-eight. Not too bad. At least we all get most of the same pop culture references. It seems like Matt and his friends are very big superhero geeks and they have each made a few comments tonight that the rest of us don't get. Note to self – find some sort of "Superheros for the Struggling Girlfriend" book. Is that a thing? It should be a thing! He's learned makeup and skincare for me so I should try to figure some of this out. The reaction from him when he saw me in my costume was pretty exciting. What would he say if I actually picked up on some of the references in the next Marvel movie?

Carter and Max (the other bartender) are having fun getting creative with the limited amount of mixers and liquor available. They've been sharing a few specialty drink recipes with Luca and Johnathan for them to try on their next time out. I've challenged them to find me a few more coffee recipes to play with. I may be slightly obsessed but having fun drinks like that at the spa nights are always a huge hit. And I can only have so many cranberry orange concoctions before I want to try something different.

I was definitely nervous about meeting Matt's friends, but they've been great. Luca is quiet like Matt is, but Jonathan pulls them out of their shells a bit more. All together, it's going pretty well. And we are taking turns at the door passing out candy.

"I am honestly surprised at how many kids we have had come here tonight." I tell Matt when I finish with the group of Ninja Turtles at the front door. It's been a new group about every ten minutes since 7:30.

"Yeah, a couple of years ago I met with a bunch of the other neighborhood homeowners and we planned a few events for the kids on the block throughout the year. Halloween became another one of those nights and now a lot of the kids bring their friends. It's a quiet street and most of us know each other so parents feel safe and the kids recognize us so it helps with the younger ones not being nervous." Matt lets us know as he refills the bowl with the chocolate mix.

"So even though you weren't a parent, you jumped in?" Carter asks. He seems unsure, which is super weird. It's a sweet gesture. I give him a look and notice that Kylie is doing the same.

Matt makes eye contact with him before he answers Carter, again, weird.

"Yes sir." Oh we are getting serious Matt, I like this. "My sister and I had that growing up and it was important to me to be one of the adults that kids and parents could rely on if needed. And when the time comes that I have kids in this neighborhood, or wherever that may be, I want to be able to have that same relationship with those here. I can't expect them to treat my kids well in five years if I am not doing the same today."

And, mic drop. Okay, I probably need to be done with the drinks. I've only had two, but that's more than my normal and I'm getting snarky. It may just be in my head, but if I'm not careful, it's going to come out. I stand up to go grab a water bottle while Kylie continues the conversation.

"So, you've thought about having kids?" She prompts him.

"I think most of us in this age group have, haven't we? I'm not in a huge rush, but I'd like to be a dad someday. Again, I had a great childhood and would like to have the chance to be a dad." He makes eye contact with me during that last bit and I slowly smile at him. Is he thinking about having kids with me? We barely started dating. We haven't even fully slept together yet. I don't hate the idea though. His eyes on a mini-Matt? Sign me up! And with the smirk he is giving me, he heard my thoughts loud and clear.

"I haven't thought about kids. I enjoy the flexibility of my job and being able to choose when we go do a weekend away. Adding kids into the mix is going to create a whole new set of challenges." Carter remarks as he sips his drink. Kylie is quiet and stands to come next to me to grab a water too.

"So, are you not wanting kids ever or just not right now?" Ashley asks him. Her and Kylie have gotten close recently and I think she's picking up on Kylie's mood shift with the current conversation.

"Not right now, for sure, maybe never. I'm not sure. I'm not thirty yet, not married, and don't want to add that into where we are in life right now. You're with me on that, right Kylie?" Oh good, he does remember his girlfriend standing here.

She nods her head slowly in agreement and I make a mental note to check with her on that later. We have talked about kids before and we were both in the "after we are married for at least a year" category, but this reaction from her tells me she might have changed her mind and I don't know what I've missed.

And with that, the doorbell rings again.

Chapter Twenty-Seven

MATT

CARAMEL PECAN LATTE

Social Post: The winning candy this year was the peanut butter M&Ms. These things are not talked about enough and they went from the basket so quickly. Now time to see if we can get rid of all of these Starbursts.

Image Description: Candy basket half-filled with various candies, mostly Starbursts and Hershey's milk chocolate are left.

As the night continues on, our friends gradually bow out. Ashley and Tilly along with Tilly's roommate, Corinne, are the first to leave since they want to get back before all the parties get out tonight. I live in a quiet area, but Ashley is bringing the others back to campus tonight before she heads home and things might get a little crazy. At least I know these three haven't been drinking.

We've settled onto the couch and a few of the chairs – Jonathan is on the floor – that man does not like sitting in chairs if a clean floor is available and it's not weird to utilize it. I never did figure out why he does that, but it's one of his quirks. I have an oversized floor pillow just for that reason so he can prop it against the wall and still be a part of the conversation.

Topics flow quickly as we go through hobbies, sports, superheros, and favorite childhood Halloween memories. I finally get to hear a little more from Sasha about her childhood.

"So, I actually didn't celebrate my first Halloween until college." She starts softly. This is hard for her to start talking about for some reason so I reach over and hold her hand, softly stroking her skin with my thumb to encourage her to continue. "I grew up in a very religious household and Halloween was seen as 'Satan's birthday' so we usually hid in the basement to avoid any trick or treaters. We didn't do any dress up things or harvest festivals either. I didn't get to enjoy a lot of things that you all probably see as staples of your childhood. When I went to college I did a lot of study into it and have gradually changed my mindset on a lot of things – including Halloween. It's usually pretty chill for me now, but those first few years, I was so nervous about dressing up and taking part in the traditions." She settles into my body a little as she takes a deep breath.

"I'm proud of you. That feels like it was hard to voice." I whisper in her ear as I move my arm to go around her shoulders and pull her into me.

"It's definitely interesting to see how each family and religion handles things like Halloween. I took a few comparative religion classes in college and had roommates that were part of different backgrounds so I was exposed to a lot over the years. How are you feeling about things now?" Max asks her.

"You mean your degree isn't in bartending?" Carter jokes with him.

"No – it's actually in Creative Writing and Journalism. I focused on modern religions and organizations with most of my assignments in college. I was always fascinated. Hence, why I would love to hear what Sasha has to say to my earlier question." Max responds with a bit of a teasing tone then directs his attention back to Sasha.

Sasha doesn't take long before she responds, "I'm still learning. Eighteen years of pretty strict religious teaching and culture is a lot to work through. It's a lot of mindset switches and understanding how I want to treat different things, not just how I was taught to think about certain things. It's a process and I'm thankful for therapy and good friends who give me the grace to try things out and then talk it out afterwards." I give her a light kiss on her temple in encouragement. I knew a bit about this before, but hearing her talk about it just shows me again how strong she is.

"Now that we are done with the deep conversations, how about we help clean up and call it a night?" Jonathan says as he stands up and starts gathering cups from the others.

We all start working on cleaning up while Kylie mans the door to pass out the last of the candy. Why there are still kids out at 9:45, I have no idea, but I don't want them to not get candy. It's mostly teens at this stage and it's good to see a few of them stop by. At ten, we are saying final goodbyes to our guests. And then, it's just us.

"Did you have a good time tonight?" Sasha asks me as she finishes wiping down the counter.

"I did. Having mostly friendly faces helped."

"Me too. It was nice meeting your friends. I hope I passed the test." She smiles at me as I come up behind her at the sink and wrap my arms around her waist, resting my head on her shoulder.

"They loved you. I've told them a lot about you so I'm glad they got to meet you. They both work a lot, so it was cool that tonight worked out for everyone." I start lightly kissing her neck and can feel her breathing hitch a bit.

"Are you ready to try messing up this lipstick?" She asks, bracing her hands on the counter a bit as I continue my exploration.

"I'd like to do a lot more than that if you're okay with it, babe." I slip my thumbs into the waistband of her skirt as I nip a little on her ear. She has a sharp intake of breath as she pushes her body back into mine.

"I think I'd like that."

"You think?" I whisper as I run my fingers up and down her side.

"Or do you know?" I slowly spin her around so she is looking at me. Her pupils are wide and I can practically see how much she wants this. God, I want this. I want her.

"I know. I want you, Matt." She responds breathily.

"So, can I take you to my room and help you get out of this insanely hot outfit?" I trace the outline of her corset with my fingers. Her breasts look incredible in this thing and I hope I get to see her in it again.

"I would love that. I may have put an overnight bag in there when I got here earlier."

My eyes come up to meet hers. "Not gonna lie, I'm not mad about that." Then I grab her hand, flip the lock on the door, and lead her down to my room.

Matt

Chapter Twenty-Eight

SASHA

ROYAL ENGLISH BREAKFAST LATTE

Social Post: I'm usually not one to promote makeup wipes, but it's a good idea to have a couple on hand in case you need to take off your makeup when you are out. I keep a couple in my purse just in case. This brand has worked really well for me. Do you have a favorite? #sashaloveslipstick #pinkeveryday #halloweenmakeup #cosplaymakeup #boldmakeuplooks

Image Description: Individual packs of makeup wipes on a bathroom counter with a chapstick and hair tie.

My heart is racing so fast right now. I didn't want to get my hopes up, but Matt has been my boyfriend for quite a while at this point. And I need him. It has literally been years since I've slept with someone. And even then, I've only been with two guys up until now. My first college boyfriend who was figuring things out at the same time as me – not ideal, but it had to happen. And then my boyfriend from my senior year in college until I turned twenty-four. I honestly thought he was going to be "the one." That's a whole different conversation though and I don't want to be thinking about other men when this one is right in front of me looking like he is about to eat me alive.

That *might be* an exaggeration.

We walk into his room and as soon as we are passed the threshold, he has me pressed lightly against his door. His hips holding me against the door. I can practically hear how hard my heart is beating right now.

"This feels familiar." I smile at him as he puts his hands on my waist again. I'm not a small girl, but having his hands grip me there makes me feel held and safe and protected. It's a small gesture, but it is one I am loving so much.

"Before we go any further, is there anything you don't want to happen tonight?"

"Um, I'm not sure. It's been a while for me though, so slow and gentle is probably going to be on the agenda tonight if you're okay with that."

"I'm okay with whatever you say, babe. I'm just honored you are here with me right now. Now I am going to very carefully take all of this off of you and mess up that makeup of yours. And you are going to enjoy it." His hands feel like they're everywhere and his lips are tracing from my collarbone to my ear and back down. The authority he conveys in that statement has my knees weak and I'm dying for his touch.

"What about you?" My fingers dig into his belt loops as I try to bring his body impossibly closer to mine. I need him close to me.

"What about me?" He breathes softly next to my ear as he kisses there and gently nips.

"Are you going to enjoy it?"

He pulls back to make eye contact with me. "Babe, you are in my room, about to be in my bed, yes, I am going to enjoy it." And with that he slowly pulls off my headband to let my hair loose by my shoulders. His hands follow my hair to rest on my shoulders then trace down my arms. "Am I going to need help getting you out of this thing?"

"It's a simple zipper closure on the back. I didn't want to have to mess with laces or things tonight."

"Thank God." He chuckles and then I feel his hands finding the zipper. His lips are on mine and my hands are helping him out of his shirt as my corset falls to the floor. Followed very closely by my skirt. Yay for elastic and easy clothing choices tonight.

Before I can even register that I'm only in my garter, thigh highs, and underwear, he has me lifted up, legs wrapped around his waist, and is walking us towards his bed. He gently lays me down and then drapes his body over mine.

Feeling his body on top of mine is my new favorite thing. I hold him close to me, feeling his body pressed against my breasts and his hand holding me steady. His chest hair brushing against my nipples is the perfect tease of stimulation. My hands are in his hair as his kiss turns more demanding. He needs this as much as I do. He begins kissing down my neck and I take the opportunity to catch my breath.

He doesn't give me much time before his mouth is on my nipple, pulling and sucking and kissing. I love the feel of him there. Why do I like this so much? I press my hips up, seeking friction, needing him in between my legs.

"Patience, Sunshine. Let me enjoy this for a moment." And then he's back on my body. His hands continue their exploration downward as he unclips my garters and then pulls down my thigh high tights.

"I love your legs." He breathes out as he takes the tights off along with my shoes. "And I can't wait to see all of you naked here on my bed."

"Well, then you better start stripping down too." I smile up at him. And I am so thankful when he doesn't make me wait. He undoes his belt and peels his jeans off and sets them with my clothes next to the bed. We are both just in our underwear now, and my garter belt. He kneels down next to the bed and begins peeling the rest of the fabric off of my body.

I have to fight to not press my legs together at his gaze on me. I can tell I'm wet. I've been thinking about him like this all day. I'm needy and so ready for this. For him.

"You are absolutely stunning, Sasha." His fingers trace up my legs as he kisses the inside of my knee. I reach down to grab the sheets under my fingers. I need to hold something. I need something. I'm not sure what. I have to fight down a whimper as he continues his teasing touches and kisses. Matt apparently knows what I need though because his mouth and his fingers continue their path up my legs. Touching, caressing, kissing, pressing, exploring, learning.

It feels like a moment and forever all at the same time before his fingers are at my center.

"You are incredibly wet for me already, Sasha. Have you been thinking about me touching you here?"

"Yes. All day." I breathe out the confession.

"What else have you thought about?"

Before I can respond, his fingers are gliding up and down my folds, from right where I want him to around my opening. Exploring. Learning. This man is studying my body. It's both the hottest thing and the most annoying thing at the same time. I am so worked up. I'm about to tell him that I need more just as his mouth descends on my center and I have to hold back an audible gasp.

His fingers are inside me now as his mouth tastes me. Embarrassingly soon, I can feel the start of my climax.

"I'm so close, Matt."

"I know, baby." And he presses his fingers further inside me and curls them as he sucks on my clit. And I am gone. It hits me hard and fast and he doesn't stop until the waves subside. I begin catching my breath just as he raises his head. I can see my arousal around his lips and on his chin. I am starting to second guess myself as he presses another kiss to the apex of my thighs and then begins his journey upwards.

"You don't get to be embarrassed about any of that. That was amazing and I am not done with you yet." He tells me as he stands and joins me on the bed. He pulls my body on top of his and I can feel how hard he is.

"That was absolutely incredible. But now I really need you inside me." I confess in a whisper.

"I can definitely do that." He rolls us over so he can grab a condom from his nightstand and then quickly removes his underwear so he can roll it on. I have never thought of a penis as beautiful, but his is. It's smooth and hard and, God, do I want him inside of me.

"Can I?" I ask him as I reach forward to grip his length in my hand. I want to feel him before he's inside me.

He passes the condom to me and it takes me a moment to figure out the right direction. He helps me get it set and then he's back between my legs.

"Kiss me please." I ask him as his fingers glide up and down my leg, touching my center on each pass. He doesn't make me ask twice.

Moments later, he is pressing slowly inside me. It's been literally years since I've felt something other than silicone or my own fingers between my legs and the stretch and pressure is incredible. Matt isn't huge, but he's enough, and he feels incredible. Six inches done right is really all I need and this man knows what he is doing.

"You are squeezing me so tightly, Sasha. This may not be very long before I come." He breaths into my shoulder.

"You feel so good inside of me. As long as this feels as good for you as it does for me, I have no complaints about quick." I tell him as I turn my head so I can kiss him. "Hopefully this isn't a one-time thing." I smirk at him and he just shakes his head lightly and chuckles in response.

His hand moves down to my breast and begins massaging me as he pulls on my nipple. I immediately feel myself coming closer to a second orgasm. His touch isn't as gentle this time. And it's exactly what I need.

"I figured you might like some nipple play while I was inside you. You are getting close again aren't you?"

"Yes, don't stop. Please."

He begins moving inside of me. Slow movements but right where I need him as he continues massaging and pulling on my breasts with his hand. His lips are on my neck and my ear and my lips and I cannot get enough of him. I can tell he's getting close when the intensity picks up in his movements.

He grabs one of my hands and positions it down to where we are joined.

"Help me get you there again, Sunshine. I know you're close. Come with me please. I need my hands on you elsewhere."

I put pressure on my clit as he puts his mouth on my nipple while his hand grabs the base of my neck and I explode. It's too much and not enough all at the same time. I feel him pulse inside of me as I begin coming down from the high. His lips continue kissing my body, the light sheen of sweat on my chest, until he meets my lips again.

"You are absolutely incredible, and that was amazing." He tells me.

"You will get absolutely no complaints from me." I smile up at him.

We stay in each other's arms for a moment and then take a few minutes to clean up and get in our pajamas.

That night I fall asleep sated and in his arms. And I know I'm going to sleep so well tonight.

Happy Halloween to me.

sasha
x
#sashaloveslipstick

Chapter Twenty-Nine

MATT

**ICED BROWN SUGAR OATMILK SHAKEN ESPRESSO
TOPPED WITH PUMPKIN COLD FOAM**

Social Post: I'm glad we kept the party simple last night. Thankful for minimal cleanup this morning. #halloween #officiallychristmasseason #happynovember

Image Description: Photo of my kitchen counter and sink with minimal dishes left over from last night and a small bowl of candy.

I wake up to the smell of berries and a wonderful weight on top of me. Sasha is draped over my body with her head right underneath my chin. I'm holding her with my left arm under her body and my right hand on her shoulder. I start gently stroking her arm and playing with her hair and just take in the morning. I love this woman. I have for a while. And she's finally here. In my bed. With me. She's mine. When I took the job this summer, I was hoping it would end up here, but whereas I can manipulate algorithms and data, I can't manipulate people. This had to be all her and me. And I was enough.

I hope I can continue to be enough for her. She has become everything to me. My parents and Ashley still take a lot of my energy, attention, and love, but Sasha has dug her way into my life and thoughts so much more than I was expecting. And I am so happy that she is there.

She finally starts stirring in my arms and gives my torso a little squeeze before she looks up at me with the most gorgeous sleepy smile.

"Good morning, beautiful." I tell her and then give her a kiss on the forehead. "How did you sleep?"

"It was perfect. I didn't realize I liked cuddling this much. We didn't do much of that in the cabin, but this was nice."

"Nice? Just nice?" I tease her as I continue playing with her hair. I love the way her strands feel in my hands and how they lay along her shoulders. She is stunning. But this sleepy, messed up look is probably my new favorite.

"Okay, more than nice. Please tell me you have decent coffee in this house, though." She starts to pull away to get up.

"Sasha – I've been taught very well by every woman in my life. I have several options for you to choose from if you would like or I can surprise you with something while you get ready. Let me know what you would like." I hope I'm not coming across as scolding her, but I got yelled at more than once by my sister as she started drinking coffee for my coffee choices.

I can still hear her chastising in my head, "That isn't coffee – it's elevated dirt in a container."

She laughs lightly. "Okay, how about you surprise me while I take a quick shower and get dressed?"

"Or I could join you?" I prompt her. I don't want to be pushy but the thought of her naked and wet in my shower has me ready to strip down and fuck her into the tile wall of my walk in shower.

"Actually, I think that sounds wonderful. But then, coffee."

"Yes ma'am. Shower, then coffee."

Her quick shower turned into thirty minutes of sensual kisses and touches. She let me wash her hair and worship her body as the water cascaded down her curves. We realized pretty quickly that shower sex probably wasn't going to be a regular thing for us. Several tries to find the right positions just had us giggling.

"I need to get a bench built in here." I mumble into her neck as we try again to get it right.

Sasha just laughs in response. "You have a perfectly good bed out there. We don't have to get crazy in here. Besides, everything is all wet and slippery – not exactly the safest place to get all over each other." She makes eye contact with me and kisses me before dragging her hands down my torso until one of her hands grips my length.

"There are other things we can do though." She confesses breathily before she slowly gets to her knees in front of me. I brace my hand on the tile wall opposite my body while the other goes down to stroke her face.

"You don't have to do that, Sunshine. I won't complain, but I'm not expecting that right now."

"Would you like for me to make you feel good, Matt?"

Why does her saying my name make me want to fuck her mouth instead of taking it easy on her?

"I would love for you to feel good. You make me feel good already, Sasha."

"Well then trust me when I tell you that this will make me feel good too. I want to give you pleasure and knowing that you get so worked up by me is incredibly arousing."

"Well then who am I to deny you?" And that's all the approval she needs before her mouth is exploring me.

Her mouth is heaven. She is exploring me like I did her last night. Kissing, sucking, playing, running her hands and her mouth up and down me. She takes me all the way until I hit the back of her throat. I can feel her constrict around me and I have to fight the urge to release immediately. She is good at this.

She pulls back slowly and looks up at me. "You don't have to be gentle with my mouth, Matt. Take what you want."

"Are you sure?"

"Completely." And with that, her mouth is back on me and her hands are gripping my thighs and ass and holding me in place as she gets back to work.

"Squeeze my leg if it gets to be too much." And that's all the warning I give her before my hands are both in her hair. I hold her still as I slide in and out of her mouth.

"Take me all the way to the back of your throat. I know you can take it all." I grunt out while I continue to chase my own release. Her mouth feels so good. I'm going slow to start with and she is taking advantage of the pace to drag her tongue along the underside of my dick when I slide out and then sucks on me when I enter back in.

"Are you ready for more, love?" Her eyes meet mine and she nods gently, her lips pulled tightly around my length. The look of her swollen lips and her eyes fighting back letting the tears fall unleashes something in me and I take what I want – what I need.

I stop holding back and fuck her mouth like I wanted to claim her pussy last night. I find my release a few moments later as I hit the back of her throat and empty into her mouth. She waits until I stop pulsing and pull out before she looks back up at me. When she notices my eyes on her, she opens her mouth to show me she got it all on her tongue.

"Why is that so hot, baby?" Her only response is a smug grin as she swallows it all down and then she leans forward to lick me clean.

"Do I get that coffee now?" She asks as she stands up next to me and places a kiss on my cheek.

"You get whatever the fuck you want now, Sunshine." I chuckle as she turns off the water. She grabs a towel and we make quick work of getting dressed and heading to the kitchen to see what I have available.

It doesn't take her long to find the coffee cabinet. Yes, I have a full cabinet of coffee and then a similar one with tea in it. I had a lot of this already for my mom and Ashley, but since working with Sasha, I added some more options to my syrups and extras that I know she would love. It looks like a mini coffee shop in my kitchen and I am not mad about it.

"This is incredible. I could come over here every morning for coffee and have almost all of the combinations I drink at the coffee shop."

"I won't complain about that." I smirk over at her. "Hot or iced?"

"Hot please."

Chapter Thirty

SASHA

ICED PUMPKIN SPICE LATTE WITH CHOCOLATE SYRUP AND CARAMEL DRIZZLE ON THE WHIPPED CREAM

Social Post: It's officially holiday season!! It's early November so that means it's fall décor outside and Christmas décor inside. And I've pulled out the deeper shades of lipstick to go with it. Have you started decorating for the holidays yet or are the Halloween decorations still up? #sashaloveslipstick #falldecor #countdowntochristmas #coloradogirl

Image description: Fall wreath on my apartment door.

The beginning of November comes and we fall into an easy routine of date nights, coffee mornings, and continued work meetings. There are a lot of phone calls and following up with resources for brands now and not just social media. But I am so excited where things are going. I've spent the night with Matt a few more times and it just keeps getting better. The relationship we have built has been absolutely incredible and he knows my body better than I do in some ways.

It's the second week of November when I get an email from a cosmetic company based out of New York City while I am with Matt for our weekly meeting. I take a moment to open it and read it before reacting. If this is just one of those emails with an exciting header to get me to open it and then is just another sale, I don't want to get my hopes up. This is the brand I've had at the top of my wish list for a collaboration since I figured out the difference between BB and CC cream.

Matt must realize that my energy just shifted because his gaze is fixed on me as I continue reading. And then reading through it again.

"Can you read this and make sure this says what I think it says before I totally freak out and make a complete fool of myself in this coffee shop?" I ask him as I pass over my laptop.

He moves things around so he can take my laptop and begins reading. Out comes the notebook as he jots down a few things. When he finishes, he looks up at me over the screen and smiles.

"Well, it looks like it says that you are going to New York for the Christmas release from Natalie's new makeup line and are going to be their featured influencer and will get to do some behind the scenes content before attending a special dinner as they officially partner with you and COBeauty for their endeavors in sustainable cosmetics."

So I did read that right.

"So, this is real. This is happening?"

"Yes it is, love. Are you ready to turn in your notice at Home Depot?"

"Can you help me write the letter after I accept this?"

"Would you hate me if I said it's already done and it just needs your signature?" He asks me. And yes, I am shocked, but I can't even process that fully right now.

"Hand it over."

Wait, did he call me 'love'?

Sasha
x
#sashaloveslipstick

Chapter Thirty-One

SASHA

GINGERBREAD LATTE

Social Post: I am so excited about this announcement!!! As soon as I get the official approval from the brand, I will be sharing about a new collaboration and a travel date coming soon for me! Thank you to everyone who has been a part of this journey so far. Oh, and I'm turning in my notice today! #sashaloveslipstick #twoweeksnotice #nomoreorange #morepinkplease #coloradogirl

Image Description: New purple water bottle with a #sashaloveslipstick sticker on the side next to an envelope with the words "Thank you Home Depot" on the front

I turned in my notice today.

I did it!!! Before the December fifth deadline that I gave myself. My last day is going to be November 29. I didn't want to leave before Black Friday, because it's retail and I'm not going to do that to my team. And that way I can start helping with the transition. I told one of my managers back in August that I was looking to leave before the end of the year and they have been working with me to train my replacement since then. So this should be a pretty seamless process for that side of things.

The collaborations have been coming in steadily and I've been able to do some consulting for a couple of brands and small spas and businesses to increase their outreach to the community and have some more "ready to use" products for their target demographics. I never thought this would be something I would be doing aside from makeup, but the process has been perfect and I love the brands and locations I have been able to work with. The community outreach for so many of them has increased and it is more than just selling products.

And the paychecks have followed too. The free product has definitely increased for myself, as well as Ashley and Tilly, who has joined us in doing a few promotions and campaigns with us too. But being able to have a paycheck alongside it means that I can be confident in stepping away from my job. There are a few paid classes and resources on my site that are generating several hundred dollars every week too. And that will just keep growing as we add more to that section of the business for both consumers and businesses. And creating those is a lot of fun.

Natalie is launching a new line of cosmetics for her Christmas launch that was inspired by my "Pink Every Day" campaign so she is bringing myself, Ashley, and the founders of COBeauty out to New York to strategize on a few things before the launch. There will be a small launch of social media only beginning this December and then there will be a full collection in the spring. They were already planning a small product launch this holiday season so didn't want to totally change that on their team. So this will be a secondary one that starts a new line and initiative for her brand.

I'm hoping this is the start of other major cosmetic companies doing something similar. It won't just be a new cosmetic line but a new community outreach initiative too. She is calling it "Pink Every Day x Natalie" and has already told me she would like for me to be able to do this with other brands with just changing the collaborative name at the end.

So much is happening so fast but it is working so well! And it feels so right!

Matt and I have a meeting tonight and then tomorrow I have a Zoom call with Natalie and her team as we work out the social media plan for the next month until I will be in New York for a few days. It's going to be a fast and busy end of the year, but this is so incredible. What started as me being nervous about that first farmers market meeting has turned into me meeting with CEOs and brand partners for major collaborative efforts.

How is this real life right now?

I'm meeting Matt at his house today to go over things since we are going to be dealing with some confidentiality documents and NDA's that need to be signed and I don't really want to go over legal jargon with everyone around me. With how fast this has all happened, I need to be able to just lounge around a bit and focus on relaxing after we go through all the documents.

It was a comfy clothes day for me so I get to Matt's a little after six in a pair of black leggings and a long sleeve tee. It's a sapphire blue color and it does amazing things for my skin tone and my eyes. Jewel tones are my favorite and the cooler months mean I can really lean into that coloring with my wardrobe and my makeup.

Matt opens the door before I even make it up onto his porch and helps me with my bags. I brought an overnight bag just in case. I have a drawer over here now so I don't have to stress about all of my extras or for the nights that I fell asleep watching a movie. We have been dating since August and things are feeling really good with him.

He sets my bag into his bedroom then comes to meet me at the kitchen table. He greets me with a kiss and then we get everything set up.

"I ordered dinner and it should be here in about twenty minutes. Do you want to tackle some work before food or save it for after we eat?" Matt asks as he organizes some papers next to his laptop.

"Can we take care of things before dinner please? I know we may not finish it, but I want to get through what we can. I don't know if I can do all of it tonight. I'm already feeling a little overwhelmed and don't want to push it."

"Absolutely. Let me grab the critical papers first and then we can take a break for dinner and then go from there." Matt pulls out a folder with my branding on it. "I may have had some things made up for you."

"How did you get all of this in so fast?" I ask him as he continues pulling folders, binders, pens, pencil cases, and even a makeup bag out of a box that I hadn't noticed before.

"So, I might have actually ordered this stuff back in August. I wanted to surprise you with it once you hit the point where you would need some professional items to go along with what you are doing." I gape at him, realizing how long he has had all of this.

"But what if it didn't work?" I find myself asking him. I have been doubting myself so much these past few weeks. Is this all some big fluke and I'll lose it all in a few months? Did they mean to reach out to another influencer? Is this really happening?

Matt must sense me spiraling because he comes up to me and rests his hands on my shoulders before dragging them down my arms to my hands. He interlaces our fingers and then waits for my eyes to meet his own.

"You are absolutely incredible, Sasha. I knew from before I even sat down with you at that coffee shop that you were going to do amazing things. And I just prayed that I got to be around to see it and begged to be a part of it – even if my part was small. I needed you to succeed and knew this was all meant for you. Being able to have a part of it on the back end and to encourage you to pursue what you love, this has been the most incredible year for me, because of you. And I know that this will work. Because this is yours. You put in the work. This is all you babe. And thank you for letting me have a part." I choke back tears as he presses a kiss to my forehead. It's tender and close and I feel like he is giving me some of his confidence through the touch.

I lean back a little so I can see his eyes again. "I could not have done this without you. I hope you know that."

"You could have done this and more without me. I just helped speed up the process a little bit." He winks at me. "Okay, let's chat NDA's."

We sit down at the table and begin going through paperwork

and signing on more pages than I feel is necessary, but Matt went through this with an attorney he knows and wanted to make sure I am set for this next chapter. Once Natalie announces the collaboration, there's a chance that other brands will follow suit and we don't want them taking the name or the model without proper channels being utilized.

Matt surprised me right before dinner arrived with another folder.

"What's in this one?" I ask before opening it up.

"Open it and see." He has a mischievous grin in his eyes.

And I gasp when I open it. Not only do I now have a bunch of amazing business supplies with my name and brand all over it, I now am the owner of Sasha Loves Lipstick and Pink Every Day as copyrights and Sasha Loves Lipstick as a trademark too. The business model is also laid out on the papers I am flipping through. Everything is here. The ideas that we talked through last week about Natalie are typed up and laid out in a seamless order from marketing to email campaigns to outreach opportunities for their core product lines.

As I keep going through everything, there are similar papers for more brands. All done.

"What is this?" I breathe out.

"I got everything ready for you for when other brands reach out too. I did a mix of smaller companies, economy brands, and major and luxury brands. So you can use these when you finalize campaigns with them and can go into those meetings ready to share the process and sign on the dotted line. The trademark for Pink Every Day is in the works and hopefully that gets finalized soon too."

"Matt, there are thirty companies here! How long did this take you?"

He seems to be trying to work out the correct answer when the bell rings and he goes to grab dinner. I am shocked. This is intense! I know he doesn't sleep much, but this is so thought through. There is so much here. I reach over and grab the next folder on the stack. It's a bunch of numbers – breakdowns – data. What the heck?

I flip through it, it's the sales reports, website hits, and wholesale numbers for Natalie from the last three years, and projections for the next two years – with my collaboration and without. This is more than intense. Matt is still in the other room so I grab the next folder. It's the same thing, with a different company. Another one on my wish list to work with. But the numbers that include my collaboration don't start in January like Natalie's does – this starts in April of next year. Just as I'm reaching for the next folder, Matt comes in with the food containers.

"What is all of this, Matt?"

"Just something I was playing with a little bit. I like numbers and so I was running some options for what could work if we used this same idea with other companies – nothing major." He says casually. It doesn't sit right with me and I feel like there are other questions I should be asking, but I can't place what those questions are.

"Let's put this away for a bit and eat and then we can go over your questions and proposals for the Zoom call tomorrow." Matt closes the folders and stacks them back up and I follow his lead.

Dinner is quiet. My head is so full of numbers now that I am overwhelmed again. Matt suggests that we call Ashley and go over things with her since she will be attending the meeting tomorrow too. I will be the one heading up this campaign but she is doing a lot on the back end with me now and I want her to have a part of this with me. Ideally, we will be doing this together in the coming years with other brands so I want her with me the whole time.

Going over options for Natalie together gets me back in a good creative headspace. Numbers stress me out but glitter definitely doesn't. We are toying with the idea of creating a separate "Pink Every Day" social media when Ashley says she needs to call it a night.

"Everything okay?" Matt asks her. Big brother mode has been engaged apparently.

"Yeah, it's just getting late and I have a meeting tomorrow morning with one of my teachers that I don't want to miss."

"Which teacher? Are you having issues with your classes?" I ask her. We haven't talked much about school recently and I kick myself internally for it. I'm supposed to be mentoring her and that includes stuff like school and her social life too. I want to be her friend too.

"Prof. Johnson. It's nothing major. I have to write a paper on color theory and I want to do a different approach to it than what is laid out in the syllabus so I need to meet with him to pitch my idea and get it approved. He has his office hours early tomorrow and I was able to get a meeting scheduled. I would prefer to talk it out than try to email it."

"Okay, well let us know if you need help with anything and good luck with the pitch. And I will see you tomorrow at three for our Zoom right?" I ask her.

"Yep, I'll head over to Matt's right after my last class and work on things there so I'm ready when it's time for the call. Goodnight guys!" She hangs up and I turn towards Matt.

"I have not done a great job of keeping up with her on things outside of work recently. I feel bad about that. I see her as my friend and my business partner, but I've had my focus split the last few weeks," I tell him. I really am upset about this and part of me wants to try to schedule something for us over the break between semesters. I reach for my phone so I can jot myself a note.

"The last few months have been a lot of transition times for you and her. She understands. And she has some new friends this semester that she has been able to work with too. I know you are bummed about not knowing about her projects and things, but next semester a lot more of this is going to be automated and we will be able to give her some more attention on what she is working on. No stress babe." He reaches for my hand and puts my phone down.

"How about we call it a night so we can take it easy tomorrow morning and finalize what we need for the meeting? Do you want some tea before bed or do you need something else tonight?" Matt asks me as he rubs my hands gently. This man seriously gives the best massages, even the simple hand ones where he works the tension loose in my fingers and wrists.

"I think tea sounds perfect. Can we put on a Disney movie and just chill until I fall asleep? I just want comfy clothes and one of your big blankets right now."

"That's it?"

"Well, and you of course." I smile up at him as he heads into the kitchen. I feel unsettled right now and I don't know why. I need to sleep and reset. I'll stress about this tomorrow.

Sasha
x
#sashaloveslipstick

Chapter Thirty-Two

MATT

ICED CHAI TEA LATTE, PUMP OF BROWN SUGAR SYRUP, ONE PUMP OF VANILLA, SWEET COLD FOAM CREAM, CARAMEL DRIZZLE

Social Post: I think Colorado missed the memo that Thanksgiving is next week. #coloradolife #fallincolorado #noco #wheresthesnow

Image Description: Screenshot of weather forecast for the next week – all in the mid sixties.

We take things slow in the morning. I run out to grab breakfast at the coffee shop so we don't have to worry about cooking this morning. And I want to get Sasha a specialty coffee. I don't have a full espresso machine yet so I can only do so much until I get that in. I'm debating chatting with Luca to build a custom cabinet or something so I can get her fully set up with her coffee things. I may surprise her for that for her birthday. I pull out my phone to add a reminder to my notes app when I get a notification from my tracker app.

I haven't used it in a while, but have a few alerts set up for different things. Things for Ashley for if she needs help – like whenever she calls for a ride share or transfers money to someone. I usually text her when she opens those apps to see how she is doing and make sure she doesn't need anything. I think she knows I installed something on her phone so I can make sure she's okay. She bugs me about it occasionally, but for the most part, she lets me do what I need.

This notification is for Sasha. I have different notifications set up for her. It's on her phone and laptop. This one is on her laptop. I stop right outside my front door to see what she is doing.

She is on a basic Google search engine, but what she is looking for has my heart racing.

"How long does it take to get a trademark established?"

I take a deep breath and then step inside.

Matt

Chapter Thirty-Three

SASHA

COOKIE BUTTER LATTE

Social Post – All the good vibes appreciated today. Big meeting happening today and then hopefully I can share more soon! #sashaloveslipstick #readyformore #coloradogirl #noco

Image Description – Calendar screenshot of blocked off calendar today for a meeting with Ashley and "blocked out name."

The morning started slow and cozy. The weather has just a bit of a nip in the morning, but it's still getting pretty warm every afternoon. I'm ready for all the time "sweater weather." At least I can justify my oversized cardigans in the morning.

Matt had left to go get coffee and breakfast while I got ready. After a quick shower and getting dressed, I go back to look at the papers on the table. I smile as I look at all the pretty branded gear that Matt got for me. He had also gotten me a necklace and water bottle with my logo on it. I flip through until I find that trademark paperwork again. I cannot believe he got this done for me. This is a big deal and definitely makes me feel super official. This is actually happening.

I wonder if I can get him one too for his business. He may already have one. A quick Google search says that he doesn't have one for himself yet. I wonder how much of a process this is. Maybe I can surprise him with it for Christmas.

"How long does it take to get a trademark established?"

Google doesn't take long to populate an answer.

"The trademark process can take twelve to eighteen months to get approved, but the time it takes depends on many factors. The process is complex and technical, and involves the application moving through several stages. For example, the USPTO examines the application, then issues a letter if the mark should not be registered. The applicant must then submit a response within three months, and the…"

Wait. What? I clear the search and do it again. And again. A year? I go back and look at the paper in front of me to see when it was received.

Mailed to Matt Carter, August 18 of this year. That means, it had to have been submitted in August of last year at the earliest.

Why did he submit for a trademark for my brand over a year ago? I didn't start working with him until six months ago.

Can this be fast-tracked or expedited?

I'm about to continue my search when Matt steps inside. I stand up from the table and make eye contact with him.

And somehow, I know that he knows that I know. And I cannot even appreciate the pop culture reference at this point because what is happening?

He sets the bag down on the counter and just looks at me.

"So, I'm the one starting this conversation?" I ask him. I don't like the accusatory tone that I have, but I honestly don't even know what to do right now.

"If you want." He replies softly. He doesn't seem angry. He is very calm. And I do not feel very calm right now.

"I'm kind of freaking out right now, Matt. What is this?" I

point to the screen. "A trademark takes a year to get established. A freakin' year! When did you do this? I don't understand."

He takes a moment before he takes a deep breath and responds. "I filed for it two years ago."

"Two years ago." I repeat back to him softly. What do I do with this information? "Why?"

"Do you want to have this conversation now or do you want to wait until after your meeting with Natalie and her team today?"

"I don't know, Matt. I need you to give me something because I am spiraling right now and I don't know what is happening. Please, just give me something."

He walks towards me and hands me my coffee then motions to the chair next to me. I sit down and look again at the paperwork in front of me. Now I see it, the submission date is listed in the midst of all of the legal jargon. He did submit this two years ago.

"Why?" I ask again. I am struggling to hold the tears back at this point and I'm thankful I skipped the eye makeup this morning.

He takes a deep breath and starts talking and the more he shares, the smaller I feel and the more anxious I become. When he finishes, I quietly pack up my things and start heading towards the door.

"I will tell Ashley to come to my apartment for the meeting."

"Sasha, please, don't go. What are you thinking right now?" He is broken. Not as broken as I am though.

Chapter Thirty-Four

MATT

I think I fucked that up.

Chapter Thirty-Five

SASHA

TOASTED MARSHMALLOW ICED COFFEE

Social Post: Even for a virtual meeting, I like to get fully dressed in something I feel put together in. Yes, even down to the shoes. #sashaloveslipstick #poweroutfit #businesswoman #pinkeveryday #wfhstyle

Image Description: Mirror selfie with my outfit for today: black slacks, an oversized emerald green sweater and gold jewelry.

Twenty minutes after I leave Matt's house, I am sitting in the middle of my bed staring at my wall. I hear a soft knock on the door and then hear footsteps. The bed moves a little next to me as Kylie sits down next to me.

"What happened? Matt is blowing up Carter's phone and Ashley is blowing up mine. We haven't answered yet but are getting the idea that something happened."

"I don't even know where to start, Kylie. I turned my phone off when I got home. I feel so overwhelmed right now. Like my entire existence is a lie. Nothing was real."

"What are you talking about? Just start at where it makes sense. I'm here to listen. My phone is in the other room and yours is off. I'm here babe, let me in."

The floodgates open and I relay the story to Kylie.

EARLIER THAT MORNING

Matt sits down next to me and reaches for my hand. I pull it away and just glare at him.

"I need you to talk right now, Matt. No touches, no excuses. What the hell did you do?" I level my stare at him. I am starting to feel angry and I need him to know that. He can't talk his way out of this. I need to know what happened.

"A little more than two years ago, Ashley started following you on social media. She would share your posts to her stories and would send me things when she wanted to try a new technique or a product line that you were featuring. After a few weeks, I saw you in person for the first time. You were at the coffee shop behind me talking to Kylie. You were the most beautiful person I had ever seen. Your content on social media didn't do you justice. You took my breath away. I recognized you immediately.

"I think you had 10,000 followers at the time. You were having fun with your channels and even though you weren't focusing on it at that time, you loved it. And it showed. And I knew I wanted to help you then. I just didn't know how. I said hi when you grabbed your coffee next to mine and you smiled at me before walking away."

"I don't remember you." I confess after taking a moment to try to remember the interaction.

"I wasn't expecting you to. You were in the middle of a conversation and it was early in the morning. I think you were going hiking with Kylie afterwards."

"So, then what happened?" I prompt him to continue

"I just kept watching for a while – just on social media. I never came to your house or even tried to figure out where you lived. I needed to keep that separate and didn't want to come across as creepy."

I have to hold back a grunt at that point. "This is feeling a little creepy, Matt," I scoff at him.

"I know. Just, let me get this out, please. The next week I saw you again. You had been invited to participate in an event as a makeup influencer and you had declined it. You were talking to Kylie about your social anxiety and how you hated going to new places, especially if you didn't know anyone. While you talked to her about the event and how you wish you could have made it happen, I pulled up the invite."

"How???" I ask a little louder than is probably appropriate.

"I don't always use fully above-board procedures for helping my clients, Sasha. I hacked into the system for the company who was hosting the event and looked at the guest list. And you were right, you didn't know anyone that was going. I knew that if I wanted to help you, I was going to have to take a longer approach to it and make sure you met the right people in a way that you felt comfortable and then gradually go from there. Hopefully, your confidence would grow as the invites continued to come in.

"The next week, I sent a coupon for someone I knew at a local nail salon to go into Home Depot. You helped her in the aisles. You started the conversation and talked a bit about the work she does. That was all you. She came in a few more times to finish her project and you were the one she worked with. Again, that was all you. About a month later, you got an invite for a girls' night out at her nail salon. She had been wanting to do one for a while and asked me to help with the email blast. I added a photo of her so you would know who it was coming from and made sure you were on the email list. That was the first event that I helped make sure you got to go and were comfortable saying yes to the invite."

"The first one? How many were there?"

"Eight in total before we started working together."

"What else did you do?"

"I filed for the trademarks after you attended that first event. I knew you were someone that would do well with a business, you just needed the support to get there. I added you to a few emails that would help you increase engagement and give you ideas for things that were trending, and a few things that were in the pipeline for companies that hadn't been released yet. That way you would be posting about certain trends in line with releases. I never did anything to hurt your business or your engagement. All I did was support what you were already doing."

"Why not tell me? When we started working together and then when we started dating?"

"I didn't want to freak you out."

"Well, consider me totally freaked out, Matt. Was there anything else?"

"I set alerts on your devices so I could adjust your algorithm, send myself notifications, and bump your content to certain brands."

"Alerts? Did you clone my phone?" My heart is racing again. This is so much to take in. I've read about this level of involvement in some of my dark romance books but I didn't realize people did this in real life.

"Yes. One of our first coffee meetings. I cloned your phone and then I downloaded a tracker onto your devices from there. Again, I never meant to hurt you. I just wanted to help you. I love you, Sasha. I have for a while."

"You don't get to tell me that right now." I am crying now as I stand to walk away. I pace in his living room. "I need some time to go through all of this. Was any of my success my own? Or was all of that manipulated by you? This whole thing with Natalie, does she actually want to work with me or have you done all of that too? What about Ashley, does she know?" I'm spiraling and I know it. I'm about ten seconds from hyperventilating.

"Ashley didn't know. I kept her outside of everything. And this was all you, Sasha. You are the one behind the brand and behind the campaign. This was you."

"But it wasn't, Matt. You put things in place that I wasn't ready for. You did all of this. So I'm guessing all of those times that I saw you outside of our meetings wasn't coincidence either was it?" I walk back over to the table and grip the back of the chair.

He drops his head softly before he meets my eyes again. "No, it wasn't a coincidence. I believe fate brought us together, Sasha. Brought me to a place where I could help you. And yes, I knew who you were before you met me. I have loved you longer than you've known my name. But I have always been your biggest supporter. I want to see you succeed. And I want to be by your side while you do it. You are the most incredible woman I have ever met and I say that with all of my heart. I love you, Sasha. Please let me show you how amazing you are."

"I don't know if I am ready to hear those words, Matt. I don't understand and I am trying not to totally lose it. I have that meeting with Natalie this afternoon and I am supposed to be doing this major campaign. Can I actually do this without you manipulating things on the back end?"

"I know you can."

"Then let me."

And with that, I grab my bags and walk away.

meeting with Sasha
Agenda:

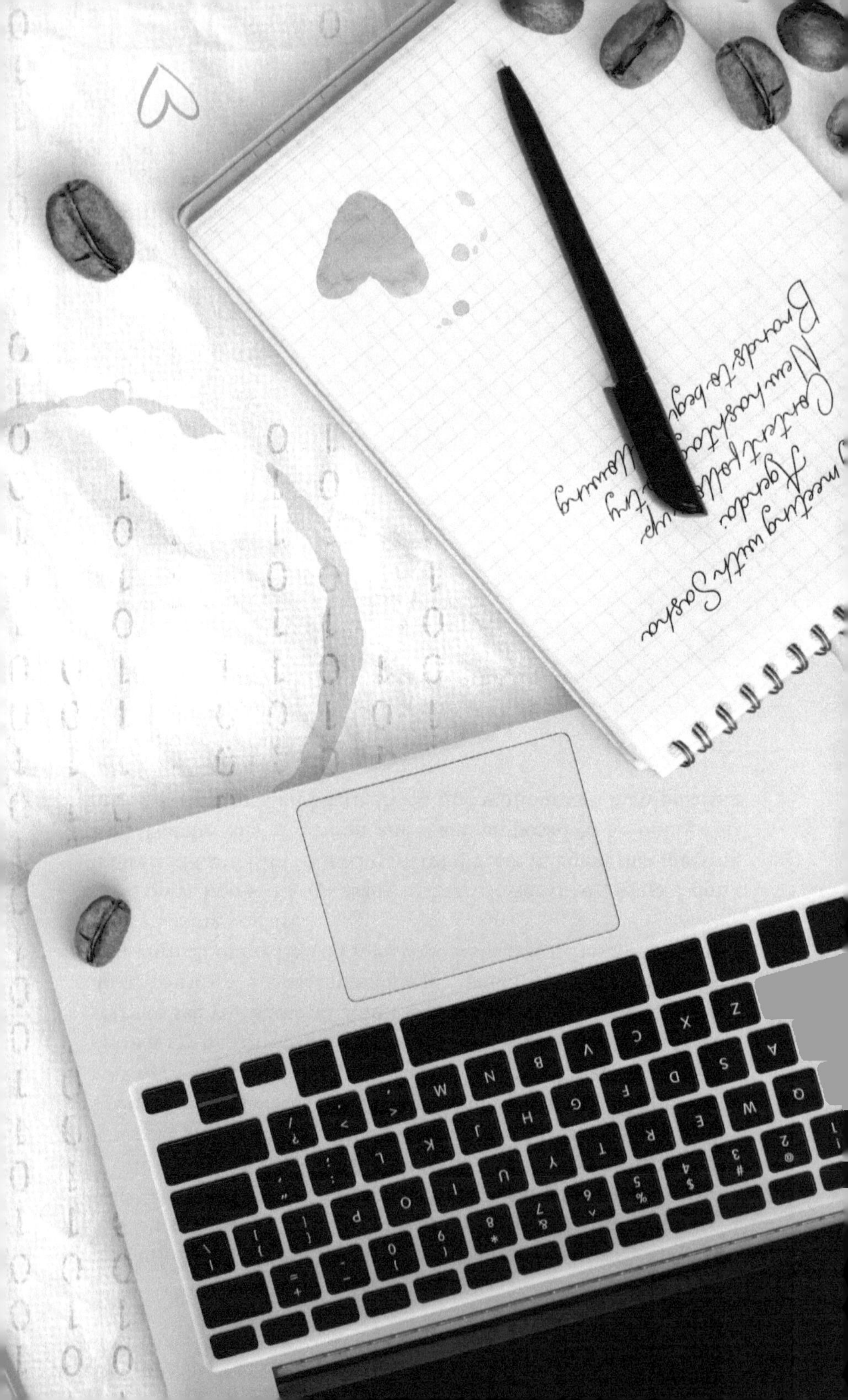

Chapter Thirty-Six

MATT

MAPLE CINNAMON LATTE

Social Post: I think it's time to start thinking about helping my parents with Christmas decor...wondering what the theme is going to be this year... #christmasincolorado #holidayseason #keepingbusy

Image Description: Throw back photos of old decor at my parent's house for the past couple of years.

It feels like it's only been moments since Sasha walked out of my home. I am praying she didn't just walk out of my life. But I honestly don't know. I knew she was going to be nervous about what I had done, maybe a bit self-conscious about everything, but I wasn't prepared for that level of confrontation from her. I'm about to reach for my phone when I hear the front door opening, maybe she changed her mind.

But Ashley is the one to come inside. And she does not look happy. Apparently I've been sitting here for several hours and not just the moments I thought it had been.

"How was your meeting?" I ask her, wondering if this is because of the meeting with her professor if Sasha has already told her how awful I am.

"Nope. Not going there with you right now. What did you do?" She says. Actually, she accuses. She shouts. She throws. 'Says' is not the right word for the way she is talking to me right now.

So, I tell her. I tell her everything.

"You are smarter than this. Did you really think this would end well?" She asks as she sits next to me. She's exasperated with me, and I can't say that I blame her.

"I just wanted to help her. I wanted to help you. She needed support to be all she could be, and I could provide that. I fell in love with her along the way. I can't lose her, but I will do what she needs."

"Dude, we have this call with Natalie in just a few hours and you basically just showed her that she didn't do anything on her own. She went from thinking she could run a major collaboration with one of the top luxury brands in the country to not sure if any of her content can reach one hundred views without you manipulating things."

"I understand that. What should I do?"

"You start by sending her an apology and letting her know you will give her the space she needs. Then, you will turn off all of those alerts and other things you have done so she can see that she can do this on her own."

"What if she realizes she doesn't need me?"

"You are stronger than that, Matt. Be there to support her, in the capacity that she lets you."

And with that, she walks away to go meet Sasha for their meeting.

Matt

Chapter Thirty-Seven

SASHA

APPLE CRISP MACCHIATO

Social Post: I'm going to New York!! I'm so excited to announce the collaboration with COBeauty, Natalie, and myself. The "Pink Every Day x Natalie" collection and initiative will be coming soon and we can't wait to tell you more! #cobeauty #sashaloveslipstick #nataliecosmetics #pinkeveryday #coloradogirl #newyorkbound

Image Description: Sasha Loves Lipstick logo layered with the COBeauty and Natalie logos.

That call went incredibly well. Considering that I went into it faking it like crazy and then immediately broke down crying again when it finished, I think it went really well. Ashley got to my apartment about an hour before the call so we could get in the right headspace together and go over our information and questions. Apparently, she had no idea that Matt was doing all of that. She figured he was adding some things on the other side of things to boost my content more, but didn't realize the length that he had gone to before we met.

"I'm pretty sure he has a few alerts on my phone to make sure I'm safe, but not to that level. I'm so sorry that I didn't realize what was happening and say something sooner." Ashley tells me as we finish wrapping things up after I finally stopped crying.

"Girl this isn't on you. I'm just having a hard time wrapping my mind around everything he did and how much of this success is actually because of what I did. How do I know he actually is going to be done manipulating things now?"

"He pulled everything while I was over at the house with him before I came here. He's done changing things. All he is going to do moving forward is actually legit and what you hired him for. That's it. I think you need to let him sit for a bit though before you try to go over things with him again. He crossed a line and he needs to know that's not okay. I know he cares for you, but this was too much."

"Did he tell you that he told me he loves me?" I have to hold back another sniffle. I can't believe he spilled that in the midst of everything else this morning. How was that conversation just this morning? It feels like today has been two weeks long.

Kylie joins in the conversation here from her spot in the living room, "He did what??!"

"Yeah. I told him he wasn't allowed to tell me that right now and I don't even remember what else before I left. It was all just too much. I wish I recorded the conversation."

"That probably wouldn't have helped anything babe. And he didn't tell me that, but honestly, I'm not surprised. My brother has been absolutely in love with you since our first meeting together and that was obvious even to me. He just took his time to start pursuing you in that way."

"Was any of the business stuff even something he wanted to do or was all of this just some massive ploy to get me to be his? To sleep with him? What was he trying to do here?" I feel another cry session coming soon. I don't know what to do with this and I'm second guessing my entire life for the last two years now.

"It's been two years. Two years of him watching and doing

things behind the scenes. Do you understand how violated I feel?" I confess to the girls.

"I get it. And you definitely need to let this sit for a bit. Focus on the collaboration. If he says anything, ask for the space you need. What he did wasn't okay, but I genuinely think he was trying to help you. It seems like he had a plan for making sure you were comfortable with connections and gradually helped you step out of your comfort zone. I'm not condoning what he did at all, but I get his thought process." Kylie adds to the conversation. She is the voice of reason here and is great at helping me settle my thoughts.

"Ashley, can you ask your brother to please give me some space for a bit? I haven't turned my phone back on yet and don't want to deal with it tonight. I need to focus on this trip that we have next month and what that means for us moving forward."

"I can do that. Is there anything else you need from me tonight before I head out?"

"No. Just know that I still want to work with you and Tilly and what we have been working towards. I still see you as a friend and someone I value with this collaboration and our content. I don't want this to hinder our goals at all. It may just be slowed down a bit without the extra push from Matt, but I really need this to work on our own."

"I get it. Thank you, Sasha. I'm here for whatever you need. Can I come over tomorrow after class so we can work on things a bit more? We head for New York in two weeks and with Thanksgiving coming up, I don't want us trying to rush through it all."

"Yeah, that should be fine. I'm probably calling out of work tomorrow. And I need to call Chelsea with COBeauty to go over what we are going to do locally to support this. I'll probably email her to set something up and then call it a night."

"And I'm going to go run you a bath. Have a good night, Ashley." Kylie adds in and then heads down to the bathroom.

"Oh, how was your meeting this morning? I totally spaced it with everything else happening. I'm sorry, Ash." I stand up and ask Ashley as we walk to the door together.

"It was okay. He had me go over quite a bit of my thought process before he okayed the project but I think it will be a good fit for the class and what I'm working on. I want to make sure my projects are aligned with what I want for my career as much as possible. There were several other students waiting to see him so I'm glad I got in when I did. I should be able to complete it before we go to New York." She smiles at me and I can see that she is more settled than she was yesterday before the meeting. She was really nervous about this.

"Sounds good. Let me know if I can help at all. I can't wait to read it when you're done."

With that, I give her a hug and lock up the door. Then I grab a glass of rosé and head to go soak my sorrow away in the tub – hopefully with lots of bubbles. Kylie is just turning off the water when I enter the bathroom.

"Okay love, have some quiet time and holler if you need me, but otherwise I will see you in the morning." Kylie says as she begins walking towards my door.

"Thank you so much," I pause for a moment, remembering something else I haven't talked to her about yet, "Can I ask you something about the Halloween party?"

"Sure, what's up?"

"You felt a little off when Carter brought up the whole marriage and baby thing. Did something happen?"

Kylie's face falls even more than it was before and now I'm second guessing asking her about this. "We had a pregnancy scare a few months ago. I was just coming to terms that I might be ready to be a mom and he was so excited when it was negative when I finally was able to test. He then went off a little bit on how he may never want kids and now I think I may want them. So I'm just processing through things and trying to figure that out. Especially with his promotion things are a little weird right now so I'm hoping that we can give it some time and then talk about it again."

"I'm sorry hon, I can't even imagine. Why didn't you say something sooner?"

"I didn't want to bother you over something that wasn't actually happening. But it's going to be okay and we now have to focus on getting you rested and ready for New York so go enjoy that bath and wine and I will chat with you later, okay?"

"Okay. Thanks Kylie. Love you babe."

"Love you too."

Thanksgiving comes and goes with no issues. I get a text from Martha asking how I am doing and reminding me that I have an open invite at her house. I haven't heard from Matt since the day of the meeting. The day I found out everything.

Things have been quiet, but it's been good. I have been pouring my energy into this project and getting things ready for New York. I cannot wait to start this initiative on a bigger scale and see what we are going to be able to accomplish together.

Black Friday was nuts, but that was to be expected. I opened so I was at the store at 4 AM for the 5 AM open. Hardware is one of the biggest departments because of all the power tools and we exceeded my goals. Going out with a bang was the goal and we hit that! My team did a great job and a lot of my customers came in to say hello since tomorrow is my last day officially.

I've told management and the person taking over for me that I am a phone call away if they have questions during the official transition. Luckily, there won't be mass quantities of new product coming in for a while so he will have some time to adjust to the layout before he has to do any big changes.

Saturday morning comes sooner than I am ready for it. I have been so excited for my last day at Home Depot for months. And it's finally here. But part of me is so nervous. Can I actually do this? Stepping into this role of influencer, consultant, and business partner is happening officially when I go to New York. And I know I can't manage a job and those commitments. I have to choose.

Ready or not, here we go.

Chapter Thirty-Eight

MATT

HONEY CHAMOMILE TEA LATTE

Social Post: Looks like it's finally decided to snow. Time to switch the fall décor to something a little more festive. #coloradochristmas #whitechristmas #novemberpics #noco

Image description: Snow dusting on the pumpkin on my front steps.

It took everything in me not to show up at the store this morning to congratulate Sasha on her last day. She asked for space and I needed to give her that. I want to give her that. But I miss her so much. She has been my entire world for the last two years. Hell, she still is. My parents were not happy to learn that I had crossed some lines (okay, a lot of lines, but they don't know that) with Sasha and her business. Thanksgiving at their house was a little intense. Sasha was supposed to be there with me. At least Ashley was there and we had a good dinner together.

I sent a bouquet of flowers for Sasha at the store and am currently watching the delivery tracker. She is supposed to be clocking out in about thirty minutes, so they should get there right before she has to leave. I have a mix of a lot of local flowers – even though it's cold out – there are several indoor nurseries not too far away that offer Colorado flowers all year long. And I hope she loves these. This is the first time I have sent her something since she asked me to give her space. I hope I'm not overstepping, but I miss her so much and I need her to know that I am thinking about her.

I've written to her every day. It's all in a notebook that I keep at home. Part of me wanted to use regular letters and send them to her but I don't want to come across like a lost puppy. Am I a lost puppy without her? Absolutely. I just don't think she needs to see me like this right now. She is focusing on the trip coming up and I am doing what I can to support her, within the boundaries she laid out for me. Doable? Yes. Fun? No. But I'm doing my best with it.

I get the notification that the flowers are on site. I cross my fingers and pray that she accepts the delivery. Or hopefully the front desk will. I included a simple card with it. Just in case someone else read it before handing it to her. I didn't need any more possible blow ups in regards to our relationship. Ashley is supposed to meet Sasha tonight for dinner so I'll ask her if the flowers are at the apartment.

Since there's not much for me to do here at my house, I head over to my parents to help them with their Christmas décor. My mom goes all out with the decorations and I know my dad could use some help with the lights and garlands. And whatever theme my mom chose for this year.

An hour later, I am covered in tinsel and pine needles and I smell like a mix of cinnamon and dust.

"Which set are you using for the main floor this year, mom?" I ask her. We have all the totes down from the attic so she can look through her options and pick her flow for the year. My parents have been increasing their Christmas décor since they got married so now she has a lot of options and can have a cohesive look throughout the house. Christmas is my mom's hobby and she goes all out every year.

"I think let's do the bronze and red sets on the main floor this year. And then we can do the gold and silver sets outside and upstairs. Keep it simple this year."

So glad that's what she said. Last year she did a Mardi Gras theme and the colors were all over the place. Because most sets didn't come with all of those colors, we had to pick and choose through so many totes. When it was all done, it was spectacular, but it was not a fun process to get everything out – or put away.

We get to work outdoors first since the weather is decent. It takes us a couple of hours to get it all set and the timers scheduled. Then we go next door to help one of the neighbors do the same. It looks like everyone else is waiting before they set their lights up.

Around dinner time we head inside to get cleaned up and see how mom is doing.

"Wow, it smells good in here." I say to mom once we get back to the kitchen.

"First day of Christmas means homemade soup. I went with a lemon, chicken, and orzo soup today. It's not as heavy as some of the other options but it's not too cold out yet so I wanted this one."

"It's a favorite." Dad says before going over and kissing mom on her cheek and then helping to dish out the soup.

"Have you talked to Sasha yet?" Mom asks once we sit at the table and start eating. I didn't realize my fingers were so cold until I held my bowl in my hands for a minute. I take a moment before I respond.

"Not yet. I did send her flowers today with a note, so I'm hoping she accepts those and I can start working on apologizing. I knew she wasn't going to be excited about everything, but I didn't think she would block me out this much."

"When do the girls leave for New York?" Dad asks as he uses his bread to get the rest of the broth out of his bowl.

"They leave on Tuesday. Meetings with the company on Wednesday and Thursday and then there is a dinner on Friday. They are set to come back on Sunday so they will have a quiet day or a tourist day on Saturday. It'll be a good week for them to get everything done. And Ashley was able to take her finals early so she can focus on the meetings and events and not school."

"Are you going?" Mom is hopeful with her question.

"I honestly haven't decided yet. I want to be there – for both of them. But I don't want to overstep or go against what Sasha has asked for. I miss being with her and seeing or talking to her every day, but I want her to succeed more than I want to be selfish or hurt her further."

"Well then, it's time to start groveling, son. Actions speak louder than words, so let's get planning."

So that's what we spent the rest of the night doing instead of finishing Christmas décor. The mistletoe can wait until I get my girl back.

Matt

Chapter Thirty-Nine

SASHA

CHAI WHITE HOT CHOCOLATE

Social post: Last day in the apron is officially done. Thanks for the experience. Time for the next chapter! See you soon, New York! #nomoreorange #lastday #sashaloveslipstick

Image description: Apron laid out on the table with a few loose stem florals next to it.

He sent me flowers.

I'm not sure what I was expecting today. I think part of me wanted to see him today, but I am glad he respected what I said. The bouquet is gorgeous. And huge. I love that he planned ahead to have it delivered right before I left. It definitely made me feel special knowing that he was still thinking of me. I do miss him, but I need to know that I can do this on my own. My numbers on social media this week have been pretty steady. There was a slight dip on Monday and again on Thursday, but I expected that with the holiday. And it bumped right back to my normal the following day.

"Sasha, you are going to do amazing things. I hope these make you smile. Know that I am so proud of you and can't wait to see what this next chapter brings you. I love you, Matt."

The note with the flowers was simple, but was just what I needed to see. It's been more than a week since we've talked. I miss him about as much as I expected. I keep reaching for my phone to see if he called or texted me. And I find that I am equally upset and relieved. I'm glad that he is respecting what I asked, but I miss talking to him. I decide to send him a quick text just to say thank you and show him that I got the flowers.

Me: Thank you for the bouquet. It is beautiful. <image attached>

Matt: I'm glad. I wanted to get you something special to celebrate you today. I hope you had a good last day.

I don't respond, but it feels good to hear from him again.

Time to get set for New York.

Sunday is spent planning wardrobe and finalizing schedules with Ashley. Dinner shows up right at six from our favorite local restaurant. We didn't order anything, but there is a note from Matt on each of the take-out containers.

"Don't add hot sauce to this one – it's spicy enough and you won't eat it if it's any spicier."

"This is a new menu item. I think you'll like it."

"This is for lunch for tomorrow."

"I remember the first time we went to this restaurant together."

"You wore your blue cardigan and pink lipstick t-shirt."

"You got sauce on the shirt, but it was on the lipstick tube so the stain was hidden."

"I love it when you wear that shirt."

We chuckle together about the notes. But it's perfect.

Me: Thank you for dinner. I'm actually wearing that shirt today. <image attached>

Matt: You look beautiful. Enjoy.

Monday is insane. We pack and have phone calls with Chelsea and Natalie's team. We check in for our flights and make sure we have everything printed in our folders for hotel and car rental and contact numbers. I am zipping up my last duffel that I will use as my carry on and the zipper pops completely off.

"You have got to be kidding me!" I whisper shout at my bag. This thing is insanely old and I knew it would happen soon. But I was really hoping it would hold out for this trip. I didn't want to try going to any stores this week. Everyone is holiday shopping, and it's going to be crazy enough at the airport tomorrow.

"Kylie, do you or Carter have an extra duffel bag that I can borrow?" I shout down the hallway.

"No, I'm sorry. Carter let one of his friends borrow them to move this week. I have literally zero luggage on the premises." She comes into the room to tell me. "How much more do you have?"

"Just my overnight stuff. I wanted a couple outfits and my base makeup bag in this bag just in case checked luggage gets lost or delayed."

"Makes sense. Have you asked Ashley?"

"Not yet, let me call her." I take out my phone and give her a quick call.

"Hey, Sasha, what's up?" She responds. I can hear her moving things on the other end and assume I'm on speaker while she is packing up her things too.

"Hey. Just finished packing my carry on and my bag just broke. Do you happen to have an extra bag I can borrow? I really don't want to run to the store if I can help it."

She's quiet for a moment and I wonder if her mom is helping her pack and they're communicating on the other end.

"Yeah, I've got you babe. I'm still planning to come over tonight to spend the night so we can leave together in the morning so I will bring it with me then, is that okay?"

"Yeah, that's perfect."

"Do you need anything else before I finish up here and head over there in a little while?"

"No, I think I'm all set. See you soon."

I breathe a sigh of relief. One less thing that I need to worry about.

A couple of hours later the bell rings. I go to answer it thinking that it's Ashley, but it's actually a couple of boxes from Macy's. They're addressed to me and there's a note taped to the top one.

"Sasha, I hope these options work for what you need. I was in the room when you called Ashley and I told her I would take care of getting you a bag. You are going to do great tomorrow. Sleep well tonight."

I smile softly as I grab the boxes and come back into the living room. I needed one bag. What is all of this?

Box one has two different duffle bag options. Both are purple and absolutely gorgeous but still professional. Box two has a set of silk pillowcases and a sleep mask with a note that says "for the hotel." I chuckle to myself – I hate using hotel pillowcases. I have no clue why, but they freak me out. I'm fine with the blankets and everything else, it's just the pillowcases. Box two also has a travel coffee mug, my favorite lip balm, and about fifty different pens.

Me: Thank you so much for all the goodies. Quick question though, why so many pens?

Matt: I didn't know what you would be in the mood for this week so I checked off all the boxes with the options.

Me: They're great. Thank you, Matt.

Matt: You are very welcome. Sleep well, Sasha. Be safe tomorrow. You're going to do amazing!

Me: Thank you again. Good night, Matt.

Just then the bell rings again, and this time it is Ashley. She just smiles when she sees all the boxes.

"How did I know it was going to be more than just a bag?"

Chapter Forty

SASHA

TIRAMISU LATTE

Social Post: Airport fit. Also, why is it so cold here? TLDR: Welcome to New York!! #allthesass #nybound #sashaloveslipstick #ootd #coloradogirl Image Description: Mirror selfie of me and Ashley.

Tuesday is non-stop! The flight was smooth and we didn't have any bag or car issues so we are in our hotel right on schedule. We are sharing a room at the Double Tree in the city and it's absolutely perfect. The cookies upon check-in were still warm and we were able to have help getting everything to our room. We both overpacked a bit because we don't know how many "dinner meetings" will be happening this week and it's always easier to pull from things you already know that fit than try to go shopping. Especially in a big city right before Christmas.

The room is beautiful! It's light and clean and there is a massive basket of goodies on the beds. They have our names on them so we know which one is for each of us. I tip the bellman as he leaves the room after helping us unload the bags from the cart.

No surprise at all when we see that the baskets are from Matt.

"I think my brother's love language is gift giving."

"It's mine too." I respond quietly as I take in the basket. It's massive! It's filled with masks, bath salts, coffee mixes, tea, mints, pens, notebooks, a couple of books, fuzzy socks, slippers, and snacks. He thought of everything.

I snap a quick picture and send it to Matt.

Me: This is perfect. Thank you so much. <image attached>

Matt: You're welcome, Sunshine. Thank you for letting me take care of you in this way even when I am not with you. How's the room?

Me: It's great. We had help up to the room and everything looks great. We have a quiet night so I think we are going to just do room service for dinner. We have our first meeting tomorrow at ten so we have a little space for the time adjustment.

Matt: Don't worry about dinner. I already have that taken care of.

Me: Of course you do. :)

Matt: Let me know if you need anything. You're going to do great tomorrow. Enjoy the goodies tonight so you are refreshed after the trip.

Me: Will do. Sleep well, Matt. Thank you.

Seven on the dot, there's a knock on the door with dinner. Ashley squeals behind me when she smells the pizza. New York bucket list item number one is now checked off.

Wednesday morning is perfect. The meeting with Natalie and Chelsea is perfect and very conversational. Most of what we needed to discuss was done over Zoom before we got here, so we are able to tour the facilities and film some content today as we meet different facility members and see how things are made. Luckily, we don't have any meetings in the afternoon or a dinner meeting today. Natalie knew after the travel yesterday that we would need a quiet day and we are so thankful for that. The four of us plus Natalie's husband and a few others from the company go out for an early dinner at an Italian restaurant in the city.

It's only 5:00 when we get there so it isn't super busy and we are able to be seated right away. The food is great and the conversation is even better. We are all going to work great together and I can't wait to see how the rest of this week goes as we start implementing things for the collection and the initiative.

"So are you all ready for the gala on Friday night?" Natalie asks us once we finish dinner and are just sitting down enjoying our coffee and tiramisu.

"Gala? I thought it was just a dinner." I ask. I did not pack for a gala. And by the look on Ashley's face, she didn't either.

"Oh, I'm so sorry about that. It should have been sent out to you last week with the full itinerary. We are doing a gala and there is a women's organization that is hosting the full event. They are doing several awards and grants during the event so we are hoping to get some good connections with the Pink Every Day initiatives amongst those in attendance. I will be presenting as part of the evening alongside other new community outreach endeavors. I actually wanted to see if you would like to split the presentation time with me since this was your brain child."

I have no words. This is so much to process. I am not ready

for this. Hosting a girls' night out or a spa meeting is one thing – presenting to a gala is something else entirely.

"How many people will be in attendance?" I ask, trying to mask the nervousness in my voice.

"We are expecting around 1,500 guests including the mayor and a few other political and societal figures. They will be giving away over two million dollars in grants and awards to different charities and organizations. We officially got invited last week when we made the campaign public and you were specifically named on the invitation." Natalie responds and Ashley reaches over to rest her hand on my knee under the table. She knows how important this could be for us but how insanely nervous I am.

"I'd be honored. Can we add this to the itinerary tomorrow to go over together?"

"Absolutely. Get some rest tonight and we will see you at the office at nine tomorrow."

With that, Ashley and I grab an Uber back to the hotel – the whole time I am trying not to spiral into a panic attack. I can't do this. I have to do this. But I can't. This is too much.

I don't even realize that we have made it to the hotel and are back in our room. I have been so focused on the previous conversation that I haven't paid attention to what is around me.

"Dresses. We need to go get dresses. Where are we supposed to get gowns in the time we have before the gala?" I breathe out once I sit on the edge of my bed. Ashley is already on her laptop.

"I found a place that has open appointments for rentals tomorrow at four. Can we make that work?"

"I think so. Do we need anything else?"

"Probably jewelry and shoes and stuff but they have all of that. We can do our own hair and makeup so we don't have to worry about that. Do we want to try to get a nail appointment?"

"If we can. Worst case scenario, we can grab a bottle of polish and do that on our own on Thursday – having another person do them is best but we can make do. I need to go take a shower and reset myself a bit. I am already freaking out about this thing and we still have so much to do this week."

"Okay. Take a few minutes and breathe. It's going to be great.

You know what we are doing and why we are doing it. I know this was a surprise, but you are amazing and the fact that they asked for you tells me that they have every faith in you that you can do this."

I nod and go into the bathroom. I miss Matt. I feel so alone even with Ashley here. I make quick work of taking a shower and then getting ready for bed. I add a few extra steps to my nighttime skincare routine so I can really take the time to prepare mentally for bed. When I peek out into the room, Ashley is sleeping.

I take a deep breath and stare down at my phone. I may regret this, but I need to talk to him.

Chapter Forty-One

MATT

BLACKBERRY LAVENDER WHITE MOCHA

Social Post: I've been learning how to add @sashaloveslipstick grounding practice into my routines too. Having the time to just be still has made a big difference in the moments when I normally get overwhelmed with all the things I can be working on. #sashaloveslipstick #groundingpractice #entrepreneur #mindset

Image Description: Notebook open on desk with a few affirmations listed.

My phone rings at eight while I am working on staining the new coffee cabinet from Luca. He did a great job on this thing and I hope I will be able to show Sasha when she gets back. I had asked him to make this for me before she found out everything and it's been nice to work on something while my girls are gone.

I wipe off my hands and glance over to see that Sasha is calling me. I momentarily think the worst – it may be Ashley calling me because something happened.

"Is everything okay?"

"Um hey, Matt. Yeah, we're good. How are you?" Her voice is quiet. She sounds scared.

"I'm okay. Working on some house stuff. Sorry for the initial start to that. I freaked out for a second. It's good to hear from you. What's wrong? You sound nervous." I make my way to the kitchen to rinse off my hands and then go sit on my couch. I've missed talking to my Sunshine so much.

"I just found out that the dinner on Friday night is actually a gala. 1,500 people, Matt. And I've been asked to speak. I have to present and tell people about Pink Every Day and what I am hoping to accomplish and how am I supposed to do that? I am not qualified for this. I can't do this. I'm not that girl. I'm just a social media influencer who wants to help other people out. I'm not a business woman or CEO or celebrity. This isn't me."

"Hey, love. Take a moment. You are absolutely all of that. You are a makeup influencer. But you are so much more than that. You have taken your platform and position to do so much! Over the last two years I have seen you step into your confidence on your channel as you reach out to more people. You have taught new influencers how to find their voice. You have empowered businesses to start community efforts to support other people. You have encouraged new moms to take care of themselves and reminded them that self care isn't selfish. You have shown companies that they don't have to cut corners in order to keep customers happy." I take a breath and continue, she needs to hear this from me.

"And you have shown me how absolutely incredible you are every moment of every day that you have allowed me to be in your presence. You can get on that stage. You can share your heart. Because that's exactly what you will be doing – you are sharing your passion. Don't think of it as a pitch or a presentation. Think of it as you sitting at your makeup desk, chatting with your followers about what you love and what you hope to accomplish. That is the Sasha everyone loves. Show them who you are. I love you for that person. And they will too."

She's quiet for several moments and I know she is taking it all in. I didn't mean to totally monologue on her but she needed to hear that. I needed her to hear that from me.

"How do you always know what I need to hear?" She finally whispers.

"Because. I know you, Sasha."

Chapter Forty-Two

SASHA

OATMEAL COOKIE CHAI LATTE

Social Post: Need a confidence boost? Pick your favorite lipstick and pucker up, babe. Here we go! #sashaloveslipstick #pinkeveryday #coloradogirl #nytrip #womenscollectivegala #galanight #blacktieready

Image Description: Selfie in the mirror with me applying my favorite pink lipstick.

Okay, I can do this. I'm just sharing with my followers about my passion. In a gown. In front of 1,500 people. On a stage. With cameras on me. No biggie.

Okay. It's a big deal. But I can do this. I have repeated Matt's encouragement to me every moment from our call on Tuesday to this moment. The past few days have not given me any spare minute to overthink tonight. I just have to do this.

Matt has texted me every day to check in. I've asked him a few questions about numbers so he can verify things for my presentation tonight. Natalie decided she wants me to introduce Chelsea first and then I will come up for the bulk of the conversation. Then Natalie will wrap it up by going into the action points of the collaboration, collection, and initiative. We have a total of fifteen minutes between all of the parts and that feels like forever and a moment all at the same time.

I have eight minutes to fill. I am wearing a simple but gorgeous black gown. It's fitted to me perfectly and I feel amazing in it. My diamond jewelry is simple too and it allows for my makeup to be the star of the show. I went for a basic glam look, but I know it's my strength when it comes to makeup looks. And I love that I had the opportunity to do it. Ashley is in a jewel toned green dress that looks stunning on her. It makes her contrasting light skin and blonde hair stand out. We both went with soft curls for our hair so we didn't have to worry about maintaining an updo throughout the night.

We arrive at the venue with the rest of our group in a rented car. It is absolutely gorgeous on the outside with all of the Christmas lights and trees.

And red carpet.

And press.

And cameras.

I look at Ashley and she holds my hand for a brief moment to give me the encouragement I need.

"I know this is probably your first red carpet so here's how this is going to work. I'm going to step out first with Charlie. Once we get to that first marker, Chelsea will follow us. Once she gets to that marker, the two of you can follow. The rest of the group will come after that. You can either take pictures together on the carpet or separate or just keep walking until you get to the front door. Whatever you are most comfortable with. This was something they had talked about in the meeting last week but it wasn't finalized so I didn't want to stress you out about it if it wasn't going to happen." Natalie has picked up on my social anxiety and has been super great about easing me into things this week. I need to take a deep breath and make this happen right now though. I'm doing this for Pink Every Day, not just for myself.

A moment later it's time and I step out of the car with Ashley. There are so many lights and voices, but I just focus on the carpet in front of me and walk ahead with Ashley. We stop halfway down for a couple pictures and then finish the walk to the doors. Natalie and Chelsea along with Charlie, Natalie's husband, and a few other staff members wait for us and we make our way into the main hall together.

Here we go.

Dinner goes smoothly, no spills, and everything is going well. I've had one glass of champagne but didn't drink any more. I don't want to be nervous about tonight.

About five minutes before the presentations start, I feel my phone buzzing in my bag. I thought I turned off the vibrate.

Matt: You are going to be amazing. Just show them the Sasha that loves her lipstick. I love you.

Me: Thank you, Matt. I wish you were here with me tonight.

I leave my phone at the table when I make my way to the side of the stage with Chelsea and Natalie. We meet the emcee behind the stage to go over a few details about the mics before it's our turn. The emcee is going to welcome everyone and then we are up first. We get set up with the wireless mics and headsets so we don't have to worry about mics. After Chelsea and Natalie are set up the woman running the event turns to help me.

"So with your setup, we are going to set your mic on your desk so you don't have to worry about anything else."

"My setup?"

She moves to the side so she can show me what has been moved onto the stage.

It's a makeup desk – that looks just like mine. With an extra-large mirror and lights. And the full Pink Every Day x Natalie collection. Plus all of my favorite makeup items.

"What is this?" I ask breathily. What is happening right now?

"Here is a makeup wipe. Go ahead and take off what you want. You are going to have ten minutes out there so whatever you feel you can do in that ten minutes at your desk while you talk is what you can do."

"Wait – I'm doing my makeup while I present?" This just got a lot more complicated.

"You're not presenting, remember?" I hear another voice behind me. A voice that isn't supposed to be here. I turn around to see a smirking Matt behind me. He smiles at me as he holds up my favorite lipstick.

"You're going to go out there and do your makeup while you share your passion with your followers. And you are going to finish it off with your favorite lipstick. Go show them who Sasha is." He passes it to me then places a soft kiss on my forehead. "This is your show babe. We can talk afterwards. I'm here for you. This is where you have gotten yourself. Go tell them what Pink Every Day is all about."

I can't help myself. I kiss him right on the lips. I allow myself to settle in his arms for a moment, regulating my breathing and getting into the right headspace. I use the makeup wipe to take off my lipstick and the base face makeup I have on. All I'm doing is my makeup while recording into my phone. I can do this. It's just like when a video goes viral – I talk to the few faces I know will be watching and see it grow from there.

"Thank you so much for being here. We definitely have things to talk about but thank you for all you did for me to get here."

"You put in the work, I just built the funnel."

"The funnel to you." I smile back at him. And then it's my cue to walk onto the stage.

The End

Epilogue

SASHA

ONE YEAR LATER

Social Post: We are officially launching our third company collaboration with Pink Every Day next month! Any guesses on who is joining us this time around? Tag your guesses below or who you would like to see in future campaigns. #sashaloveslipstick #pinkeveryday #coloradogirl #christmasincolorado

Image Description: Lipstick from Pink Every Day collection lined up on my makeup desk.

I t has been a full year. And I wouldn't change any of it. Christmas is next week and I am officially moved in with Matt. We kind of started our relationship over after the gala last year and it has been wonderful. We did the whole dating thing again and completely separated it from the work we did together. He isn't doing consulting anymore, instead he is working alongside me as my business manager and will be in the same role for Ashley when she is ready.

Ashley has jumped in and is doing more work alongside our Pink Every Day brand now and it has exploded. We don't do a ton of just makeup tutorials anymore, but still put out new tutorials a few times a month along with our current favorites and trends we are loving. The platform is so much more than we thought it would be eighteen months ago.

But it's gotten us to an amazing place.

I didn't fully get to a space where I trusted Matt again for a while, but I told him I loved him last Valentines' Day. I know it's cliché, but it was perfect. And I was ready. I moved in with him at Halloween this year. It fit for our relationship. And I wore my Spider Gwen outfit again. He didn't complain. The coffee cabinet that he worked on with Jonathan was such a wonderful surprise and I worked with Jonathan to get some custom pieces made for my makeup items and the awards we have received. Yeah, multiple. I won my first award at the Women's Collective Gala last year. And Matt and I have been recognized a few times since then. I received my fifth award last week at the second Women's Collective Gala. I didn't need to hide behind a makeup desk that time. I was the keynote speaker. And I had my man right there at my side.

Matt is no longer manipulating algorithms or email campaigns. He's settling well into his role as Instagram boyfriend and partner. And I couldn't be happier. Things are running smoothly and I can't wait to see where the business, our community efforts, and our lives together are a year from now.

Sasha
x
#sashaloveslipstick

Epilogue Two

ASHLEY

Christmas break is finally here. We just got back from another trip to New York. There has been a lot of travel this last year with Matt and Sasha and it has been incredible. Now that I'm not buried in finals and everything that's needed for school, I can actually rest and just enjoy being home.

I ended up staying on campus this last semester. It was nice to have my own space out of the house, but I do miss the quiet of my parent's house. So, I'm taking it all in this break.

We are heading over to Matt's house for dinner tonight. I think he's getting ready to propose. But he won't tell me for sure and wants us to be surprised when he does it. I think he's nervous that I am going to spill the secret. I can keep secrets better than he thinks.

I'm getting ready to fix my hair and makeup before we head

over to Matt and Sasha's when my phone buzzes. Repeatedly. I groan to myself, already knowing what I am going to see when I pull it out of the charger next to my bed.

> Unknown: The red dress that you wore to the gala was stunning on you, baby.

> Unknown: Do I get any pictures of you in it that weren't taken by the press?

> Unknown: How was the trip home on Tuesday?

> Unknown: I wish you wouldn't keep ignoring me. You look so sad when you pretend I'm not yours.

I block the number.

Again.

I don't know who this is but they started texting and calling me when I got to college. Yes, I am halfway through my junior year, so this isn't new. They are escalating though. It started out as just a text every few months. Since the gala last year, it's almost weekly now. I don't think they've attempted anything in person. And I don't want to freak out my family if this is just some random obsessed person on social media. Thankfully, we are sharing less personal stuff on social media now that we have the Pink Every Day foundation starting up officially.

I just need to get through the holiday break and then I can immerse myself back in school in the new semester. Less time at home means less time where I let my mind wander about who this is and what they want. I finish getting ready and head to my car to drive over to my brother's house. My parents are already over there so they could help finish dinner.

There is an envelope taped to my windshield wiper. I grab it and get in my car and immediately lock the doors.

"Aren't you tired of ignoring me yet, baby girl? I'm getting tired of you pretending I'm not here."

I look around but don't see anyone on the street.

Okay, deep breaths. This may not be the same person. This was meant for someone else or is a harmless prank from the teenage boys down the street.

I am fine. I am safe. This isn't happening.

I turn on my car and get ready to back out of the driveaway.

My car Bluetooth picks up an incoming text message:

"Text message from Unknown contact: You look beautiful in green baby girl. Have fun at your brother's tonight."

This isn't happening to me.

Ashley's story coming soon.

THANK YOU SO MUCH FOR READING SASHA AND MATT'S STORY.

Subscribe to my newsletter at nikkigrantwrites.com to hear first about when Ashley's story will be released as well as bonus scenes from this book!

MAKEUP AND MOCHAS SERIES

The Funnel to You
Book Two (Spring 2025)
Book Three (Summer 2025)
Book Four (Fall 2025)

Acknowledgments

Where do I even start? Writing this book was so therapeutic and such a wonderful journey for me. So many people had a part in bringing The Funnel to You to you.

First, my husband. Thank you, Logan, for giving me the space and encouragement to write this story. Thank you for being by my side and helping me work through my own anxiety problems. And thank you for not giving me too much of a hard time over my caffeine addiction. You truly are the perfect book husband!

Elle Thorpe – thank you for your encouragement to write my own novel. I have loved reading your books over the last couple of years and have learned so much about myself through those stories. The cowboy series, llamas, and Spiderman are a nod to you in this book. You mean so much to me and I appreciate all you have done to show real bodies in your work.

Jamie Applegate Hunter – thank you for answering my endless questions about writing, events, and content.

To my Alpha and Beta readers – Kaylie, Alyssa, Marie, Bethany, Dani, Ely, Tiffani, and Tori – Thank you for your input, encouragement, and criticism. You helped me make this project better!

Autumn, Justine, and the Bookish Bubbly PR team – thank you for your support and encouragement. You have been such a huge help with keeping me on track and promoting The Funnel to You.

To my street team and ARC readers and other hype people on my content – thank you for all of your encouragement. Knowing that I was writing this for you has made such a huge impact on me already!

And to all of the other authors, PAs, and readers out there that have had a part in encouraging me to finish and publish The Funnel to You – thank you.

Until next time!

Love and sparkles,
Nikki